Sooner or later Alexandra would likely be married.

She would be vulnerable, open to the same hurt and betrayal her mother had suffered. And she was afraid.

Not all men were like her father, Alex reassured herself.

Or like Rafe Garrick.

Only a short time ago she had come up from the beach and gone into his room. She had stood beside his bed, her eyes tracing the strong, stubborn lines of his face, the wave of dark chestnut hair that tumbled onto his forehead. A warm sense of possession had stolen over her. Hadn't she saved him from the sea? It was almost as if part of his life belonged to her.

Then Rafe had awakened, banishing all her illusions. He was not the kind of man to be possessed by her or by anyone. He was arrogant. He was quarrelsome. For all she knew, he could be out of his mind. And she would be out of her own mind as well, Alex told herself, if she had anything more to do with him.

* * *

On the Wings of Love
Harlequin® Historical #881—January 2008

DON'T MISS THESE OTHER
NOVELS AVAILABLE NOW!

#879 THE VANISHING VISCOUNTESS—Diane Gaston

Can the Marquess of Tannerton prove the innocence
of a notorious fugitive—or will his fight to save
her bring an English lord to the gallows?
*RITA® Award winner Diane Gaston visits the gritty
underworld of Regency life in this thrill-packed story!*

#880 MAVERICK WILD—Stacey Kayne

War-hardened cowboy Chance Morgan needs no reminder
of the guilt and broken promises of his past. But Cora Mae's
sweetness soon begins to break down his defenses.
*Warmly emotional, brilliantly evoking the Wild West,
Stacey Kayne is an author to watch!*

#882 HER WARRIOR KING—Michelle Willingham

Patrick MacEgan gained a Norman bride through blackmail,
so he refuses to share her bed! But beautiful Isabel
is determined to be a *proper* wife....
*This sexy Irish warrior is the third MacEgan brother
to fight for the heart of his lady.*

WINGS of LOVE

ELIZABETH LANE

TORONTO • NEW YORK • LONDON
AMSTERDAM • PARIS • SYDNEY • HAMBURG
STOCKHOLM • ATHENS • TOKYO • MILAN • MADRID
PRAGUE • WARSAW • BUDAPEST • AUCKLAND

ISBN-13: 978-0-373-29481-7
ISBN-10:   0-373-29481-6

ON THE WINGS OF LOVE

www.eHarlequin.com

Printed in U.S.A.

HIGH FLIGHT

Oh! I have slipped the surly bonds of Earth
And danced the skies on laughter-silvered wings;
Sunward I've climbed, and joined the tumbling mirth
Of sun-split clouds,—and done a hundred things
You have not dreamed of—wheeled and soared and swung
High in the sunlit silence. Hov'ring there,
I've chased the shouting wind along, and flung
My eager craft through footless halls of air...

Up, up the long, delirious, burning blue
I've topped the wind-swept heights with easy grace
Where never lark, nor ever eagle flew—
And, while with silent, lifting mind I've trod
The high untrespassed sanctity of space,
Put out my hand, and touched the face of God.

—John Gillespie Magee, Jr.

Thanks to the family of John Gillespie Magee, Jr.
for permission to publish this poem

The characters in this story are fictional, except for one. This book is dedicated to the memory of a real-life heroine, Harriet Quimby.

Acknowledgments

I'm indebted to the authors who provided me with the research needed to write this book. Most notable among my sources were *The Pioneers of Flight* by Phil Scott (Princeton University Press, 1999), *Picture History of Early Aviation, 1903-1913* by Joshua Stoff (Dover Publications, 1996), *Long Island* by Bernie Bookbinder (Harry N. Abrams, Inc., 1998) and *Nassau County, Long Island, in Early Photographs* by Bette S. Weidman and Linda B. Martin (Dover Publications, Inc., 1981).

Special thanks go to children's author Linda Granfield, who graciously helped with copyright information for the poem "High Flight." Her fine book *High Flight* tells the story of the poem and the young pilot who died soon after writing it.

Finally, I'd like to thank my editor, Demetria Lucas, for her patience and wisdom in helping me transform an unwieldy epic into a love story.

Prologue

Long Island, New York
June 16, 1911

The wind struck without warning out of a calm summer sky. Sharp gusts buffeted the wings of the fragile biplane, causing the craft to pitch and heel like a stricken dragonfly.

Rafe Garrick cursed as he fought to stabilize his lurching aeroplane. His right hand clutched the lever that raised and lowered the ailerons. His feet shifted frantically on the rudder bar as he wrestled for control of his precious machine.

Blast! He'd checked the weather reports carefully before taking off from the aerodrome at Hempstead Plains. This was to be the last test of his engine prior to next week's big air meet—he was counting on that event to make all the difference. The sky had been flawless, the day pleasantly warm. There'd been no sign of wind. Not this kind of devil wind, at least.

Two hundred feet below, the waters of Long Island Sound rose and curled. White-winged sailboats rode the cresting waves off Matinecock Point, their wakes trailing foam. Rafe would have to get the aeroplane down at once. But for that he needed solid ground beneath the wheels. The field at Hempstead was too far to fly in this accursed wind. He would have no choice except to head straight for the nearest landfall and pray for a long, smooth stretch of beach.

On his right, the north shore of Long Island extended along the horizon. He should have known better than to fly so far out over water. But the sky had been a deep crystalline blue, the summer breeze a perfumed siren, luring him onward and upward. Drunk on sunlight, he'd surrendered to the call. Now it was time to pay.

Easing down on the rudder bar he banked the craft sharply to the right and swung it in a wide arc toward the land. Wind clawed at the canvas-covered wings, threatening to rip the varnished fabric from its lightweight wooden frame. The engine coughed, sputtered, died for a breathless instant, then roared to life as Rafe jerked the throttle full out.

Blast! What was wrong with the damned thing? Was it the wind or some vital weakness his inspection had missed?

He had no more time to ponder the question as another gust struck from behind, catching the rear elevator and sending the nose of the aeroplane plummeting toward the waves. Rafe wrenched the stick backward, launching the craft into a steep climb. *Easy…easy now,* he warned himself as he leveled out. *The beach was only a couple of miles. If he kept a cool head he'd be fine.*

He'd be bloody fine….

He was whistling "Annie Laurie" between his teeth when the engine started to sputter again.

Chapter One

The champagne had gone flat. Alexandra Bromley took a sip, grimaced and sighed. She dreaded these lavish summer parties her parents gave for their wealthy friends. She hated the pretense, the show, the banality of small talk. And she resented that she had to be here when she'd rather be galloping her horse along the beach or sneaking out to test the speed limits of her father's new Pierce-Arrow on Glen Cove Road.

As she stood on the terrace, her face fixed in a rigid smile, she felt the appraising eyes of people who passed. Alex squirmed inwardly, even though she was long accustomed to stares. She was tall to the point of stateliness. Her face, framed by clouds of gold-brown hair, was the sort that could have graced one of Charles Dana Gibson's famous magazine covers. But she had one glaring flaw. Hours of walking on the beach and riding in the sun without a hat had burnished her skin to a most unfashionable brown. She was as tawny as the Indians whose lodges had stood here on the north shore of Long Island before Europeans came.

After soaking her in lemons to no avail, Alex's mother had come up with a gown calculated to hide the defect. It was of ruffled lavender voile, with long sleeves and a collar of Cluny lace that came all the way up to Alex's chin. An elaborate tulle hat sat atop her upswept hair like a huge dollop of whipped cream.

Never one to pay much mind to fashion, Alex hadn't argued with her mother's choice. It was not until minutes before the party, after she'd been bathed, perfumed, combed, laced, pinned and dressed, that she'd stood in front of the big hall mirror and faced the truth. Lavender was definitely not her color. And the style of the dress was much too old for her. She looked like a gangly child playing dress-up in her grandmother's clothes.

For a moment she held the champagne glass to her mouth. Her tongue slid thoughtfully along the blade-thin crystal rim as she surveyed the party from the terrace of her parents' twenty-eight-room Edwardian house. Long tables, spread with linen, had been set up on the vast emerald lawn. Men in white summer gabardines and women in butterfly hues of organdy and silk georgette flocked around the tables, helping themselves to Smith Island oysters, fresh clams and Lobster Newberg, wild-rice croquettes and dainty Swiss crackers spread with Astrakhan caviar and pâté de foie gras. An elaborate glass dolphin spouted pink champagne; a matching one on another table flowed red with rum-laced Roman punch. In the distance, beyond everything, the waters of Long Island Sound glittered in the afternoon sunlight.

Idly she watched her parents' guests stuffing themselves like pedigreed cattle milling around the feeding trough. The men were big, bellowing bulls flaunting their money and power. Their wives were placid heifers with ropes of pearls around their necks.

Were these women happy? Did they care about anything beyond money, status and the broods of children they produced? Heaven forbid, there had to be more to life than that! In this day and age, females were doing things that Alex had only dreamed of—climbing mountains, working as journalists, marching in the streets, exploring the world! Why couldn't she be one of those women? Why did she have to be a prisoner of her family's expectations?

With ruthless detachment, she appraised her own situation. At twenty, she was of an age when young women were expected to marry. The fact that she was her father's only child and heir to the fortune he'd made in the firearms business made this an imperative. That's why she was being trotted out on display this summer, for sale to the most promising bidder.

Maybe it was time to pack a suitcase and run away.

Alex handed the champagne glass to a passing servant. At least Mama would have some things to be pleased about. For a summer party the turnout wasn't bad, and the guests represented some of New York's better families. Papa, on the other hand, was growing impatient with these soirees. All Buck Bromley wanted was to see his daughter married to a man he deemed suitable.

Alex picked out her father's hulking shoulders among the crowd. She knew what he wanted. He wanted the son he never had—another Buck Bromley, with money and connections, who'd take her in hand and sire a pack of bullheaded grandsons to take over the company one day. He wanted to forge her life like one of his custom-made hunting rifles. Well, she had news for him. She wanted a life of her own.

"Alex, for heaven's sake!" It was her mother, approaching with swift, nervous footsteps. Maude Bromley was a thin, plain woman, as pale as wallpaper. Her hands fluttered like dry leaves as she spoke. "How can you stand there when you should be mingling with our guests? This is your party, too, you know."

She took her daughter's hand and led her down off the terrace onto the lawn. There the guests, plates teetering with food, were seating themselves around umbrella-shaded tables.

"My dear, I'm so delighted to see you!" Alex found herself smothered against the ample bosom of a woman whose name eluded her. Most likely she was a Whitney or a Vanderbilt, or a member of some other clan whose founders had come to the Colonies and made their fortunes early. Most of the families who lived on Long Island's Gold Coast were Old Money, part of the American aristocracy.

Buck Bromley, on the other hand, had married into a modest gunsmithing business and expanded it himself.

Burnsides and Bromley was now the largest firearms manufacturer on the East Coast. Buck was wealthier than some of the Old Guard people. Still, in terms of social standing, the Bromleys were nouveau riches, practically bourgeois.

Alex extricated herself from the woman's arms. Her mother had darted back to the kitchen, leaving her on her own. She sighed, feeling adrift. Most of the party guests were friends and neighbors of her parents' generation or business associates of her father's. Her own friends had married and moved away or gone abroad for the summer. Alex had begged to go abroad herself, but her father had insisted on keeping her at home. He didn't want to risk her eloping with some fortune-hunting French fop, he'd said, only half joking.

Alex had never felt comfortable in crowds. She was walking faster now, down the slope of the lawn. People pressed around her, sweating, talking, eating. She fought the urge to break loose, to run to the sea like a lemming and plunge into the cold white surf.

"Alex!" She stiffened at the sound of her father's voice. Buck Bromley turned away from the two men he'd been talking to. "Come here, girl," he boomed. "I want you to meet my friends!"

Alex turned slowly, her face assuming a mask of polite cordiality. *All he wanted was to show her off, to whip her out of the chute and run her around the ring like a prize heifer. That's all she ever was to him anyway—breeding stock!*

Buck Bromley grinned. He was a powerful man,

bull-necked, barrel-chested and hard as hickory. His unruly brown-gold hair matched his daughter's, but his features were blunt where hers were fine. His blue eyes gleamed like the flame of a gas jet, where hers were almost purple and as cool as the distant ocean.

"Come here, girl!" He repeated the order with a jerk of his head. He was not a handsome man, but his jut-jawed face exuded vitality. Men admired and followed him. Women... Alex preferred not to think about that now.

"Yes, Papa," she said mechanically.

"These are colleagues of mine." Buck indicated the men who stood beside him. "I invited them here for two reasons. First, I wanted them to see that I wasn't just bragging about the beauty I'd fathered. And second, I wanted you to meet them."

Alex glanced at the two men. They appeared to be in their forties, with thickening waists and thinning hair. The younger man was blond and vain-looking with a waxed moustache that curled upward at the tips. The other man had a florid face framed by bushy sideburns. Both were turned out in a manner that exuded wealth and arrogance.

Their names and accomplishments slid past Alex as each, in turn, took her hand. The blond man had evidently made a fortune in shipping and had just returned from an African safari. The one with the sideburns owned the biggest sporting goods business in the state of New York.

"Joe Templeton," he introduced himself, squeezing her hand till it hurt. "Buck told me he had a pretty daughter, but I hadn't figured on meeting a goddess!"

"Thank you. It's always an honor to meet my father's friends," Alex lied in a formal voice. "Now, if you'll excuse me, I need to get back to my other guests. Please enjoy yourselves, gentlemen."

She turned to leave, but her father caught her arm. "Walk with me a little," he said. "There's something I've got to say, and I want you to hear it."

"Can't it wait?" Alex asked, though she knew better. Buck Bromley never waited for anything.

"Come on," he said, gripping her elbow and propelling her away from the party, in the direction of the beach. He didn't speak again until they were out of earshot.

"Well, what did you think of them?" he demanded, stopping beside a blossoming honeysuckle bush.

"I assume they're single."

"Single and damned well-off, both of them. You could do worse, girl."

"Really, Papa, they're old and stodgy. What makes you think I'd like them?"

Buck Bromley shoved his hands into his pockets and stared toward the dunes that edged the whitecapped water. "Because they know what they want and they're not afraid to go after it. They know how to take charge. They're real *men!*"

Alex felt a flash of anger. For a moment she struggled to hold it in check. She tried to shift her concentration to the sights and sounds of the party, to the kaleidoscopic movement of forms and colors, the tinkle of crystal and silver, the muted cacophony of voices, and something else—a faint, mechanical, droning sound, coming from nowhere, fitting nothing, making no sense at all.

"Papa," she snapped, "you have your own ideas of what a man ought to be. I have mine, too, and they're not the same! A real man is somebody who cares about other people, somebody who's gentle and loving and not afraid to show his feelings!"

"Damn it, girl!" Buck rumbled behind clenched teeth. "Don't you ever think of anybody except yourself? Look at me! I built Burnsides and Bromley from a two-bit gunsmithing shop to one of the biggest operations in the country. It took blood, guts and sweat. For years I worked sixty, seventy, eighty hours a week. But I wasn't doing it just for me. I was doing it for the sons and grandsons who'd come after me, who'd take over the company and keep it going!"

He took a deep breath. "Even after you were born, and we found out your mama couldn't have any more babies, I didn't give up hope. I knew you'd get married one day—and I counted on it being to a man who'd run the company with me and give me a brood of strapping grandsons to take over when I was gone. Now, damn it, girl, it's time for you to choose the right kind of husband and give me some peace of mind!"

Alex fought for self-control. The droning sound was louder now, like a throbbing inside her head. "Papa, we've been through all this before," she said icily. "I'm not ready to get married. There are other things I want to do."

Buck's face was dark red. Alex could see the subtle twitch of a vein in his left temple, the herald of an explosion. She was dimly aware that the droning sound had stopped. The sudden silence was oddly frightening.

"Please, Papa, not here!" she whispered.

"Listen, girl," he muttered through his teeth. "Your selfishness is ruining—"

He was interrupted by a shriek from one of the female guests. "That aeroplane! It's going to crash!"

The party was forgotten as everyone turned and stared upward. There was the aeroplane, less than a hundred feet above the beach, as fragile as a mosquito against the sky.

Alex had seen aeroplanes before, though not many. This was a biplane, with a wide double wing, and it was clearly in trouble. She could see the frantic motions of the pilot as he tried to restart the engine. She heard the motor cough once, then die again into terrifying silence as the plane started a downward spiral.

"He's got one chance," a man behind Alex said. "If he can level it out, he might be able to glide in. Otherwise—"

"Good God!" exclaimed Buck. "He's trying to pull out of it! What a fighter! Come on, man!"

A cry lodged in Alex's throat. Time slowed to a nightmarish crawl as she watched the spiraling plane and the pilot struggling with the controls. For an instant it appeared that he'd be able to right the plane for a landing. But for that he needed power, and his engine was dead.

He was still pulling on the stick when the fragile craft angled in toward the beach and vanished behind the dunes.

The watchers stood stunned, unable to believe what

they'd seen. But Alex couldn't stand still. She felt herself breaking into a run. Her shoes flew off as she raced down the long stretch of lawn toward the dunes. The wind tore away her tulle hat and plucked at the pins in her hair. Her skirt caught on a low bramble, ripping the ruffles as she heedlessly ran on.

Others were running, too, now, but Alex was ahead of them all. She was the first to reach the sand, the first to scramble up the landward slope of the dune and the first to sight the wrecked aeroplane.

The aeroplane had crashed nose-down near the water's edge. Its double wings were twisted, its tail askew. The front end was partly buried in the sand. Waves eddied around it as the tide moved onto the beach.

Where was the pilot? Alex spotted him as she tore down the side of the dune. He was hanging out of the plane, his legs caught in the wreckage, his head dangling in the water.

Fearing he would drown if the crash hadn't killed him, Alex plunged into the surf. The waves were swirling around her waist by the time she reached the aeroplane. A ripple washed over the pilot's goggled face. Then Alex had her arms around him. She lifted him, feeling the heaviness of his upper body. He was a big man, rock solid. She cradled his head against her breasts while she waited for help.

"Is he alive?" Buck was beside her in the water now, his strong arms supporting the pilot's shoulders.

"I don't know." Alex ran a finger along the man's neck, searching for a pulse. He was bleeding from a gash on his temple. The blood made wet red streaks down the front of her gown. "I can't feel anything," she said, fumbling with the leather chinstrap.

By now, other men had reached the aeroplane and were trying to free the pilot's legs. Alex held his head steady with one hand while the other hand tugged at the stubborn buckle.

Finally the strap came free. Alex pulled away the helmet. The goggles came with it. Underneath was a square-jawed face—a face that was young, yet somehow not young at all. The hair, plastered damply against the head, was dark reddish-brown. The nose was crooked, as if it had once been broken. The eyes were closed.

She pressed his neck where the strap had covered it and caught the faint throb of a pulse. "He's alive!" she exclaimed, weak with relief. "Hurry! Get him out!"

At the sound of her voice the pilot's closed eyelids twitched. The wet lashes fluttered upward. Alex found herself staring into a pair of riveting, green-flecked eyes.

He blinked, trying to focus on her face. "Don't worry," she said, feeling the warm pressure of his cheek against her breast. "You're safe. They're just trying to get your legs loose."

As she spoke, the rescuers suddenly pulled the man's legs free of the wreck. With a sharp moan of pain, he lapsed back into unconsciousness. Alex glanced over her shoulder and saw that one of his high-topped leather boots was grotesquely twisted. His leg, she realized, was badly broken.

"Let's get him to the house!" she shouted. "Careful—support that leg!"

"We'll take him," Buck said. "Alex, you run on ahead. Get somebody to call a doctor."

"No, I've got him." She cradled the unconscious head, refusing to let go. She had found him. She had reached him first and saved him. It was as if, somehow, the young pilot had become hers.

Most of the party guests had lined up along the top of the dune to watch. Alex felt their eyes on her as she backed out of the water, her skirt dripping and encrusted with sand. Hands reached out to support the weight of the pilot's torso. He stirred against her breast, his lips forming words she couldn't hear.

Alex's mother struggled down the slope toward her, walking sideways to keep from sliding in the loose sand. "What a sight you are, Alexandra!" she gasped. "I almost fainted when I saw you out there in the water."

"The pilot's hurt!" Alex said. "Have someone run to the house and telephone Dr. Fleury!" She cradled the man's head, ignoring her mother's outstretched arms. "Please, Mama, I'm fine!"

Her mother stared down at her, still hesitant. "But your gown—you're covered with blood!"

Alex glanced down at the ugly lavender dress. The bodice and skirt were blotched with crimson. A little shiver went through her as she felt the pressure of the pilot's firm jaw through the thin fabric. Her head went up. "Yes," she said. "But it's not my blood. It's his."

Chapter Two

Rafe awoke with a body-wrenching jerk. He had felt himself falling, spinning downward in a ripping descent that seemed slow only because it had no bottom. Now he felt the starch-crisped softness of a pillowcase against his cheek and realized he'd been dreaming. The dream had merged with reality until he was no longer sure where one left off and the other began.

Keeping his eyes tightly closed, he tried to piece together the fragmented memory of the crash—the plummeting plane, pulling on the stick until his hands bled, the water rushing upward to meet him. Then blackness, broken only by a flash of lucid pain.

Even then he'd been hallucinating, Rafe reckoned. Those violet eyes looking down at him could not have been real. Only angels had eyes like that. Or devils, maybe. And considering the life he'd led, Rafe would have been less surprised to find himself in hell than in heaven.

Not that it mattered. No body that ached as much

as his could be dead. He was still among the living. But where?

Rafe forced his leaden eyelids to open.

The first thing he saw was sunlight streaming through a tall, cane-shuttered window. It was so bright that he had to close his eyes again. *The hospital,* he thought. *That's where he was. And running up the bloody bill, most likely. When they found out he wasn't rich, he'd be out on the street.*

He turned his head to one side, even that small motion hurting. Lord, what had he done to himself?

Concentrating, he willed his eyes to open again. This time he could see more of the room—a large teakwood armoire with oriental hardware; a richly woven Turkish carpet on the floor; a four-foot brass vase trailing the fronds of a huge, lacy fern. On the wall above the vase—Rafe gasped when he saw it—was the snarling, mounted head of a Bengal tiger.

A hospital? "Not bloody likely," Rafe muttered out loud.

Burning with curiosity, he raised himself on one elbow and tried to sit up. Pain shot a searing path up his right leg as he twisted it. Broken, Rafe concluded dourly even before he felt the heavy splint. Broken nastily. It would be many weeks mending.

Blast! Rafe cursed his luck. Next week's big air show, with $100,000 in prizes, was to have been the turning point of his life. He was gambling everything on the chance that he would find a backer to invest in the aeroplane he'd designed and built. He'd had a chance. A good chance. Now his aeroplane, his leg and his dreams all lay shattered.

Slowly Rafe sank back onto the pillow. He would rebuild the aeroplane, of course. And he would fly again. But he'd lost the season. He had missed his big chance. *Damn!* He glanced around the strangely exotic room again. Where in hell's name was he, anyway? And where was his aeroplane?

The sound of approaching footsteps outside the half-open door broke into his thoughts. Instinctively Rafe froze. Life had taught him to be cautious. Even in a place like this, you could never tell who might be slinking around the halls. Once, in a perfectly respectable New Orleans hotel, he had gone to sleep and almost lost his life to a wallet-snatching bellhop with a stiletto in his boot. This place looked too ritzy for such shenanigans, but all the same…

Hinges creaked softly as the door swung all the way open. Rafe lay still, his eyes closed, as the footsteps padded across the carpet toward him. They were light and swift—a woman's, Rafe guessed, relaxing a bit. Though a woman could be just as dangerous as a man. What would she look like? he caught himself wondering. Would she be young? Pretty? And what would she be doing in this room? He let her come closer, playing the game as long as he dared.

Now he sensed the light press of her body against the side of the bed. She was looking down at him. Rafe could feel her eyes, like sunlight on his face. His heart drummed against the wall of his chest, so loudly that he wondered if she could hear it.

She leaned closer. Rafe could hear the soft, feminine whisper of her breathing. He smelled no perfume, though. That was a bad sign. A perfumed woman approaching a man in bed usually had just one thing on her mind. That would be easy enough to manage, even with a broken leg—with a little cooperation from the lady, of course. But this female didn't seem bent on seduction. She was too quiet.

Whatever her game, it was time to end it. Rafe opened his eyes. At the same instant, he moved, striking with the speed of a diamondback. Before the girl could even gasp, he had seized her arms in his two hands. He jerked her down and forward, bringing her face to a level with his own.

Startled eyes stared into his—violet-blue eyes, as cool and translucent as sapphires, and strangely familiar. Maybe he hadn't been hallucinating after all. Or maybe he still was.

"Let me go!" she gasped.

"Not until you tell me where I am," Rafe said.

She tried to pull away, twisting hard against the grip of his hands, but he was too strong for her. When she saw that she couldn't escape, she stopped struggling. Her eyes glared at him through the tumble of her loose, tawny hair.

"Why, you stupid, addle-brained son of a baboon!" she said in a low voice. "If you want to know where you are, all you have to do is ask! There's no reason for you to behave like an animal! Now let go of me, Mr. Garrick, before I scream bloody murder!"

Half amused, half embarrassed, Rafe let her go. The little spitfire was right about his behavior, he admitted grudgingly. If anyone in this place had meant to harm him, they could easily have done it while he was still unconscious from the crash. He had acted out of instinct. Acted rashly.

"How did you know my name?"

"It's written on the lining of your jacket." She had taken a couple of steps backward, giving Rafe his first real chance to study her. She was taller than he'd first realized. Prettier, too, with a windblown mane of hair and a face that could have been stamped on an ancient Greek coin, or used to launch a thousand ships. But she was dressed like a child, in a white middy blouse and a rumpled pongee skirt. Grains of sand clung to her bare feet. Innocence was written all over her. Rafe sighed. He liked his women experienced and eager.

"I've been down on the beach watching our grounds-keepers dig your aeroplane out," she said, keeping her distance. "They were almost finished when I left to check on you." She ran a sun-browned hand through her hair, the motion pulling her blouse tight against one perfect, pear-shaped breast. Rafe felt the familiar surge of heat in his loins. Innocent or not, this female was no child.

"Not that I need have bothered," she continued in a low, breathy voice. "You seem to have your strength back, Mr. Garrick." Her straight, dark brows almost touched as she scowled at him. "What in heaven's name did you think I was trying to do to you?"

Rafe tried to laugh and winced when it hurt. Maybe

a rib or two had been cracked along with the leg. "You've got me there," he said. "I'd just awakened, you see, and I didn't quite have my bearings. I still don't have them, for that matter, so if you'd care to explain—"

"You're English, aren't you?"

"What's that got to do with anything?"

"The way you speak—you sound English," she persisted.

"All right. My parents came over on a boat from Liverpool when I was twelve," Rafe said a bit impatiently. *And they both died of typhoid eleven months later in a filthy Brooklyn tenement,* he kept himself from adding. He never made a habit of telling people his life story. People had enough troubles of their own.

"I thought so," she said. "I'm good with accents."

"Look," Rafe said, wondering if the female was stalling on purpose or if she was just naturally exasperating, "I need to know some things, like where I am and how long I've been here. And I need to know about my aeroplane. How bad is the damage? If you can't tell me, for Pete's sake, stop babbling and go get somebody who can!"

He saw at once that he had pushed her too far. Her chin went up and her nostrils flared like a blooded filly's. "You look, Mr. Garrick," she said coldly. "When your aeroplane crashed I was the first to reach it. I found you hanging halfway out of the machine with your head in the water. I held you up and kept you from drowning while the men got your legs free—and I ruined a brand-new party gown in the process. Now that you're awake and I've met you, I realize I should have saved the gown!"

With an angry swirl of her pongee skirt, she spun out of the door and was gone.

Rafe groaned. "Hey!" he called after her. "I'm sorry! Come on back!" But the silence, like the wet sand that glittered on the carpet where she'd stood, mocked him. Minutes passed, and she didn't return.

There was nothing to do but get up and investigate the situation himself, Rafe decided. Gritting his teeth, he rolled over onto his right side. Slow and easy, that was the way. Once he was on his feet, maybe he'd be able to get to the bottom of this mess.

And a fine mess it was! He remembered crashing the aeroplane, but he knew nothing about his rescuers. The girl had said the groundskeepers were on the beach, digging the aeroplane free, but what did that mean? What did these people plan to do with it, and with him? He had to find out fast.

Beads of sweat stood out on Rafe's forehead as he pushed himself to a sitting position. The pain in his ribs was nauseating. Cautiously he inspected his own body. Someone had dressed him in a pair of gray silk pajamas that were finer than anything he'd ever worn. One of the legs had been ripped open to accommodate the bulk of the splint. Under the jacket, his ribs were bound with strips of muslin. A patch of gauze dressing covered a gash on his forehead.

Well, so much for damage assessment. He could only hope the aeroplane was in better shape than he was. Bracing himself against the pain, he seized the splint with both hands and swung his legs to the floor. That was more like it. Except for his rear still being on the bed, he was almost standing. All he had to do now was get his body over his feet. Then, broken leg or no broken leg, he would walk out of here and find out what was going on.

Gingerly Rafe put his weight on his good leg and stood up. The room shimmered in front of his eyes. He forced himself to focus on the face of the mounted tiger, on the dead-cold yellow glass eyes and leathery black nose. Why would anybody hang up a dead animal anyway? Even the well-mounted ones were ghastly.

Staring into the tiger's open jaws, he gathered his resolve. The leg was well braced. There was no reason he couldn't walk on it if he was careful. Nothing was impossible. When he'd started on his aeroplane, nobody had believed he could do it. But he'd shown them all.

The tiger's face had begun to blur, its stripes curving into a moiré before Rafe's eyes. He willed the leg to move, willed himself to put weight on it. Pain was a state of mind…to hell with pain…. He leaned forward, trusting the strength of the splint. Slowly his weight came down on the broken leg….

Then pain exploded in him, shattering balance and will. The tiger's face vanished in a swirl of darkness as Rafe pitched helplessly forward. He lay still on the Turkish carpet, at the foot of the brass vase, no longer wondering or caring where he was.

Alex came out through the kitchen onto the back porch, letting the screen door slam behind her. "He's awake," she said. "I just saw him."

Maude Bromley glanced up from her needlepoint. "Oh? Is he hungry? Do you think he'd like some soup? I can send one of the kitchen girls up with a meal."

"I didn't ask him." Alex draped herself sideways across the arms of a wicker chair and fanned herself with a magazine.

"Alex, your manners—"

"He was rude, Mama. More than rude. He was awful! First he grabbed my arms. Then he told me to stop babbling. He didn't even thank me for saving his life!"

"Well, give him time, dear. He's had quite a shock. And that sedative Dr. Fleury gave him yesterday afternoon was supposed to make him sleep round the clock. You can hardly blame the young man if he's not quite himself."

"Oh, you're always making excuses for people!" Alex stormed. "For Papa, for everybody, even total strangers!"

"And for you, Alexandra. Something tells me it wasn't just Mr. Garrick who was rude. If the truth be told, young lady, you've a sharp tongue in that pretty head. If you're ever to find a good husband, you might do well to bridle it."

Maude had spoken in the gentlest of tones, her thin fingers never missing a stitch of the rose pattern she was outlining in fine, mauve wool. Alex studied her mother, trying to imagine what she had been like as a girl, long before Buck Bromley came into her life. She seemed so controlled now, as if her emotions were encased in glass. Had she ever laughed loud and openly? Had she ever cried into her pillow at night?

Maude had not married young. At twenty-eight she had been an old maid by the terms of the day, a quiet, bookish young woman who'd kept house for her widowed father and worked half days at a nearby public library. Buck had been younger than Maude, uneducated and uncouth. She had taught him how to speak properly and how to eat a six-course dinner without using the wrong fork. Aside from that, what had they ever seen in each other? Alex wondered.

"If I marry, it will be to a man who loves me as I am," she said, swinging a bare leg over the side of the chair. "Otherwise, I'll stay single, thank you."

Maude measured a strand of wool and clipped it with her tiny silver scissors. "Why should love be so important? I was in love with your father, and in the end, what difference did it make?"

The revelation caught Alex off guard. Her lips parted but she did not speak.

Maude smiled her quiet smile and resumed her needlepoint. "Some of the best marriages I know are based on suitability, not love," she said. "It's best that way, you know. When a woman is not quite in love with a man, she has…balance, let's say. She's able to keep a bit of the power for herself and look at life with her eyes open. When he hurts her—which every man does sooner or later—"

"I would never marry the sort of man who'd hurt me!"

"Time will tell, dear." Maude's needle slowed. "But a woman who's not quite in love can bear the hurt. She can tend to her own affairs and wait for the pain to pass.

She can be sensible. On the other hand, a woman who lets herself fall in love with a man gives up everything. He gains total power over her—power to dominate, power to hurt… And he'll use it. No man can resist using it." She paused to unravel a tangle in the yarn. Her fingers trembled slightly.

"Mama—" Alex reached out, hesitated, then put her hand back in her lap.

"Never give a man all your love, Alexandra. Always hold back a little for yourself, for your own survival. I know that sounds like cynical advice, but as you grow older, you'll find it to be quite sound."

She lowered her bespectacled eyes as if she'd just realized she had said too much. Feeling awkward, Alex gazed at the clouds. Her eyes followed the flight of a storm petrel. Briefly she thought of the aeroplane. How fragile it had looked against the vastness of the sky. How free.

"You're wrong, Mama," she said softly. "If I ever get married it will be for love, and nothing else."

"That's your choice, dear." Maude spoke without looking up, as if she had just closed a window in her mind. "I hope you'll be very happy."

Alex shaded her eyes and gazed toward the dunes. On the beach, half a dozen men who worked for her father had spent the morning trying to free the wrecked aeroplane from the wet sand before the tide came in. Now she could see them coming up over the rise. They were bringing the flying machine with them, half dragging, half carrying the twisted wreckage onto the lawn. Seeing it now, Alex could not help marveling that Rafe

Garrick had survived the crash at all. The craft's double wings were intact, but the front struts were crushed. The rear was askew, and the engine hung precariously from the sagging frame.

"Poor Mr. Garrick!" said Maude.

"Pooh! He got out alive, didn't he?" Alex's feigned disinterest masked a sense of wonder. This shattered wreck of wood, wire and stiffened cloth had flown in the sky. Its pilot had seen the earth as she herself had never seen it—the sweep of the land, with clustered towns and pencil-line roads; the alabaster curve of beach where land met sea; the harbor, with boats scuttling like water striders on a pond. Rafe Garrick had soared over hills and valleys. He had looked down on birds and on the sun-gilded tops of clouds.

Then, like Icarus, he had fallen out of the sky.

"If he's awake, he'll want to know about his aeroplane," Maude said. "Maybe you ought to go and tell him they got it off the beach. And while you're at it, maybe you should ask if he'd like the servants to bring him some lunch."

Alex turned her head to let the breeze cool her sweat-dampened hair. "I don't want to go back in there, Mama. He's rude. I…don't think he likes me. I don't think I like him, either."

"That's no excuse, Alexandra. Anyone can learn to keep a civil tongue."

"Someone should tell Mr. Garrick that." Alex tossed her head. "I've had my turn with him, thank you."

Maude's breath eased outward in a sigh of defeat.

"You're as strong-willed as your father! All right, I'll go and talk to Mr. Garrick, and you get ready for the tea at Mrs. Townsend's this afternoon. You really ought to bathe if there's time."

"Mama, you talk to me as if I were still five years old. I'm a grown woman. I think I'm old enough to decide whether or not I ought to bathe," Alex said.

Maude tugged at a stubborn strand of wool. "Now what did I tell you about that sharp tongue, Alex? Talk to other people the way you talk to me, and you may find yourself very sorry one day." The yarn had tangled again. Maude fell silent for a moment while she worked it free. "And while we're at it," she continued, "what's this I hear about you driving?"

"Driving?" Alex parroted the word, trying to sound innocent, though she knew it wouldn't work.

"Elvira Hodge told me she saw you flying down the road in your father's Pierce-Arrow last night. She said you must have been going at least thirty-five miles an hour."

"I like driving autos. And I like going fast."

"It isn't safe. What's more, it isn't ladylike."

"Alice Roosevelt drives."

"Alice Roosevelt also smokes. Does that mean every young girl in America should take up the disgusting habit?" Maude removed her glasses, folded the needlepoint and put it back into her wicker sewing box. "Alexandra, I'm not going to sit here and waste time arguing with you. No matter what I say, you'll do as you please. I'm going inside now to see if Mr. Garrick needs anything from the servants."

She rose to her feet, tall and pale in a dress of gray batiste, her light brown hair coiled into a double chignon and covered with a net. She closed the screen carefully as she went back into the house.

Alex watched her mother go, sorry now that she had been so difficult. Maude's life was hard enough without a contrary and willful daughter adding to the burdens of it. Alex knew. She knew it all too well.

She remembered her first year at boarding school. She'd been only fourteen at the time, and racked with homesickness. On a dreary November Saturday she had impulsively caught a train home, arriving at the station just after dusk.

Alex would never forget the look of the house that evening as she walked up the drive—strangely dark and brooding, with just one light, dimly flickering in the window of her parents' bedroom. Buck's dark green Cadillac was parked at the foot of the front steps.

The door was unlocked. Alex stepped into the cavernous foyer. "Mama? Papa?"

No one had answered, not even the servants. Alex had been close to tears before she remembered that this was the night of her mother's big charity ball. Not only would she be busy running the affair at the country club, but Mamie, the cook, and Cummings, the butler, would be helping as well.

That was when she'd heard it—the creak of a floorboard in an upstairs room, and faintly, the rumble of her father's laughter.

"Papa!" she'd whispered eagerly. She was not

alone after all. Grabbing her satchel, she'd raced up the stairs.

At the landing she'd hesitated. The upstairs hallway had been dark, the door to her parents' bedroom closed. Only a sliver of yellow light had shone through the crack at the bottom.

Trembling, Alex had listened and waited. At last her hand had crept to the doorknob, then hesitated as she heard another sound, a rhythmic creaking that sounded like a bedspring.

Then, from beyond the door, a high-pitched laugh—a woman's laugh, certainly not her mother's—had shattered the darkness.

Alex had never told anyone about the experience. It remained imbedded in her soul like a splinter, as sharp and painful as the day it had happened.

Now, gingerly, she explored the tender area. She had to understand it. Sooner or later she would likely be married. She would be vulnerable, open to the same hurt and betrayal her mother had suffered. And she was afraid.

But surely she'd have the sense to fall in love with someone kind and decent, someone who would cherish and respect her. Not all men were like her father, Alex reassured herself. Or like Rafe Garrick.

She caught her breath, stunned by the force with which the young pilot's image had entered her mind. Impressions rushed over her—standing in the surf with her arms around him, his head heavy against her breast, his dark, wet lashes lifting to give her the first glimpse of his eyes. She remembered afterward, undressing in her room, standing naked before the mirror, then picking up the sodden purple gown to touch the spots that were stained with his blood.

And only a short time ago she had come up from the beach and gone into his room. He had been sleeping— or so she'd thought. She had stood beside his bed, her eyes tracing the strong, stubborn lines of his face, the oddly attractive twist of his broken nose, the wave of dark chestnut hair that tumbled onto his forehead. A warm sense of possession had stolen over her. After all, hadn't she been the first to reach him? Hadn't she saved him from the sea? It was almost as if part of his life belonged to her.

Then Rafe Garrick had awakened, banishing all her illusions. He was not the kind of man to be possessed by her or by anyone. He was arrogant. He was quarrelsome. For all she knew, he could be out of his mind. And she would be out of her own mind as well, Alex told herself, if she had anything more to do with him.

"Alex!" Maude's stricken cry from the upstairs window shattered her thoughts. "Telephone Dr. Fleury quickly! Mr. Garrick has fallen! I fear he may be dead!"

Chapter Three

"He's coming around." Dr. Henry Fleury, a portly man in his sixties with small, neat hands and a mustache like William Howard Taft's, waved a vial of ammonia under Rafe's nose. "You needn't have worried, Maude. It looks like he just fainted. Probably tried to get up too soon. He's lucky he didn't crack his skull on that armoire or do more damage to those broken ribs."

"Thank heaven!" Maude sighed. "He was so white and so still. I really feared for a moment—"

Rafe moaned sharply and jerked his head as the ammonia vapor nipped into his senses. Alex hovered over them both, bobbing back and forth in an effort to get a closer look.

"Is he going to be all right?" she asked, truly anxious.

"Don't worry, he's a strong lad. He'll mend as good as new. But I'd recommend you keep him in bed for a few more days." Fleury glanced at Alex. He'd been the family doctor for as long as she could remember, and there was little about any of them that escaped his notice. What was he seeing now as he looked at her?

Rafe moaned again, his eyelids twitching as he inhaled the pungent spirits. Maude had found him face-down on the floor. Cummings had managed to hoist him back onto the bed, where he lay sprawled, his rangy frame filling the length and breadth of the mattress.

"That's it," said Fleury. "Wake up, lad. Let's hope that fall knocked a little sense into you. You're in no condition to be strolling about."

"Oh!" Alex gave a little gasp as Rafe's eyes opened, staring not at her but at the doctor.

"Who…who the bloody hell are you?" he muttered groggily.

"Mind your tongue. There are ladies here." Fleury scowled in mock severity. "I set your leg yesterday, and I'll thank you to stop trying to undo my good work."

"Yesterday!" Rafe struggled to sit up. "What's happened? Where's my aeroplane?"

Fleury braced an arm against Rafe's chest and used his considerable weight to keep the younger man down. "Not a word," he said firmly. "Not until you lie back and promise not to move."

Rafe's breath eased out as he lay back on the pillow. "All right," he said, grimacing with the pain in his ribs. "You've got me. I'm not going anywhere. Now somebody tell me what's going on."

"Simple enough." The bedsprings creaked as Fleury sat down on a corner of the bed. "Your aeroplane crashed offshore yesterday afternoon. You were pulled out of the wreck, barely conscious. I set the leg and gave you a sedative to make you sleep. If I'd known you'd be rash enough to get up, I'd have strapped you to the bed."

"My aeroplane—" He lifted his head, straining to sit up again.

"My good man, I'm a doctor, not a mechanic. I only know that you have some cracked ribs and a nasty fracture that won't heal unless you've the patience to rest."

"Damn the leg! Damn the ribs! How badly damaged is my aeroplane?"

There was a short silence. Maude glanced warningly at her daughter, but Alex spoke anyway.

"They just brought it off the beach. It looks like a kite that's been stomped on by the town bully," she said, her eyes watching his face.

Rafe's breath hissed out as he sank back onto the pillow, looking weary and vulnerable. "Naturally," he said in a bitter voice. "One doesn't ram an aircraft down nose first and expect it to bounce back like India rubber. Damn! If only I could have leveled it out in time!"

"You ought to be grateful you got out alive," said Fleury. "Aeroplanes can be replaced. People can't."

Rafe scowled. "People heal. Aeroplanes don't. This was the only one I had. I designed and built it myself, and there's not another like it in the world."

"The wings look all right." Alex's tone had gentled. "It's the front end that's smashed the worst. The engine's hanging loose, and the rear parts are out of kilter—"

"I want to see it!" Rafe began to struggle again. "Blast it, somebody help me up!"

"No, you don't," said Fleury, using his weight again to press him back onto the pillow. "You're to stay right here."

"How long?" Green fire flashed in Rafe's eyes. He was clearly not a man who liked being given orders.

"Until I say it's all right for you to get up." Fleury knew how to be as implacable as his patients. "A couple of days at least, maybe longer."

Rafe sighed with resignation, but his eyes glared like a tethered hawk's. Alex pressed close behind the doctor. She was leaning over his shoulder when Fleury suddenly turned toward her mother.

"Maude," he said, "you're as pale as a ghost. Come on out of here. We can sit in the parlor, you and I, while Mamie brews some good strong tea. Alexandra here can keep an eye on the young man for a while." He turned to Alex and hardened his rubbery face into a scowl. "Watch him," he ordered. "See that he doesn't move."

With that, he offered Maude his arm and escorted her out of the room, leaving Alex and Rafe alone.

"What's your name?"

Rafe Garrick's bold-eyed gaze made Alex want to squirm like a bashful child, but she forced herself to remain composed. The wretch probably wanted to make her feel uncomfortable. She would not give him the satisfaction of knowing he'd succeeded.

"My name is Alexandra Bromley. This house belongs to my parents," she answered, posting herself like a sentry at the foot of his bed.

"I'd hardly have taken you for one of the servants." His eyes glinted sardonically as he looked her up and down, openly taking stock of her face and figure. Rafe Garrick was clearly no gentleman. "Is the rest of the house as exotic as this room?" he asked.

"This is one of the guest rooms. Since most of the guests are friends of my father's—" Alex cleared her throat. Her gaze swept the room, coming to rest on the mounted tiger head, which had given her the horrors for years. She shrugged. "My father has his own tastes, as you see."

"I see." He flashed a sudden, boyish grin that was like the sun coming out. Alex steeled herself against a sudden onrush of warmth. She could not allow herself to like this man. Even the thought of liking him disturbed her.

Rafe looked at the tiger, shaking his head. "Did your father actually shoot that thing?"

"Oh, yes! From the back of an elephant, six years ago!"

"He's a big-game hunter?"

"No. Just a rich man who uses his money to buy excitement." *In more ways than one,* Alex thought, imagining for a moment how the heads of Buck's female conquests would look in a mounted collection above the fireplace. "He makes firearms. Guns and such," she said.

"Of course!" Rafe's eyebrows shot upward as the realization struck him. "Bromley and Burnsides!"

"Burnsides and Bromley—though father is all of it now. Joshua Burnsides, my grandfather, died fifteen years ago, when the company was still a small one."

Rafe didn't reply. He was gazing straight at her, his eyes as intense as two burning coals. "Help me get up,

Alexandra Bromley," he said. "I want to see my aeroplane. I *have* to see it!"

The passion in his voice was so commanding that Alex stiffened where she stood, fighting the strange impulse to do as he demanded.

"No," she protested. "The doctor ordered you to keep still, and he told me to watch you."

"Where is it?" he persisted, stirring restlessly beneath the bedclothes. "Isn't there a window, or maybe a balcony where I could at least get a look? If I can see how bad the damage is, and decide whether it can be fixed—"

"You heard me. Make one move to get out of that bed, and I'll scream for the doctor!" The ridiculousness of the situation was beginning to dawn on Alex, but she could not back down now.

"Rubbish! I'm not a prisoner. Which way is the beach?"

"Don't be a fool. It's only a machine. It will be there tomorrow."

They glowered at each other, separated by the length of the bed. "Only a machine!" he exclaimed in a low, rasping voice. "For your information, Alexandra Bromley, that tangled wreck out there is my life!"

When she only stared at him in silence, he sank back onto the pillow. "You don't know what I'm talking about," he said. "You can't know, if you've never flown. The freedom of it…the wonder…"

"And the danger?" Alex curled one hand around the bedpost. Almost against her will, her gaze traveled down the length of his body under the sheet—the broad shoulders and powerful chest, the narrow hips and lean, hard belly. Her eyes lingered on the intriguing bulge at the top of his thighs, then shifted guiltily away.

"The danger's part of it, yes. But it's more than that." His face was flushed, his eyes alive. "When you're in the sky, it's as if you've left the whole dirty world behind. There's nothing up there but you, the birds and the fine, clean air. You look down and you see the earth for what it is—little houses, little fields and factories, little people with little problems. It's like…like—"

"Like being God?" Alex's blasphemous whisper rang loud in the room.

Rafe laughed, deep in his throat. "Maybe. In a very precarious way—though I like to think that God doesn't have engine trouble or get caught in downdrafts."

"Tell me," said Alex. "When you're in the sky, don't you ever have the urge to just point the nose up and keep going, higher and higher? But no, that would be very dangerous, wouldn't it?" She laughed uneasily, conscious of his eyes on her and wondering what he was seeing. His gaze seemed to burn through her clothes. No man had ever looked at her like that. Not openly, at least.

"I did that once," he said quietly. "I climbed, and kept on climbing. It was wild, like being drunk on sunlight. I didn't want to stop, but the air began to get cold and very thin. I started to lose control—that was when I knew I had to get down." He fell silent for a moment, as if focusing on something inside himself. "I want to see my aeroplane," he said. "Just a look. Then I'll know how soon I can be flying again."

Something broke loose in Alex—a reckless, impulsive urge that had been building since she entered the room. "There's a balcony at the end of the hall," she said. "You can see it from there."

"Will you help me?" His green-flecked eyes engulfed her.

"On one condition." Alex took a deep breath. "I noticed your aeroplane has a second seat. When you're able to fly again, you must promise to take me up with you."

He scowled. "It's too risky."

"Not for you."

"Your father would have my hide."

"My father wouldn't have to know."

"And what if something were to go wrong?"

"Then neither of us would be in a position to care, would we?" Alex shrugged with feigned disinterest. "Promise me or lie there and rot. It's up to you." She turned her back on him and took a step toward the door.

"Wait!"

Alex spun around to find him laughing.

"Why, you stubborn little chit!" he exclaimed. "You'd really leave me, wouldn't you? All right. One very short flight. As soon as my aeroplane and I are mended. Now, come here and help me get up."

Alex hesitated.

"Please," he said.

She came to him, bending over the bed so he could slip his arm around her shoulders. His skin was warm beneath the thin gray silk of Buck's pajamas, his muscles solid and sinewy. His clean, leathery aroma reminded Alex of the dark brown jacket he'd been wearing when she lifted him from the water.

"Easy now," he said. "Watch the ribs." His arm lay lightly about her as he used his own strength to sit up and slide his legs off the bed. Alex was acutely aware of his closeness, the warm weight of his arm across her back, the slow, even rise and fall of his breathing.

"Here goes!" he muttered, pulling himself to his feet. Alex braced herself to steady him. Standing, he was even taller than she'd realized. Her own head did not reach the bottom of his ear. He took one step, then another, leaning on her to ease the weight on his broken leg. "You make a fine crutch, Alexandra Bromley!" His laughter stirred her hair. "Would you care to stick around till my leg mends?"

Alex groped for a clever retort and came up empty. Most of the time she felt at ease with men. She could be flippant and bitingly funny, especially when she didn't care what they thought of her. Why was it that now, when she so wanted the upper hand, she felt like a tongue-tied dolt?

Together they made their way through the door and down the thickly carpeted hall. Rafe was silent, concentrating on each step, wincing when a movement hurt him. Once he stumbled, and Alex's arm went around his waist to steady him. He was, she realized, wearing nothing at all under the thin silk pajamas.

A glass door at the end of the hallway opened onto a small balcony that overlooked the back lawn. Maude had decorated it with potted palms, hanging asparagus ferns and a pair of white wicker chairs.

"There!" Alex pointed as they reached the railing. "See, there's your aeroplane at the far end of the lawn!"

Rafe let go of her, braced himself with one arm on the railing and used his free hand to shade his eyes. "If I were only closer!" he muttered.

"Can't you tell anything from here?"

"Not enough. You were right about the wings. They don't look badly damaged. And the rear elevators can be fixed. But the engine and the propeller…" He shook his head. "I'd have to see them up close."

"Why be so concerned? You built it once. You can build it again."

"Yes. But how much time will it take? How much money?" He turned bitter eyes on Alex. "You've no understanding of what's involved—people like you, with everything at their fingertips. You don't know what it's like to go without heat in the winter, to go without cigars and haircuts and decent meals just so you can buy an engine piece by piece and put it together, so you can afford the right kind of wood for the braces, the right kind of wire, the right kind of linen canvas." His knuckles whitened on the railing of the balcony. "Damn it, how can anyone who's always had whatever they wanted understand that kind of love?"

Alex had listened quietly to his outburst, but her own indignation was building. "That's the most arrogant crock of nonsense I ever heard!" she stormed. "You think you're better than I am because you've had to struggle! You think that building an aeroplane qualifies you for some kind of sainthood! Well, maybe it does!

Maybe you are an expert on that kind of love! But let me tell you something, Rafe Garrick! You have no tact at all, no gratitude, no consideration for people at all! There are other kinds of love, and you don't seem to know anything about them!"

She whirled away from him and started for the door that led back into the hallway. Let him stay there. He could crawl back to bed by himself or shout for help. She wasn't putting up with his self-righteous arrogance another second!

She had almost reached the door when he caught her. His hand seized her shoulder with the strength of an iron vise and he whipped her back toward him. "Don't tell me what I don't know!" he muttered, jerking her hard against his chest.

His kiss arched her backward over his arm. Alex struggled against his strong hands and brutally seeking lips. Then suddenly, incredibly, she felt herself responding. A ripple of fevered excitement coursed through her as she softened against him and felt the hard contours of his aroused body through the thin silk. Her lips went molten beneath his. Her fingers dug into his flesh, clinging, demanding. Madness. It was running away with her and she couldn't stop it—didn't want to stop it.

No! Something in her was still fighting him, still struggling for control. This was insanity. He had no right!

He released her, and she spun away from him. They stood a pace apart, both of them breathing heavily. As Alex stared at him, she felt panic welling up in her body. She'd wanted a life in which there was no question of her being in control. Now, suddenly, she felt threatened. Rafe Garrick was all the things she despised in a man, all the things she had spent her life protecting herself from. And he had just violated her safe, well-ordered world.

Rage and fear exploded in her. Her hand came up and she struck him with all her strength across the face. The force of her own blow sent her staggering backward.

He did not move. He did not laugh, scowl or even wince. Only his eyes mocked her anger as he spoke. "If it's an apology you're wanting—"

"No!" Alex spat out the word. "I'd never accept anything of the kind! Not from you!"

He laughed then—bitter, knowing laughter—as she whirled toward the door. It was as if he saw through her anger, as if he knew how deeply he had stirred her, and how frightened she was of her own emotions. Damn him. Oh, damn him!

Slamming the door behind her, she hurtled down the hall. Her face burned. Her eyes stung. She wanted to hide. Damn Rafe Garrick! She never wanted to see him again!

At the landing she almost collided with her father.

"Alex, are you all right?" Buck gazed at her in surprise. He had spent the morning in the city and was dressed in a dark business suit, white shirt and bowler. He smelled of the expensive Havana cigars he smoked.

"I'm quite all right, Papa." Alex smoothed her skirt in an effort to compose herself. "Your fallen angel, Mr. Garrick, is all right, too. You'll find him on the balcony. Dr. Fleury said he should stay in bed, but I think he's well enough to leave!"

She brushed past him to go to her room, but he stopped her with a hand on her arm. "You're sure you're all right? You look flushed."

"I'm fine, Papa. A little too much sun on the beach, that's all. I was just going to my room to freshen up."

"Well, you might want to hurry it a bit. Your mother mentioned something about tea at the Townsend place this afternoon."

"Oh!" Alex gasped. "Oh, drat!" She'd completely forgotten about that ridiculous tea, but she had no desire to further upset her mother. "Tell her I'll hurry!" She flew down the long corridor to her room.

Through the glass panel in the door, Rafe saw the husky, well-dressed man staring after Alexandra for a long, thoughtful moment. Then the stranger turned, strode down the hall toward the balcony and opened the door. "So you're on your feet already!" he boomed.

Rafe was still leaning on the rail of the balcony. "You might say that," he replied. "Though I'm still not up to walking without a crutch. I was just trying to figure out how to get back to bed by myself. You'd be Mr. Bromley, right? Your daughter's got your eyes." The last was a lie. Alexandra's eyes were unlike any he had ever seen.

"Yes, I'm Bromley. You can call me Buck."

They shook hands. Buck Bromley's grip was bone-crushing in its power, as if he'd exercised his hand to strengthen it. "So you've met Alex," he said. "She was the first one to reach you in the water. I was the second."

Rafe rubbed his chin, which was shadowed with

whisker stubble. "I'm much obliged to you for taking me in after the crash," he said.

"We could hardly have left you lying on the beach," Buck laughed. "Besides, I'm a curious man, and I'm intrigued by you and that machine of yours. I wouldn't mind keeping you around until you and the aeroplane are both mended. It would be worth it, just to see what makes the thing fly."

Was this an invitation? Rafe wrestled with his pride. He'd been keeping his plane in a small hangar at the Hempstead aerodrome. He could make minor repairs there, but its cramped space wouldn't do for rebuilding the craft. And there was his tiny flat in the Bronx with its shared bathroom, as well as the motorcycle he wouldn't be able to ride to the airfield until his leg healed. Staying here would solve any number of problems. But he'd be damned if he'd ask for charity.

"I owe you a debt," Rafe said. "I repay my debts. I don't like being obligated to anyone."

Bromley's eyes narrowed appraisingly. "If you're talking about money, forget it," he said. "As you see, we're not exactly paupers here."

Rafe shook his head. "Most of what I have is tied up in that aeroplane out there. But I'm not useless. I can work."

"With a broken leg?"

"I had two years at M.I.T. Mechanical engineering. I'm good with engines. Got fine marks in draftsmanship—"

"You've no family?" Buck interrupted him.

"None. I was fourteen when my parents died. I've been on my own since then."

"M.I.T., you say." Buck's tone was cynical. "I never went to college myself. Never needed it. But why only two years?"

"Time. Money. I wanted to build my own aeroplane and fly it. I couldn't do that, work to support myself and still go to school. I had to make a choice."

Buck followed Rafe's gaze out across the sun-splotched expanse of lawn to the rise of the dunes where the aeroplane had been dragged and abandoned. "Was it the right choice? Was the end worth it?"

Rafe's jaw tightened. He didn't answer.

"Come on," said Buck. "I'll help you back to your room. Tomorrow we'll go out and look at your machine, eh? We'll see how much of it can be salvaged."

He took Rafe's weight on the right side and they moved off the balcony and through the door, into the hallway. In spite of the pain and difficulty, Rafe strove to move mostly under his own power. He had never been one to lean on others.

They had almost reached Rafe's door when Alex came out of her room at the far end of the hall. She was dressed in pale yellow organdy trimmed with ribbons that fluttered when she moved. Her hair, freshly brushed, shimmered loose over her shoulders. Rafe caught his breath as, ignoring them both, she swung around the newel post and skimmed down the stairs in her low-heeled slippers.

Bromley, he realized, was studying him again, with that slit-eyed gaze of his. "So you like her, do you, lad?" he murmured. "Of course you do. What man wouldn't?

She's beautiful...intelligent...spirited, and heiress to everything I own. Isn't that right?"

Rafe swallowed, taken aback by the man's bluntness. "She's all that, and well beyond my reach, sir," he said carefully. "As a pilot and a man, I know where my limits lie."

"Do you, now?" Bromley's left eyebrow slid upward. "Judging from the way you look at her, I'm not so sure you do. My daughter isn't to be trifled with, Garrick. I'm saving Alex for a man who can keep her in style and keep her in line—a man who'll breed grandsons to run my company someday. And since he won't get a penny of her fortune, he damned well better have money of his own—preferably old money and plenty of it. Do I make myself clear?"

"Perfectly." Rafe had no problem with anything the man had said. He'd had his share of experience with rich, spoiled, beautiful girls. They liked playing around with the bad boy from across the tracks, but in the end it came down to one thing—money. Alexandra Bromley was prettier than most, but she was no different from the others and this was no time for games.

From here on out, Rafe resolved, he would put that blistering kiss out of his mind and give the girl a very wide berth. For him, Buck Bromley's daughter could be nothing but trouble.

Chapter Four

Maude's white-gloved hands clung helplessly to the side of the open-topped Pierce-Arrow. "For heaven's sake, slow down, Alexandra! You're going to get us both killed!"

Alex eased back on the gas pedal of the elegant black automobile. "I was only going thirty miles an hour, Mama. It's a perfectly safe speed."

"Not on this road. You can't see around the curves. You could hit a cow or a horse or even a child. And you're throwing up dust all around us. Use some sense!"

Alex sighed. Since Felix, the chauffeur, had gone home sick, it had fallen to her to drive herself and her mother to tea at the Townsend mansion. Ordinarily she would have been pleased. But after her encounter with Rafe Garrick, she was in no condition to sit behind the wheel of a dangerous machine.

"What's bothering you, dear?" her mother asked. "I've never seen you in such a state."

Alex's only answer was a tightening of her jaw. The

yellow ribbons on the shoulders of her dress streamed out behind her like battle flags. Her heart was pounding like the pistons on a runaway locomotive. She could still feel the burn of Rafe Garrick's kiss on her lips and the raw, masculine pressure of his body against hers. Heaven help her, she didn't want to feel this way. She didn't want him, or any man, to have this kind of power over her. Anything would be better than ending up like her mother—a faded ghost of a woman, cowed and emotionally frozen.

She swerved to avoid a white leghorn rooster that ran squawking out of her path. The auto lurched as its left front wheel hit a pothole. Alex cursed. Her mother gasped.

"Alexandra! Wherever did you learn to talk like that?"

"Where do you think?" Alex sighed and eased back on the gas again. The engine slowed to a chugging purr. "Maybe you should learn to drive, Mama. It isn't hard at all. In fact, it's fun. I could teach you today, on the way home from the tea."

"Goodness gracious!" Maude shook her head. "I could never do that! What would people think?"

"They wouldn't have to know. Papa wouldn't even have to know. It could be our secret."

"The very idea! What will you think of next, Alexandra?" Maude sank lower in the seat, adjusting her protective veil as if she didn't want to be recognized. "It strikes me that you have too much time on your hands and too much energy for your own good. A husband and babies would take care of that. Elvira Townsend's nephew will be at the party today. He has excellent prospects, and he's keen on meeting you. Promise me you'll be nice to him."

"All right, Mama. I promise not to scratch or bite or spit."

"You're impossible!"

"Yes, I know." Alex swung the auto through the wrought-iron gate and up the long drive toward the palatial neo-Roman-style house. Her organdy gown felt damp and itchy, and her lips burned where Rafe Garrick's stubble had roughened her skin. She could feel the beginning of a headache moving upward from the clenched muscles at the back of her neck.

It was going to be a very long afternoon.

Rafe was sitting up in bed, wolfing down a late lunch of cold ham, deviled eggs and fresh, buttered rolls when Buck Bromley strode into his room.

"Feeling better?" Buck placed a bottle of Jack Daniel's and two crystal glasses on the nightstand. Then he sat on a leather-covered side chair next to the bed.

"Much better, thanks," Rafe said, trying not to talk with his mouth full. "Maybe I was just hungry." He put his fork down and gazed levelly at his host. "I meant it when I said I didn't like being obligated to anyone. I plan to pay you for every bite of this meal, and all the rest as well."

"All in good time, lad." Buck leaned backward, clasping his broad, hairy hands around one knee. His tan trousers were cashmere, Rafe noticed, and the white shirt he wore with the sleeves rolled up was exquisitely tailored linen, the monogram on the pocket sewn in ecru silk.

"Cigar?" Buck opened a drawer in the nightstand and produced a gold case, monogrammed with the same ornate *B* that graced his pocket. "After you've finished your meal, of course."

"I've just finished, thanks." Rafe put his tray to one side. It had been, literally, years since he'd had a really good cigar between his teeth. That was just one of the sacrifices he'd made to get his aeroplane built.

"Here." The golden lid swung open at a touch. The molasses-sweet aroma of expensive tobacco filled Rafe's nostrils. He selected a cigar and balanced it between two fingers for a moment, enjoying its weight, its perfect symmetry. Then, with exquisite deliberation, he placed one hand between his lips.

The match flared in Buck's hand. Rafe inhaled, feeling the mellow, bittersweet sensation trickle through his body. He closed his eyes, savoring the moment.

"We hauled your aeroplane into the old carriage shed out back," Buck said. "From the looks of it, I'd say you're damned lucky to be alive."

Rafe's eyes opened. Buck was watching him intently, the way a cat watches a bird. Rafe sucked pensively on the cigar, meeting the older man's gaze head-on. Life had taught him to be wary, and right now his instincts were on full alert.

"I looked at the engine," Buck said. "Can't say as I know horseshit about aeroplanes, but I do know engines. I've never seen anything like it."

"It's a rotary engine," Rafe said. "You can buy them in France these days, but I built this one myself, with my own improvements. It's the best of its kind. I only hope it's not ruined."

"It's hanging loose from its mountings, but aside from that it doesn't look too bad." Buck lit his own cigar. The smoke obscured his face as he puffed on it. "If you can fix the framework, your aeroplane ought to fly again."

"No matter." Rafe tried to sound disinterested, though inwardly he sensed that his whole future could be teetering in the balance. "I could build another one from the same design. I could build a hundred if I had the resources."

"The design is your own?"

"All mine." Rafe directed a puff of smoke toward the ceiling. "I've got others on the drawing board, mind you, including a monoplane, but this is the only one I've perfected."

"Perfected?" Buck snorted with laughter. "Then why the hell did it fall out of the sky with you?"

"I don't know. But as soon as I'm able, I mean to find out." Rafe tapped the end of the cigar into a black onyx ashtray. "For whatever it's worth, that flying machine out there has taken me as close to heaven as it's possible for a man to get!"

"Not as close as a few of the women I've known could take you, I'll wager."

"Have you ever flown?" Rafe asked earnestly.

"Not in an aeroplane!" Buck's strong white teeth flashed in a devilish grin.

Rafe put the cigar down on the edge of the ashtray.

"My aeroplane's built to carry a passenger. Why not let me take you up after it's repaired? I promise you, it's an experience like you've never—"

"Oh, no. Not me, lad. Flying is for young fools with nothing to lose. Me, I've got responsibilities. I've got plans. Listen." He leaned toward Rafe. His eyes gleamed like the eyes of the mounted tiger head on the wall behind him. "Last fall I made a trip to Germany. Shook hands with Kaiser Bill himself, the cheeky bastard! But that was the least of it. The real high point of the trip was a visit to Essen and a tour of the Krupp Works!"

Buck puffed furiously on his cigar, sending up volcanic clouds of smoke. "Lord, you'd have to see it to believe it! Miles of factories! More than fifty thousand workers! It was a city in itself—a damned kingdom! The Arms of Krupp!"

Rafe knew something of the world. He knew that the Krupp family had built their empire on the finest Bessemer steel ever made. Though they produced everything from railway wheels to razors, the fame and glory of the Krupps was vested in one thing: the manufacture of weapons.

Buck's eyes glazed for a moment, as if the mind behind them were making a brief journey to some secret place. Then, chomping down on his cigar, he impaled Rafe with a gaze that was frightening in its intensity.

"That's my dream, lad," he rasped. "An empire. A family dynasty like the Krupps. That's why I can't go risking my neck in some damned flying machine. I want to live to see that dream come true!"

He paused long enough to twist the stopper off the bottle of Jack Daniel's and pour two fingers of whiskey in each of the glasses. He handed one to Rafe, who was staring at him in disbelief. The man sounded slightly mad. But madmen with money weren't to be taken lightly.

Buck took a swallow of the amber liquid. "Sounds damned far-fetched, doesn't it? But I know a few things you don't." Buck paused long enough to wet his lips. "Between you and me, I'm just wrapping up a deal with Uncle Sam. Burnsides and Bromley will be making rifles for the United States Army! What do you think of that?"

"Impressive," said Rafe.

"But that's just the beginning," Buck continued. "My engineers are already drawing up plans for light and heavy artillery pieces, mortars, shells and rockets."

"Pity for you there's no war going on," Rafe remarked cynically, at once regretting his words. War had never made much sense to him, but the last thing he wanted to do was antagonize this man.

"True." Buck had taken Rafe's comment at face value. "But mark my words, the way things are going in Europe, there will be. Get a real man like Teddy Roosevelt back in power, instead of a fat pantywaist like Taft. That's when you'll see America show her fighting spirit!"

"And that's when you'll build your empire."

"That's right. I'm already expanding my factory. If war comes—*when* it comes—we'll be ready to produce more than rifles! We'll be cranking out motor-mounted artillery, howitzers, shells, bombs—"

"Have you thought about the role of aeroplanes?

They could be useful for reconnaissance in a war." Rafe spoke casually, letting the words drop as if they weren't of vital importance. There, he'd opened the door. The next move would be Buck Bromley's.

Buck leaned backward in his chair and studied Rafe through narrowed, calculating eyes. Maybe his mind was formulating questions, Rafe thought. Maybe he was pondering the use of the aeroplane in modern warfare. Maybe—

Buck spoke, and his words caught Rafe completely by surprise.

"What do you think of my daughter?" he asked.

"What?"

"Alexandra. You look like a man of the world. What do you think of her?"

Rafe took a deep gulp of whiskey. Its mellow fire burned its way down his throat as he thought of Alex in his arms. He remembered the supple curve of her back as she struggled against him, the warm pressure of her hips against his groin, the rush of passion that had brought him to a throbbing arousal in an instant.

He remembered her soft, full mouth, resisting at first, then clinging to his in wild surrender. He remembered the fury in her violet eyes as she struck him, the sting of her palm on his cheek. He had deserved that slap, Rafe knew. He should never have crossed the forbidden barrier between them. He should never have touched her. But, by heaven, he wasn't sorry.

What did he think of Buck Bromley's daughter?

"Well?" demanded Buck.

Rafe drained the glass. "We were talking about aeroplanes."

"I know. And I asked you what you thought of my daughter."

"Oh, she seems to be a bright girl," Rafe said cautiously. "A bit headstrong, but I suspect she gets that from you."

Buck laughed, a hard, humorless sound. "Forgive me, but I'm just airing my fatherly frustrations. You do find her attractive, right?"

Rafe stared down into his empty glass. "Yes, in a coltish sort of way. Frankly, I prefer my women a bit more…shall we say, ripe?"

"Aha! I understand," said Buck. "I'll even admit to liking them that way myself. But Alex is hardly what you'd call a child. She's twenty—old enough to be married and cranking out the next generation."

Rafe willed away the urge to mention the aeroplane again. Clearly, this was a time to listen.

Buck opened the whiskey again and refilled both glasses. "The girl's driving me crazy. You'd think she'd have suitors swarming all over her. But she doesn't show any interest in the men she meets. I've begged her, threatened her. She claims she doesn't want to get married. She wants to live her own life. Live her own life! Can you imagine? What would you do with a girl like that, Garrick?"

"Maybe you should stop pushing her so hard," Rafe suggested cautiously. "Give her a little more time to come around."

"More time? What the hell for?" Buck's fist came crashing down on the nightstand. "Damn the girl! She doesn't give a rat's ass about my sweat, my blood or the future of the company! She wants her own life on her own terms. The selfish little—"

His words fell off into muttering as he rose to his feet and began pacing the carpet. Abruptly, he stopped.

"Never mind. My daughter's my own problem." He sat again and picked up the whiskey glass. "Garrick, I'm not a man who believes in mincing words. I have a business proposition for you!"

"Business?" Once more Rafe was caught off balance. They'd been discussing Buck's daughter, not his business dealings.

"I'm a fair judge of men," Buck continued. "There's something you want from me, and I'm pretty sure I know what it is. Maybe I can help you out."

Rafe waited, trying to look disinterested. Inside he was churning. If Buck was talking about the aeroplane, then the dream he'd worked for, starved for, for so long, could be within reach. He felt light-headed, afraid that if he reached out everything he wanted so badly would be snatched away from him.

"I'll get to the point," said Buck. "The empty carriage shed where we stashed your aeroplane has a furnished room on the second floor. It's yours while you work on your machine. You can take your meals with the family, or in the kitchen if you'd rather not stand on formality."

Rafe weighed the offer. It wasn't what he'd hoped for,

but it was bloody tempting. If he accepted, he wouldn't need to rent new work space and move the aeroplane or dig into his hard-earned savings to live while his leg healed. But at what cost? Nothing in this world came free, especially from a man like Buck Bromley.

He picked up the cigar, studied it a moment, then put it down again. "Thanks for your generosity, but the answer is no. I won't be a charity case."

"Charity has nothing to do with it," Buck said. "I'd like to buy your aeroplane with exclusive rights to its design and any others you might create. You'd be working for me."

Something dropped in the pit of Rafe's stomach. This wasn't what he wanted. He wanted backing for his own company. He wanted the freedom to manufacture and sell his aeroplane under his own name and to improve the design as he went along, like Glenn Curtiss and the Wright brothers were doing. But maybe that was never going to happen. Maybe this was the best he could hope for. Right now everything he owned was tied up in a pile of twisted wreckage. His back was against the wall, and Buck Bromley knew it.

Rafe toyed with his whiskey glass, trying to look nonchalant. Behind that facade, all was turmoil and chaos. He wanted the success of his aeroplane more than he'd ever wanted anything in his life. He ached for it, hungered for it, and now it was within reach. All he had to do was grasp it.

But he was a proud man with a sense of his own worth. He knew the value of the aeroplane he'd built, knew its power, knew its beauty. He knew the sweat and sacrifice that had gone into its making.

Buck Bromley knew none of those things. To him, the aeroplane was just a pawn to provide him with the means of getting what he wanted—the services of someone who might otherwise emerge as a competitor. For a pile of garbage, Buck's offer would have been the same. And what he had in mind would be like making a deal with the devil. Rafe would never be his own man again.

"Well, what's your answer?" Buck's manner was cocky. He seemed sure of what Rafe's reply would be.

Rafe took a deep breath. "Wouldn't it be smarter to wait and see how the aeroplane performs?"

Buck's eyes narrowed.

"You hardly know anything about my aeroplane," Rafe said. "You don't even know if it's any good. The risk you'd be taking—"

"What the hell has risk got to do with it?" Buck snapped. "I'll make you a fair offer, and if the damned machine won't fly you'll make one that does. What's wrong with that?"

"Just this," Rafe said. "You're welcome to back my aeroplane as a partner, but it's not for sale. Lord knows I could use the money. But I want to be my own boss, not an employee. I won't bargain away my future, and I won't be bought. Not for any price."

Now he'd done it. Rafe braced himself, waiting for the explosion. But Buck only laughed.

"Proud young whippersnapper, aren't you? I wasn't so different at your age. But I had the sense to recognize an opportunity when it came along. That, and hard work, got me where I am today." He poured another two fingers of Jack Daniel's into each of the glasses. "Take your time, then. The shed's yours in any case, and I can give you some kind of work if it'll ease your fool pride. My offer stands open in case you change your mind."

"That's very generous of you, sir." Rafe picked up his glass and swirled the golden liquid cautiously.

"It's Buck, not sir. Hell, I'm as common as you are!"

"All right, Buck," Rafe said, knowing he might be making a fatal mistake. "You've been very good to me. But since I won't be working for you, I think it best that I move myself and my aeroplane somewhere else. As soon as I can get out of this bed on my own, I'll do just that."

Buck's florid color darkened. "You're afraid that if I can't buy the design I might steal it from you? Is that what you think?"

"Frankly, that hadn't even occurred to me." Rafe set his glass on the nightstand. "I just feel that since we can't come to an agreement, I shouldn't impose on your hospitality any longer than I need to."

A vein twitched in Buck's temple. "Of all the mule-headed—"

The words froze on his lips as Maude Bromley stumbled into the room. Her face was chalky. One hand hovered at her throat.

"Buck." Her voice quivered. "The police are downstairs. They just brought Alexandra and me home."

"What the devil—?" Buck gasped.

"The auto. She wrecked it—ran it off the road five

miles out of Glen Cove. It's mired to the running boards. You'll need to go and see about getting it out."

Buck was on his feet. "Is Alex all right?"

As if in answer to his question, a tattoo of light, rapid footfalls echoed along the upstairs hallway, followed by the impassioned slam of a door. Buck glanced in the direction of the noise, then rushed headlong out of the room. His wife bustled after him, closing the door behind her and leaving Rafe alone.

Rafe picked up his whiskey and drained the glass. His head ached, his leg throbbed and he felt as if he'd crashed into the middle of a lunatic asylum.

If he didn't get out of here soon, he'd could end up as hell-ridden as the Bromleys.

Chapter Five

The aeroplane lay in the cavernous space of the warehouse like a crumpled bird in a child's pasteboard box. The sight of it jerked a knot in Rafe's stomach. Compared to this utter calamity, his fractured leg was nothing.

A week after the accident, Rafe had dragged himself out of the Bromley mansion and paid his friend Jack Waverly, who ran a construction firm in Queens, to haul the shattered aeroplane by wagon to Minneola. They'd been lucky to find this empty warehouse with an office and bathroom facilities inside. The rent wasn't cheap but since Rafe could move out of his tiny flat and live here for the duration it would be affordable enough. Best of all, he wouldn't need to worry about traveling back and forth.

His leg and ribs still pained him. It wouldn't be easy getting around the place on his crutches, but at least he'd disentangled himself from the Bromleys. Now he could concentrate on his work.

"How long will it take you to fix it?" Jack, who was

blond, husky and affable, gave Rafe work when he wasn't flying. Now he stood beside Rafe with his hands in the pockets of his coveralls.

"That'll depend partly on how the engine's fared. I won't know until I've tried to start it up. But the framework's wrecked. I can salvage a lot of pieces, but it's going to need a complete rebuilding and new canvas to boot. I'll start on that as soon as you bring my tools and spare parts."

"I'll bring your clothes and bedding and a few groceries along with the rest," Jack said. "I'll bring your motorcycle, too, but you won't be able to ride it anywhere with that cast on your leg."

"Thanks. I'll get better over time. It's the aeroplane I'm concerned about."

"Well, the damned aeroplane won't get fixed if you starve to death. I'll wager you got spoiled staying with those rich folks, all that champagne and that caviar on those fancy little crumpets. Now you'll be living on beer and cheese sandwiches, if you even remember to eat."

"I'm just glad to be out of there and well enough to work."

"Well enough is debatable, friend. But I know you've got a one-track mind, so I'll be off now to get your things. It'll take me a couple of hours. Sure you don't want to come with me?"

Rafe shook his head. He needed some time alone before he pulled himself together and went to work. It would take a calm, clear mind to transform a twisted mass of wreckage into a creature of the sky once more.

As Jack's wagon rolled out of sight, Rafe sank onto a wooden crate. The past week had been draining. The crash and his injuries, the long hours of inactivity and the constant tension in the Bromley household had left him with frazzled nerves. The work of rebuilding his machine loomed as all but insurmountable. But he was grateful to be back in action again. If he could move, he could work. If he could work, he could accomplish whatever was needed. He was going to be all right, damn it, and so was the aeroplane.

"Hello."

The throaty voice startled Rafe, but only for an instant. He knew without turning around who had spoken. "Hello yourself, Miss Alexandra Bromley," he replied. "After what you did to your father's fancy new motor car, I'm surprised your parents would let you out of your room."

"I'm not a child," she said, leaning her bicycle against the door frame. "And the auto wasn't that badly damaged, just stuck in the mud. All it needed was a good scrub and polish. What a pity your own machine won't be so easy to fix."

Rafe turned the crate around to look at her. She was wearing a divided skirt with a plain white blouse that clung damply to her skin, showing glimpses of the lace camisole beneath. Her cheeks were flushed, her hair tousled by the morning breeze. He had the distinct impression that if he were to bury his face against the warm hollow of her neck, her scent would be the pungent, earthy aroma of a woman's sweat. He let his gaze roam up and down her body, not caring whether she noticed.

"You've come a long way just to argue," he said. "It's a pity you're not a man. I could put you to work."

She answered him with a toss of her head. "Don't let my being a woman stop you. There's nothing here that I'm not smart enough to learn."

Rafe squinted up at her, dazzled by the light that fell through a high window to play on her caramel-colored hair. "Cocky little chit, aren't you? I could be tempted. But your parents would skin me alive if you came in with grease stains on those dainty hands of yours."

"Dainty? Ha!" She extended her hands for Rafe to see. They were large for a woman's, the fingers long and tapered, the nails cut short, the skin tanned to a golden apricot color. "These hands can saddle and bridle a horse, drive an automobile and do a lot of other things that I have yet to try—maybe even fix an aeroplane. Or maybe…" Her violet eyes impaled him. "Maybe even fly one. So don't sell me short, Mr. Garrick, or you might be very sorry."

Rafe chuckled, warmed by her outrageous cheekiness. He'd sworn not to go near her, he reminded himself. But on this anxiety-ridden afternoon, with his spirit shrouded in gloom, Alex Bromley was a ray of pure sunshine.

"Come here and make yourself useful," he said, struggling to stand. "I need a close look around the aeroplane and these crutches are murder on cracked ribs."

She eyed him suspiciously, the color rising in her

cheeks. "Haven't we been down this road before? As I recall, the last time I did crutch duty, you ended up getting your face slapped."

"I earned that slap fair and square," Rafe said. "But this time I promise to behave. On my honor."

"Your honor!" She cast him a scathing look. "I'd count more on a he-goat's honor than on yours!"

"Then resolve to live dangerously, Miss Bromley." Rafe proffered his arm.

She hesitated, head high, nostrils flaring. "Will you let me help work on your aeroplane?"

"Your father would have me skewered."

"My father doesn't have to know."

Rafe sighed. "Maybe a little. No promises."

"No promises?" Her eyebrows shot up. "Well, then, goodbye, Mr. Garrick. Have a lovely day." She turned on her heel and strutted toward the door, her hips twitching in a way that almost made Rafe groan out loud. He cursed under his breath. Let the brat go, he admonished himself. But even as he willed himself to heed the warning he heard his voice calling out to her.

"Blast it, Alex, come back here!"

She turned slowly, her violet eyes sparkling with mischief. "Will you show me how your aeroplane works—without snarling at me even once?"

Rafe exhaled sharply. "Come on, then. Help me over there."

The task that had loomed as tedious with Buck became something entirely different with the man's daughter. Alex's frame fit perfectly beneath Rafe's arm as she took his weight. The warmth of her softly curved body, resting against his side, was pleasantly arousing. But it was her intelligence that intrigued him most. Her questions were insightful, her grasp of scientific principles swift and sure. Pity she was a mere woman. Otherwise Buck Bromley's only child might have made one hell of an engineer, or even an aviator.

They made a slow half circle of the wreckage, Rafe thinking aloud as he assessed the damage to his precious machine. The rudder and rear elevators were fully intact. But everything forward of the wings was hopelessly shattered. The wings themselves would need new ailerons and a complete rebracing. Maybe while he was at it, he could improve the warping mechanism, making the craft easier to maneuver in the air.

The engine appeared worse off than he'd hoped. He wouldn't know how much damage it had sustained until he could take the thing apart. To say the least, he had his work cut out for him.

"You don't look very happy." Alex was gazing up at him, her eyes deep violet in the shadows. "Can you rebuild it?"

"I'll have to. The only question is how much time and money it will take. Right now the picture's not a pretty one."

"Papa would help you with the money if you asked him to. He has his faults, but stinginess isn't one of them."

Rafe's sharp intake of breath triggered a jab of pain along his battered rib cage. He clenched his teeth, waiting for the agony to pass. "I've been down that road with your father, thank you. He offered to buy the aeroplane…and me. I turned him down."

"You turned him down!" She stared up at him, amazement written across her face. "Why, for heaven's sake?"

"I won't be owned. Neither will my aeroplane. I want to start my own company, under my own name, like Glenn Curtiss here in New York, or Louis Blériot in France. My dream. My designs. My decisions. That's what I'd be giving up if I were to accept your father's offer. Does that make sense to you, or do you think I'm crazy?"

She pursed her very kissable lips. "Knowing Papa, I'd say you were very brave. Get on his bad side, and he'll eat you alive."

They moved on around the aeroplane, her body warm, damp and fragrant against his side. Rafe struggled to ignore the ripples of awareness that shimmered through his body. Despite his good intentions he was becoming aroused. "Your father's been very generous," he said. "I'd like to find a way to repay him. But as for the rest, I'm on my own now."

Her eyes narrowed. "I'm sure he'll think of something. Papa usually finds a way to collect what he's owed. Have you seen enough?"

"Just get me back to the crate and you can go. I could use some quiet time to think. Besides, it might not look so good, your being here with me. The last thing I'd want is to sully your reputation."

"My reputation?" She gave a derisive little snort. "Don't be so quaint, Rafe Garrick. This is 1911, not the 1860s."

He was leaning on her shoulder as she turned back

toward the wheelchair. The sudden shift threw them both off balance. Stumbling, they reeled sideways toward a dusty workbench that was built along one wall. They came to rest against its edge, their arms clutching each other, their legs entangled and their faces a hand's breadth apart.

Rafe could feel her trembling, but she didn't pull away from him. She seemed to be waiting, her eyes like purple smoke, her wet lips slightly parted. His heart had begun to race, pumping blood and heat to his already swollen groin. He fought to stay clearheaded. This had to stop. It had to stop now.

"I could kiss you silly right now, Alex Bromley," he muttered. "But you're not going to let me try. You're going to help me back to that crate. Then you're walking out of here, and you're not coming back."

She drew away from him with a gasp. "Of all the insolent, presumptuous—"

"Listen to me!" he rasped. "I'm not in your class of people. If I were to lay so much as a hand on you, it would drag you right down into the mud. So get out of here! Go live your privileged, pampered life and leave me alone!"

"Oh, you—!"

For an instant Rafe thought she was going to slap him again. Instead she spun away and stormed out of the warehouse, leaving him perilously balanced against the workbench. He watched her go, flashing glimpses of white and khaki as she pedaled away. It was for the best, he told himself as he hobbled painfully back toward the crate. The fastest route to ruin would be for him to get caught dallying with Buck Bromley's precious daughter. For Alex, the consequences could be even worse.

Buck was right. It was time she found some nice blue-blooded boy, got married and started raising the next generation of Bromley heirs. Her ripping beauty and untamed spirit made her a magnet for trouble, and right now the girl had far too much time on her hands.

Alex's hair had come unpinned. As she pedaled blindly through the trees one flying lock snagged on an overhanging limb. The sudden pain jerked her to a halt.

Battling tears, she reached up to unsnarl the mess. What was it about Rafe Garrick that always incited her to fury? The man had no more manners than a wild bull, let alone any regard for her feelings. Whatever thought crossed his mind, he spoke aloud, even if it was rude and hurtful.

She should have slapped his face again, harder this time. But the effort would have been wasted. Rafe would never have given her the satisfaction of knowing she'd hurt him.

Alex struggled impotently to free her hair, jerking on the sharp twig and tightening the tangle. Why did this have to happen now, when all she wanted was to get away from the miserable man.

He probably thought she'd come looking for *him*. But it was the aeroplane, not its pilot, that had compelled her to ride all the way to Minneola and find the warehouse.

She'd been awestruck from the first moment she'd seen Rafe's flying machine. In the days that followed, after the broken frame had been dragged into the carriage shed, she'd stopped by each morning to gaze at it and touch it as if trying to discover a hidden magic power. Then Rafe's friend had come with his wagon and hauled the wreckage away. When she'd asked, he'd told her where he was going. On impulse, she'd decided to follow. Maybe she would find Rafe there. Maybe he would help her understand how a framework of wood and canvas and a metal engine could carry a man into the sky.

Walking around the aeroplane while Rafe explained its mysteries had been pure bliss. Alex had imagined herself working at his side, stringing the wires, tightening the screws, applying varnish with loving strokes of the brush. But her dream had met with a cruel awakening. She was a woman—and that was the only way Rafe's tradition-clouded eyes would ever see her.

How like Rafe it was not to understand her. To him, she was nothing but a silly, decorative creature, flirting with the lower classes for her own amusement. He was blind to what burned inside her—the hunger to learn, to experience, to feel.

Something in her loved the aeroplane—every curve, every angle, every junction of its parts and the way they came together in gravity-defying beauty. The flying machine had captivated her. She would never be satisfied until she'd ridden it into the clear, free air.

How could she explain all that to a man like Rafe?

Frustrated, she seized the snagged lock of hair in her fist and yanked hard. Her eyes welled as it ripped free of the limb. Damn Rafe Garrick. If he'd understood her, or even pretended to, she would have fallen in love with him on the spot.

When she'd tumbled against him, her arms clutching him for balance, his knee thrusting between her legs, her belly had clenched with hot, wet need. The hunger to be kissed by him, to feel and smell and taste every part of him, had been like a cry inside her. Only when he'd turned her away with a coldness as brutal as a blow had she come to her senses.

Rafe had the power to break her heart. If she let him, he would destroy her, just as her father had destroyed her mother. And like her father, he would not even be aware of what he'd done.

Dragging her feet, she walked the bicycle back toward her house. By now the sun had burned away the last of the morning fog. A flock of kittiwakes rose and circled above the Sound. Through the trees came the faint clatter of the gardener's boy mowing the grass. Another soul-numbing day had begun—a day of yearning to be in the one place where she wasn't welcome.

She would never give up her dream of the aeroplane, Alex vowed. Let Rafe Garrick do his damndest to drive her away. She would wear him down with sheer persistence.

If there was one thing she was good at, it was getting what she wanted.

What she wanted now was the sky.

Rafe's leg was slowly growing stronger. The doctor had insisted that he wear the heavy plaster cast for at least two months. Now, after nearly three weeks, he was getting used to its cumbersome weight. The soreness in his ribs had eased as well. He was able to hobble around the carriage shed with the aid of a single crutch.

Jack had brought all his things here from the grim little flat in the Bronx—his books and papers, his tools, his clothes, his drafting table, the spare parts for the aeroplane and his motorcycle. The latter sat idle now in the corner of the warehouse, covered with a canvas tarp.

By day he worked on the aeroplane, sweating rivers in the midsummer heat. At night he hunched over the lamp-lit drafting table, sketching plans for Jack's construction projects. Rafe was good at his work. But the urge to fly was a fever in his blood. Earthbound, he counted the long summer days with impatience. Only when his aeroplane and his leg were whole would he be free to take to the skies.

Work on the aeroplane was crawling along at a frustrating pace. The fragile craft was broken in so many places that it would have been easier to build a new framework from scratch. Even the engine would require straightening and welding before it could be filled with petrol and tested.

What made everything worse was his own bloody awkwardness. If some needed part or tool happened to be out of reach, maneuvering to get it could take precious minutes. Rafe did his best to stay organized, but on some days he spent more time fetching than fixing.

Now, on a molten July afternoon, Rafe paused in the tightening of a wheel nut to wipe the sweat out of his eyes. Even with the large doors open, the warehouse was an oven. Only the pump water he drank liberally from a nearby bucket kept him from fainting in the heat.

He glanced up to see a flash of green coming down the road. Warning bells went off in his head as he recognized Buck's older Cadillac, which Alex often drove.

Moments later she appeared, dressed in immaculate tennis whites and carrying a wicker picnic hamper on one arm. Her face was flushed, her hair curling in damp tendrils around her face. She looked healthy and clean and so beautiful that Rafe was almost afraid to breathe on her.

"Hungry?" She opened the hamper and waved it enticingly, letting the mouthwatering aromas float toward him. "I've got fried chicken, potato salad, watercress sandwiches and lemon tarts. Are you up for a picnic, or are you too busy working on your precious machine?"

The growl that rumbled from the depths of Rafe's stomach reminded him that he hadn't eaten since dawn. But spending time with Alex was an open invitation to trouble. He sighed.

"I'm too busy and way too dirty for company, thanks. But if you don't mind leaving some of that food in a napkin on the workbench, I'll wolf it down when I get to a good stopping place."

Her eyes danced with mischief. "Oh, no, you don't. It's a picnic or nothing. And since you obviously have better things to do, I'll be on my way. Ta." She swung back onto the path and walked away with that hip-twitching strut that made his blood boil. Damn it, he was starving. He was at her mercy and the minx knew it.

"Alex!" Her name roared out of him. She took three more steps, hesitated, then turned around very slowly.

"Did you want something, Mr. Garrick? Don't tell me you've changed your mind."

He glared at her, knowing he'd been shamefully out-flanked. "You win, lady. Just give me a minute to clean up."

Alex wrinkled her nose at him. "I really should make you beg," she murmured.

The bucket was nearly full. Rafe picked it up, raised it high and let the water trickle down over his hair, his face, his bare shoulders, his bare chest…

Alex watched him, her stomach fluttering. Building up the courage to approach him had taken weeks. Even now it was all she could do to keep from flinging down the picnic hamper and bolting back to the car. She kept her eyes on him, her face fixed in a confident smile. The last thing she wanted was to let him know how nervous she was.

Prickles of heat flowed into her thighs as she watched him. His ivory skin was lightly dusted with freckles. Beneath that skin, his muscles rippled like a panther's. Where the cold water ran over his chest, his nipples had shrunk to taut mauve beads. Droplets glistened on a virile dusting of reddish-brown hair that broadened across his pectorals, then narrowed to an intriguingly thin path that vanished beneath the line of his worn leather belt.

Something clenched low in her body, a warm, liquid weight that pulsed and tightened, leaving her breathless. As Rafe sluiced the water off his skin, she forced her gaze toward the aeroplane. After all, wasn't that her reason for being here?

The flying machine lay like a patient in surgery, its parts scattered over the crumbling concrete floor. With Rafe's impaired leg, working alone was bound to be difficult. Maybe by now he'd be ready to accept her help. That hope had brought her here today, with a peace offering from the Bromley kitchen.

Slicking back his hair with his fingers, Rafe reached for the chambray shirt he'd tossed on the workbench. The faded indigo fabric clung to his wet skin, outlining the contour of every muscle. Alex willed herself not to devour him with her eyes.

"So have you figured out where we're going to have our picnic?" he asked, fastening two of the buttons and leaving the rest open.

"I have. There's a patch of shade out back. Take your crutch and come with me."

He hobbled alongside her as they circled the outside of the building. In the back was a grassy strip overhung by willows. The shade looked deliciously cool.

"Here we are. Wait…" She pulled a light cotton quilt from one side of the hamper, shook it open and spread it over the grass. "There, now. Have a seat."

He lowered himself awkwardly toward the quilt, using the crutch for balance. For a moment he teetered and almost fell. Instinctively, Alex reached out to steady him. His eyes blazed so fiercely that her hand dropped to her side. Getting what she wanted from this man wasn't going to be easy.

She took her time spreading the feast on the picnic cloth. He watched her hungrily, a bead of water trickling down his unshaven cheek. He looked wild and dangerous, a wounded creature ready to attack or fly at the slightest provocation.

"So how was your tennis game?" he asked as she handed him a plate of food. "Judging from your outfit, I'd guess that's what you've been up to."

"Fine. I played at the club against Allen Throckmorton. Beat him three times. Do you play?"

He snorted as if she'd asked him whether he liked to crochet. "Never had the time. My parents died when I was fourteen, and I've earned my own keep ever since."

"So how did you end up building your own aeroplane?" Alex nibbled at her potato salad.

He shrugged, taking the time to wolf down a hunk of chicken breast. "It took years. As soon as I heard what the Wright brothers had done I wanted to fly. But I was barely grown, a lad with no money and no prospects. By the time I'd worked my way through two years of engineering school, I knew that if I waited any longer I'd be left in the dust. I had a mountain of notes and drawings. I'd spent time hanging around airfields to get my pilot's license and study the different kinds of flying machines. I knew how they worked, and I knew I could make a better one. Eventually I did. But I could only afford to build one aeroplane. What I need is the backing to build multiple models, each one an improvement over the last, enough of them that a single crash won't set me back months—months I can't afford to lose."

Alex nodded her understanding. She could only imagine the pride that had forced Rafe to turn down her father's offer.

Lifting a bottle of blackberry wine from the hamper she filled two small crystal glasses and handed him one. "How's the work coming along?" she asked cautiously.

He muttered a curse and quaffed the wine in a single swallow. "It's this damned leg that's holding me back. When something I need is out of reach and I have to hop or hobble or crawl to get it…" He shifted restlessly. "What I need is a pair of ten-foot arms. That would do the trick, wouldn't it?" He flashed her a bitter smile.

"What about your friend, the one with the wagon?"

"Jack has his own business. I might borrow him for some of the heavy work, like remounting the engine, but I could hardly ask him to stand around like a fool just to fetch things for me."

"You could ask *me*." Alex could feel her heart fluttering inside her rib cage.

"Ask you?" He stared at her. "For what?"

"To stand around like a fool and fetch things for you. I'd do it gladly, just to watch you work on the aeroplane."

Rafe refilled the glass and downed the wine in a single gulp. "Are you trying to seduce me, Miss Alexandra Bromley?"

Alex stifled an indignant gasp. "What kind of question is that?"

"A question that needs to be answered. I'm not in the market for a spoiled brat like you, and I don't have time for silly games."

"Of all the—" Alex forced herself to swallow her pride. At this point, she had nothing to lose. "It's not you I'm interested in, you conceited oaf! It's your machine. When you explained how it worked, I was fascinated. I want to know more. What's wrong with that?"

He scowled at her beneath fierce eyebrows. "You're a woman."

She battled the urge to smash the wine bottle over his thick male head. "Am I stupid? Am I helpless? I was the first one to pull you out of that wreck, and you've never even thanked me for it!"

"Your parents wouldn't like it."

"My parents are too busy to care. And today they aren't even home. I could help you all afternoon."

His gaze raked her spotless white tennis clothes. "Look at you! You'd get filthy!"

Alex had anticipated that argument. With a flourish, she reached into depths of the hamper and pulled out the permanently grease-stained mechanic's coveralls she'd stolen from the clean laundry basket.

"The chauffeur will never miss them," she announced with a triumphant grin.

Chapter Six

When the engine fired up for the first time, a flock of pigeons exploded from the roof of the warehouse. The sudden roar echoed off the walls, unnaturally loud in the cavernous space. Alex held her ears, but to Rafe the song of his engine was a symphony.

He listened to the familiar droning cadence, ears straining for the slightest discord—a misfiring piston, a loose bolt, a leaking seal. He would test it again many times, both on and off the frame, before he took the aeroplane back into the sky. If any part was less than perfect the engine's voice would tell him.

Alex was clapping her hands in triumph, shouting something he couldn't hear above the sound of the engine. He'd grown accustomed to the sight of her in the baggy coveralls, her hair piled carelessly atop her elegant head, her face smudged with dirt and grease. Even then she looked beautiful. And lately he'd caught himself looking at her far too often.

Over the past three weeks, Alex had proved herself many times over. She'd progressed from fetching and carrying to such tasks as lubing the engine bearings with castor oil and positioning nuts and bolts for him to tighten with the wrench. By now she'd begun to anticipate what was needed, almost as if she could read his mind.

On days when she was busy elsewhere, or when her father was at home, the work crawled and the warehouse became a gloomy, sweaty cave where nothing seemed to go right. Rafe often caught himself wondering how he'd ever managed without her.

Satisfied with the first test, he switched off the engine. Alex was grinning at him, her face spattered with oil.

He'd seen no sign of the petulant hellion he'd met six weeks ago. When she was working on the aeroplane she purred with contentment.

"So how did the engine sound to you?" she asked anxiously. "Is it ready for the sky?"

"Not by a long shot. But neither am I, as long as I have to clump around in this miserable cast." He reached for a thin length of scrap wood, thrust it into the narrow gap between the cast and his leg and scratched the itch that had been driving him crazy for the past twenty minutes. "I'm beginning to think seriously about bending over and chewing the damned thing off with my teeth!"

Alex giggled at the picture his words had created. "How much longer?"

"Fleury says two more weeks. Then he'll give me some exercises to make the leg stronger. It may never be as good as new but I won't care as long as I can fly.

Now, get me that wrench over there, the red-handled one on the floor. Then we'll see what we can do about this knocking piston."

She strode over and bent to pick up the wrench, giving Rafe a full view of her enticingly rounded bottom. Despite his best intentions he felt a rush of heat to his groin. Alex's behavior had been wholly circumspect over the past three weeks…and she was quietly turning him into a wild man.

Only his broken leg and an iron will kept him from charging across the floor, seizing her from behind and molding her against his fevered body with his hands clasping her breasts and his aching erection cradled between her firm little buttocks. Even that wouldn't be enough. He'd dreamed too many times of sweeping her up in his arms, dragging her into the warehouse office and flinging her onto his cot. The fantasy of having Alex under him, her long legs wrapping his hips as he thrust deep inside her, filled his nights and tortured his days.

Rafe had never had any trouble getting women. More often than not, they'd pursued him and practically hauled him into their beds. All he had to do was pick and choose. But not this time. He'd never wanted a woman the way he wanted Alex Bromley—and for all the good it did him, he might as well be living in a bloody monastery!

Alex handed Rafe the wrench, picked up the oil can and waited as he opened the heart of his engine. His hands were like a surgeon's, strong, steady and sensitive. She loved watching them. Her eyes traced the shape of each long finger, lingering on the little nicks and scars and the clipped fingernails with their neat white moons. It was his habit to start each workday with clean hands. But on most days, by the end of the first hour his palms and fingers were a road map of black lines where grease and dirt had worked into the creases.

At times like this, when they were standing close together and he was absorbed in his work, it was all she could do to keep from reaching out and touching him. She imagined stroking the back of his hand where a beam of sunlight turned the dusting of light brown hairs to gold, or placing her thumbs at the back of his neck and massaging his tired shoulders. Sometimes the temptation was so strong that Alex could barely keep her hands under control. Only the echo of Rafe's damning question held her in check.

Are you trying to seduce me, Miss Alexandra Bromley?

The memory of those cold words served as a reminder that, beyond her help with his aeroplane, Rafe wanted nothing to do with her. He had drawn a firm line between them. Cross that line and the happiest time of her life would be over.

She hadn't told either of her parents about these secret days with Rafe and his flying machine. Maude would be horrified to learn how her daughter was spending her time. And Alex didn't even want to think about what Buck would say. Since he maintained that women were put on earth to keep house and serve as vessels for a man's seed, he'd likely be livid. And of course, he would believe the worst of Rafe.

"Right here with the oil. Just a little." Rafe indicated a brass washer at the base of a stubborn bolt.

Alex complied with a few careful drops. "When will you be mounting the engine on the frame?"

"Not until the very last. And since I'll need Jack to help me hoist it, you'd best not be around to celebrate the final bolt."

Alex sighed. "But you *will* keep your promise, won't you?"

"Promise?" He shot her a sharp glance. "What promise?"

"That first day, when I helped you out of bed to see your aeroplane, you promised you'd take me flying."

Rafe shook his head. "Flying is risky business, Alex. Anything can go haywire up there. For myself, I'm prepared to take chances. But if something happened to you…no, I couldn't live with that."

"What are you saying?" Alex dropped the oil can, spilling a thin drizzle onto the stain-splotched concrete. "You promised!"

"I was out of my head that day. Sorry, but my final answer is no."

She glared at him. "It's because I'm a woman, isn't it? Would you take me flying if I were a man?"

"Not if your father was Buck Bromley, I wouldn't. What if something went wrong?"

"If something went wrong, you wouldn't have to worry about Papa because we'd both likely be dead. That's a risk I'm willing to take."

"Well, I'm not." He lowered the wrench and stood

facing her. A drop of sweat trickled down his cheek. His eyes shot flecks of green fire. "You're too important to too many people, Alex. Including me."

For an instant her heart seemed to stop. Did he mean what he'd implied—that he actually cared about her? Or was he just playing with her emotions? As things stood, she couldn't afford to give him the benefit of the doubt.

She drew herself up, her grease-smeared face inches from his own. "Of all the conniving, underhanded—"

"What the devil's going on here?" a familiar voice rumbled.

Rafe, who was facing the open door of the warehouse, had gone rigid. Alex turned around to see her father looking like the wrath of God in his cream linen suit. Alex had understood that he was spending the day in the city. Evidently Buck had decided to change his plans.

His scathing eyes looked Alex up and down. "Go home and clean up, Alexandra. Wait for me there," he said.

Alex stood her ground. "None of this is Rafe's fault, Papa. I wanted to help him. I *made* him take me on. And all we've done is work on the aeroplane. I swear to—"

"Be quiet, girl!" Buck's voice cut her off like a slap. "Get out of those god-awful coveralls, go home and find your mother. I'll deal with you later."

"Go on, Alex." Rafe tossed her a towel to wipe her face and hands. "I'll take responsibility for this."

"No, Rafe, it wasn't your doing," Alex argued. "I *wanted* to work on the aeroplane. I bribed you with food. I wouldn't take no for an answer." She swung toward her father. "Please, Papa, he didn't do anything wrong."

Buck ground his teeth. "Alex, you could wear down the Rocky Mountains. Go on, girl. Mr. Garrick and I will settle this man to man."

"Man to man! Ha!" Alex spat out the words as she spun away and stalked off to her bicycle, every step quivering with unspent rage.

Instead of going back to the house, she took a side road that led to the beach. The sand crumbled away beneath her grease-stained sneakers as she climbed the crest of a dune and huddled there with her hands clasping her knees.

Rafe had said he'd take responsibility. The wretched man hadn't even defended her. He hadn't said a word about how much help she'd been to him. He'd simply tossed her a towel and dismissed her, just as Buck had.

Run along now, like a good little girl, and we'll settle this man to man.

Alex picked up a piece of driftwood and flung it down the dune. Man to man, indeed! Damn them! Damn them both! For all she cared, they could beat each other to a bloody pulp!

Biting back sobs, she buried her face against her arms.

Buck unfolded his white linen handkerchief and laid it along the dusty edge of the workbench. Only then did he lean back and regard Rafe with narrowed eyes. A smile tugged faintly at his mouth as he reached for his inner pocket.

"Cigar?"

"Not now, thank you," Rafe said. "And I wouldn't

advise you to smoke, either. I've been running the engine and there'll be petrol fumes in the air."

Buck's face brightened. "The devil, you say! You've got the thing running? Let's have a listen!"

"In a minute, sir. First, about your daughter—"

"It's Buck, not 'sir.' And don't trouble yourself about Alex. She's an impulsive girl, and she can be as persistent as a gnat. I only wish she'd been born a boy. She has all the qualities I'd want in a son. Unfortunately…" His voice trailed off.

Rafe felt as if the ground had shifted under his feet. He'd expected a blast of fatherly rage. But Buck Bromley's responses never failed to throw him off balance. What did the man want from him? Clearly there was something. Otherwise the man would be giving him the devil for spending time with his daughter.

"You have my word that I didn't lay a finger on her," he said. "She's been helping me work on the aeroplane. That's all. And she's done a damned good job. You'd be proud of her."

"I'll be proud of her when she's married and cranking out babies every nine months. Meanwhile, it's not doing a damned thing for her prospects if she's spending her days over here working as your grease monkey. Maude tells me there's a young man who's very interested in Alex, but he complains that she's rarely available when he wants to spend time with her. Guess why?"

Rafe doused a surge of hot emotion. "I understand. And I wouldn't want to interfere with your daughter's prospects, as you say."

"I knew you'd see things my way. If you need an extra hand you're welcome to borrow one of my kitchen boys. They'd likely jump at the chance to help you." Buck grinned. "But that's not why I'm here. You turned down my first offer to buy your machine. I have a better offer for you."

"A better offer?" Rafe was instantly on alert. Accepting Buck's last "offer" would have been tantamount to selling his soul.

"I'll listen," he said. "But understand, I've had inquiries about the aeroplane. There may be other offers on the table." It was a lie, but Rafe knew he had to strengthen his position any way he could.

"Well, hear me out before you decide." Buck cleared his throat. "I've been doing a lot of reading about aeroplanes. Some pretty smart people think they're the way of the future. The industry is bound to grow fast, and the man who gets a running start with a good product stands to make a lot of money."

Rafe suppressed the urge to comment. At this point, the less he said the better.

"Here's what I'm proposing," Buck said. "I'd like to create a new division of Burnsides and Bromley—an aviation company with you in charge as a partner, not an employee. I'd put up the investment. You'd contribute your designs and your time. You'd have twenty-five percent ownership in the new venture."

Rafe willed himself not to react like a trout taking a baited hook. The offer wasn't everything he wanted. It wouldn't give him his own company and the freedom to run it as he chose. But it was a solid beginning. He'd be a fool not to take it, especially if he could negotiate better terms.

"I can do better someplace else," he said. "Fifty percent, and I keep the rights to my designs."

Buck's eyes narrowed. "Forty-five percent, and you keep the rights to anything we haven't built. Now, do we have a deal?"

Again Rafe hesitated, weighing his options. Buck's share would give him control. But that was something he wouldn't give up under any conditions. And the rights issue was only fair. All in all, Rafe knew it was the best offer he was going to get.

It wouldn't have to be forever, he reminded himself. Once the new division was doing well he could sell out his share and use the profits to start a company of his own. That was what he really wanted. This chance would give him a start on his dream. "I'd need to negotiate the fine points with your lawyers, of course," he said. "But all right, it sounds fair enough."

"Fair enough?" Buck sputtered good-naturedly. "Hell, man, you just committed highway robbery! Let's hope this venture makes enough money to keep us both happy!"

"One more thing," Rafe said. "The name."

"I take it Burnsides and Bromley won't do. Bromley and Garrick? How does that sound?"

"Garrick and Bromley. Why should you care as long as you're making money?"

Buck sighed. "What the hell. All right. I'll get my lawyers on the contract and clear out some work space for you at the factory. You can move your machine there whenever you like."

"Thanks. For now it'll be easier to work on it here. Moving it might do more damage. Once it's flying again, we can build a hangar and clear off a runway by the factory."

"Sounds fine to me. Let's shake on it." He pumped Rafe's hand, then drew back. "One thing I need to make clear. We may be partners, but Alex isn't part of the bargain. Her mother's set on her marrying somebody who can pull her up the social ladder. So don't get any ideas. Understand?"

"Absolutely. Your daughter's a fine girl, and I wish her the best." Rafe's gut twinged. He was just beginning to realize how much he would miss her.

"We're having a little party at the house next weekend," Buck said. "Just a few guests for cocktails and dancing. I'd like you to join us. We could make it a celebration for the new venture."

Rafe stifled a groan. There was no way he felt up to hobnobbing with the Bromleys' social set. "Sorry, but I've never been much for parties," he hedged. "Mostly I just stand around with my hands in my pockets, or else I drink enough to make an ass of myself. Either way, I wouldn't be fit company for your friends."

"You'd be doing us both a favor. My friends are interested in you and your aeroplane. Some of them watched you fall out of the sky. Impress them, and word will get around. Who knows where it could lead for our venture?"

Rafe had to admit his new partner had a point. "I hope it's not black tie. I have one suit, and it's brown."

Buck laughed. "Summer whites are de rigueur, as my wife would say. And it so happens that a cousin of Maude's, who's about your size, left a white summer suit in our guest room last year. I'll have the laundry maid give it a good pressing and unpick a seam to accommodate your cast. And since you can't drive, I'll have Felix pick you up. So now, what do you say we try starting that engine again? I want to hear how she runs!"

Rafe lingered in the shadows at the edge of the terrace, working up the intestinal fortitude to join the Bromleys' "little" party. From where he stood, there appeared to be somewhere between forty and fifty guests, along with a four-piece band. Strings of Japanese lanterns hung from poles set up in the shrubbery, illuminating the refreshment table and the dance floor. The brassy strains of "Alexander's Ragtime Band" drifted on the warm summer night.

One look at the crowd told Rafe he was going to feel as out of place as a turkey in a yard full of peacocks. The borrowed white linen suit was too tight across the shoulders. One of its legs showed a dark stocking and a sturdy brown oxford. The other leg parted to reveal the cast, which had become grimy over the past weeks. He should have worn his own clothes. At least he'd have looked like himself, and not some second-class pretender trying to fit in where he didn't belong.

Aside from the servants he could see no one he knew

except Maude. Gowned in faded lilac, she was deep in conversation with two other matrons near the refreshment table. Buck was nowhere to be seen.

Rafe's eyes searched for, then found, Alex. She was on the dance floor in the arms of a tall, blond young man who looked as if he'd never lifted anything heavier than a tennis racquet. Maybe he was the Throckmorton fellow she'd mentioned weeks ago, or the interested suitor who'd earned Buck and Maude's stamp of approval. Quite possibly he was both.

Alex looked ravishing. The silver threads woven into her misty gray gown caught the lamplight, reflecting rainbow glints of color. The strings of tiny silver beads that were twined into her upswept hair matched her dangling earrings. The bodice of her dress was cut in a daring V, baring her exquisite throat and neck.

She was looking up at her partner as they danced, her lips curved in an enticing smile. Rafe felt his jaw clench as he watched the pair. Since that fateful encounter with Buck, Alex had vanished from his workshop and from his life. He'd ached with missing her.

Coming here tonight had been a mistake. Rafe had sensed it earlier. Now he knew it.

"I take it you're not up for dancing. Are you up for company?" The smoky voice at his elbow startled Rafe. He glanced down to see a petite woman in black lace smiling up at him. She was no longer young—forty was his guess. But she'd taken bloody good care of what God had given her. Her china doll skin was skillfully rouged, her dark hair curled to frame a saucy face. Her ample curves were cinched and molded to hourglass proportions.

"So you're the man who tumbled out of the sky," she said. "I was there when it happened, but of course you wouldn't remember. Maybelle Hampton. Mrs. Roger Hampton the third, if you really need to know. You can call me May."

She took a sip of gin from the crystal goblet in her hand. The hefty diamonds that glittered on her plump fingers appeared real. "You can't be comfortable standing there with your crutches," she said. "There are some seats on the other side of the terrace. We can pick you up a drink on the way. What's your poison?"

"Scotch on the rocks, thanks." Rafe moved along on his crutches, allowing his newfound friend to open a path through the crowd that milled around the refreshment table. He glimpsed Buck, who greeted him with a wave and a knowing wink before vanishing among the guests. Clearly he judged Rafe to be in good hands.

And that was all right, Rafe told himself. Maybelle Hampton sounded tipsy and was likely up to no good, but he was grateful for the rescue. Anything was better than standing on the fringe of the party, grinding his teeth as he watched Alex twirl around the floor in another man's arms.

"Here we are." May indicated a wicker settee with forest-green striped cushions. "We'll have a nice view of the dance floor while we visit. Ah—and here's your drink."

A waiter had appeared like a genie with an assortment of drinks on a tray. May plucked Rafe's scotch from the selection and held it while he lowered himself to his seat. "That's better," he said, accepting the drink. "Where's your husband tonight, May?"

"Oh, Roger had other plans. He usually does." She took a seat beside him, a little closer than necessary. "I've learned not to let it stop me from having a good time. Know what I mean?" Her satin-slippered foot nudged his leg. Yes, Rafe did know what she meant. He'd lived like a damned monk since his aeroplane had crashed the Bromleys' garden party, and here was a willing, attractive woman right beside him—a woman out for a few laughs with no strings attached. Why the hell not?

The band had segued to a mellow rendition of "Moonlight Bay." Rafe saw Alex's partner draw her closer. The scotch burned a path down his throat as he swallowed. Why the hell not, indeed?

Alex stumbled over her own foot as she glimpsed May Hampton sliding a possessive hand onto Rafe's knee. Clearly there was one thing on the woman's mind—and likely on Rafe's mind as well. But then, why should she care? They were both adults, and Rafe's personal life was none of her business.

So why was she fighting the impulse to charge over to the settee and yank May's black hair out by its graying roots? Rafe was a big boy, damn him. And he was getting along fine without her.

"A penny for your thoughts, Alexandra." Allen Throckmorton's hand tightened on the small of her back. She'd met him at Mrs. Townsend's tea, and he was everything a well-bred young man should be—polite, cultured, moderately ambitious, handsome in a bookish sort of way and utterly boring. Since the tea he'd been pursuing her in his own diffident way. Maude had begun dropping none-too-subtle hints that Allen was the best catch her daughter could hope to find. Buck was less enthusiastic, but even he was ready to see her married and breeding grandsons that might inherit a spark of his own fire.

In Alex's eyes, one thing made Allen worth considering. She couldn't imagine him hurting her the way Buck had hurt her mother. He was too gentle, too decent and too well-behaved. In short, he was everything Rafe Garrick was not.

"Alexandra?" Allen had paused at the edge of the dance floor. His delft-blue eyes gazed at her adoringly. "You haven't spoken a word in the past fifteen minutes. Where have you gone off to?"

Alex blinked up at him. "I'm sorry. It's been a long day, helping Mama get ready for the party and all. I must be a little tired."

"That's too bad. Have you got a headache? Can I get you some punch? Do you want to sit down?"

She shook her head. "If I sit down I might fall asleep. Let's just keep dancing."

"Your wish is my command, my princess." He chuckled at his own witticism and swung her into the dance once more. Over his shoulder Alex could see Rafe on the settee with May. She was leaning toward him, her dark head tilted like a pretty little bird's. Whatever she was saying, Rafe seemed to be lapping it up. Well, fine. If he wanted to get cozy with an older, experienced woman who made no bones about the state of her marriage, it was no skin off her nose.

But why did he have to do it here, right in front of her and all creation? Didn't the wretched man care that he was making her miserable?

May's diamond-encrusted hand was edging up Rafe's leg, approaching his crotch. Surely she would not…not in public! Alex forced her eyes away from the spectacle. For all she cared, Rafe Garrick could go to hell!

"I could do a lot for a man like you," May purred in Rafe's ear. "Push the right buttons, honey, and you could name your own terms. And I'd see to it that you had a nice apartment and clothes that didn't make you look like a fugitive from a rummage sale. Have you ever worn a really fine, tailored suit with a silk shirt and tie?"

While she chatted, her fingers did a casual spider-walk up Rafe's leg. As they neared their target Rafe gently lifted her hand aside. Whether out of simple propriety or because he wasn't responding, even he could not be sure. Maybe his real reason was the glimpse he'd caught of Alex's eyes blazing at him from across the floor. She'd looked as if she wanted to tear a strip out of his hide. In his present frame of mind, he'd be willing to let her. He'd take a furious Alex over a compliant May Hampton any day of the week.

"What is it, honey?" May had failed to take the hint. "Do you need a refill on that scotch?"

Rafe sighed. "Sorry, May. You're a right fine lady, and I'm sure you've got what it takes to make a man happy. But I'm not open to that kind of offer. I won't be kept—or owned. Not for any price. So, if you don't mind…"

She made a sucking sound as he set his glass on the pavement, fumbled with his crutches and lurched to his feet. This whole evening had been a mistake. The longer he stayed, the worse it was likely to become.

Crossing the terrace, he took the path that wound through the trees to the garage. With luck, Buck's chauffeur would be nearby. He would find the fellow and ask to be driven back to the warehouse.

Rafe had progressed a few dozen yards and was hoping he'd made a clean getaway when he heard May's voice behind him.

"Stop right there, you arrogant, self-righteous bastard!"

Rafe turned around to see her standing at a bend in the path, her fists clenched on her hips. "Nobody walks away from May Hampton!" she snapped. "Not unless they want to be very, very sorry! I've got connections, buster. One word to the right people and you won't be able to peddle that precious machine of yours to a kiddies' amusement park!"

Rafe sighed. "Don't read so much into this, May. You're a gem of a lady and we had a nice talk. Can't we leave it at that and be friends?"

"Friends?" She hissed like a she-cat. "It's that spoiled rotten little Bromley chit, isn't it? I saw the way you were looking at her, all calf-eyed and moony. Maybe you think you can marry her and tap into all that Bromley money. But she's out of your league. Buck Bromley's going to auction off his little prize bitch to the highest bidder, and you won't have a chance in hell!"

"That's enough, May," Rafe said in a taut voice. "You can say anything you want about me, call me all the nasty names in the book. But Alexandra Bromley's off-limits. Not another word."

May laughed, a harsh, humorless sound. "Why, you poor, dumb sap! You're in love with her, aren't you?"

The words hit Rafe like a gut punch. He'd been sexually attracted to plenty of women. But Alex Bromley challenged, prodded and infuriated him, stunned him with her beauty and floored him with her intelligence. Even when she was driving him crazy, he craved her like an alcoholic craves whiskey. But love her? Lord, he'd have to be out of his mind for that.

"You don't know what you're talking about," he growled.

"I know more than you think I do," May lashed out at him. "If that girl doesn't destroy you, her father will. Take it from someone who found out the hard way."

Rafe gazed down at the petite, defiant figure. The moonlight fell on her painted face, casting lines and shadows into stark relief. He had judged her too harshly, he realized. Maybelle Hampton was a wounded woman. She was fighting for her life with the only weapons she possessed.

"I understand," he said gently. "Forgive me, May. You're a wise woman and I wish you the happiness you deserve."

"Happiness is bullshit, honey. The sooner you learn to accept that the better off you'll be." She turned away and, with admirable dignity, sauntered back toward the gaily lit terrace.

Rafe stood looking after her, his gut churning. He'd taken the coward's way out, leaving the party at the first setback. He'd be smart to go back, introduce himself and please Buck by talking about the new venture. But no, he was finished for the night. If he went back to the terrace, he would spend most of his time looking at Alex, torturing himself as she floated around the floor with a suitable young man—one who was everything Rafe would never choose to be.

He would go back to his makeshift room at the warehouse, get out of this monkey suit, dig around for something to read and go to bed. With luck he might even be able to sleep without imagining Alex in his arms or remembering the sight of her grease-smeared face grinning at him over his engine.

Swearing under his breath, he dug one crutch into the gravel and used the other to swing his body around in the direction of the garage. The evening couldn't end soon enough to suit him.

He'd gone no more than a dozen paces when a slender figure emerged out of the darkness ahead of him—a figure in a flowing, silvery gown.

Rafe's mouth went dry as he recognized Alex.

Chapter Seven

Alex stood trembling on the path. After what she'd heard, it had taken all her courage to step into sight. And the way Rafe was staring at her, his body frozen in mid-stride, didn't exactly bolster her confidence.

"What are you doing here?" he asked in a none-too-friendly tone. "What happened to Golden Boy?"

Alex fought the urge to turn and flee. She should have known he'd be cruel. "Maybe the same thing that happened to Maybelle the Man-eater," she retorted with a toss of her head. "So, does that make us even?"

His breath rushed out. "You heard?"

"Yes. Everything." When she'd seen him leave, and seen May go after him, she'd excused herself from the dance to trail them shamelessly through the trees. Her heart had soared when May had accused Rafe of being in love with her, and plummeted when he'd denied it. But what now?

Her gaze swept over him. "You look awful in that suit," she said.

"I know. And you look like a goddess."

Heart pounding, she forced herself to walk toward him. His hands were gripping the crossbars of his crutches, so she simply stood in front of him and placed her palms on his chest. He gazed down at her, desperation flickering in his eyes.

"Bloody hell, Alex," he muttered.

His crutches clattered to the ground as he caught her close. His kiss was crushing, almost brutal in its hunger. Alex opened eager lips to invite the thrust of his questing tongue, drowning her senses in the wet roughness, the light whiskey taste, the warm, clean, living breath of him. Her hands circled his neck, raking the tangle of his hair as she pulled him down to her. Wet-hot with need, she pressed upward on tiptoe, arching to mold her hips to the bulging hardness that had risen between them. He moaned, curving her in against him as his mouth devoured her lips, her eyelids, her throat.

Heaven help her, she wanted him. Propriety and ruination be damned. She wanted to give herself completely to this man, now, tonight, before the chance was gone.

"Alex…blast it, Alex we've got to stop…" They were off balance now, teetering sideways as he fought for equilibrium on his one good leg. Pulling away, Alex braced him to avoid a fall. They stood facing each other in the moonlight, both of them breathing hard.

"Hand me my crutches," he muttered thickly. "Maybe if we walk awhile we'll come back to our senses."

"I'm not sure I want to come back to my senses." She gathered up the crutches and returned them to his hands.

Rafe adjusted the crutches under his arms and swung forward on the path. His silence told Alex that she'd spoken too soon.

Troubled now, she fell into step at his side. Through the darkness behind them she could hear the strains of a slow waltz. An unvoiced phrase, echoing the music, drifted through her mind.

"Many a heart that is breaking, after the ball…"

"You know we can't continue with this, don't you?" Rafe asked.

"You mean, you don't want to."

"No, I mean we *can't*. As May so astutely put it, you're out of my class, Alex. You're accustomed to the best of everything. If I could offer you the life you deserve, I'd fall on my knees and ask you to marry me right now. But as things stand, that's out of the question. Your father's told me he wants you to marry old money and the social standing that goes with it."

"You wouldn't have to marry me to have me," she said, shocking even herself.

"Don't even think about it, Alex. You're hardly the sort of girl for an affair. The last thing I'd want is to be responsible for turning you into a ruined woman."

"Why not?" Alex kicked at a rock on the path. "Frankly I've always envied so-called ruined women. They've got nothing to lose. They can do anything they please, without a care for their precious virtue."

"Now you're talking nonsense."

"Am I? If I were ruined, no respectable man would have me. I could go off to someplace like Paris or London, maybe become an artist or a writer or an explorer. Who knows, I might even take a lover. I'd be free, and I'd owe it all to you!"

"Stop it, Alex. You're thinking like a child. Maybe you should go back to the party."

"Not yet." She fell silent beside him. Did she really mean the outlandish things she'd just said, or was it only her shattered pride talking?

A breeze fluttered through the grass, lifting the sheer overlay of Alex's gown. Only when she felt its coolness on her damp cheeks did Alex realize she'd been quietly weeping.

"You can't imagine what it's like, being the prisoner of other people's expectations," she said. "You think I have everything. But Papa wouldn't even let me go to Europe with my friends this summer. I might as well be locked in a dungeon!"

"Aren't you being a bit melodramatic?" The edge in Rafe's voice cut her like a razor. "I know women who spend twelve hours a day hunched over sewing machines or cannery lines just to put food on the table. They'd be happy to trade places with you."

"There you go again!" she snapped. "You're the first person I've ever met who was snobbish about being poor! Do you think I chose to come into this world as Buck Bromley's only child?" Spinning toward him, she seized the shoulder of his jacket. "Take me flying, Rafe. Just once. If you won't make love to me, give me that, at least. Something pure and beautiful and perfect that I'll always remember sharing with you!"

"Alex—" Hesitation pulled him away from her but she was relentless.

"Please, Rafe. Is that so much to ask? If you care about me at all…"

He sagged in defeat. "All right. Just once. But only a short flight, and only after I've flown the aeroplane enough to make sure it's safe."

"You promise? For real this time?"

"I promise, blast it. You can have it written in my blood if you insist. But not a word to anyone, you hear?"

"Yes! Oh, yes!" Alex flung her arms around his neck. Rafe kept his hands on his crutches. Already he was resisting her. That, Alex knew, was not likely to change. Rafe was too proud and too strong-willed to give in to mere emotion. But at least she'd achieved one small victory. She would be going into the sky with him.

"Alexandra!" The wispy voice drifted from the direction of the terrace, barely penetrating the darkness. "Alexandra, are you out there?"

"Oh, drat, it's Mama!" Alex whispered. "I'll circle back through the kitchen and come out through the house. She'll never know I was with you."

Rafe shook his head, laughing in spite of himself. "What a little conspirator you are! You'd make a fine spy, Alex Bromley."

"I would, wouldn't I?" Alex grinned back at him, then flashed off toward the rear of the house. The rest of the evening was bound to be a bore.

But for now, the heady euphoria that swept through her with every breath was all she needed. Rafe had promised to take her into the sky. For tonight, that was enough.

By the time Rafe and his aeroplane were healthy enough for flight, summer had ripened into late August. For both man and machine, the road to recovery had been a long one. The nasty fracture, followed by eight weeks in a cast, had left Rafe's leg stiffened and weak. Even after long hours of daily exercise he walked with a limp. But as long as his feet could manage the rudder bar, nothing else mattered.

The remaining work on the aeroplane had progressed at a feverish pace. With the engine running flawlessly, Rafe had focused his energies on rebuilding the frame. The spare propeller had been honed and reshaped, every inch of its surface sanded and varnished to perfection. The wheels and skids had been replaced, and new seats fashioned from sturdy maple chairs.

Now that he could move about easily, Rafe needed less help. Much of what he did need was provided by Buck, who'd grown excited about the project now that it was nearly done. Buck's early training as a gunsmith was put to good use in the fine-tuning of the aeroplane's parts. He checked every nut, bolt, wire and screw, making sure that each connection was perfect.

Even Alex had become involved in the work once more. Although she could only come around when Rafe was alone, she'd managed her share of sanding, bracing and gluing. Knowing that he often forgot to eat, she brought him food from the house—thick beef sandwiches stacked with summer tomatoes, fried chicken, pitchers of iced lemonade and wedges of apple pie, which they shared on the shaded grass behind the warehouse. Sometimes she came with books for the nighttime reading he needed before he could fall asleep, or an armload of fresh, fragrant sheets and towels from the laundry.

Her most stunning surprise for him had been two bolts of perfect gray silk. Rafe had nearly refused her gift out of pride. But silk was the finest material to be had for the wing coverings of a biplane. Because it cost a king's ransom, he'd planned on buying linen canvas with the funds Buck had advanced him. Linen was sturdy enough but slightly rough and porous, requiring multiple coats of the thick varnish called "dope" to give it an even texture. Silk was stronger and lighter than any other material, and so smooth that the air glided easily over its surface.

In the end, overcome by the magnificence of her gift and wanting the best for his aeroplane, Rafe had capitulated. The silk was now stretched tightly over the wing framework, awaiting its first coat of varnish to seal the seams and stiffen the fabric.

"The aeroplane's better than before," he told Alex as they brushed dope onto the white pine frame of the tail section. "Everything we've done has been an improvement."

"Thank you for saying *we*." She grinned at him across the framework. "If you'd taken all the credit, I'd have gone off in a huff."

Rafe grinned back at her. He loved these times, with Alex in her grubby coveralls, her hair mussed, her face smudged with dust and grease. When she was working alongside him the rest of the world seemed to fade, leaving them alone in their small, private universe.

At times like this it was all he could do to keep from reaching out and pulling her close. Having Alex in his arms would be a taste of heaven. But he knew better than to start something he mustn't finish. Either he would have to push her away, leaving them both aching and frustrated, or worse, he might find himself unable to stop.

To her credit, Alex seemed to understand. She kept her distance, taking no risks that might fling them into the fire. But Rafe had learned to read the depths of those lovely violet eyes. She was as hungry for him as he was for her.

Still, she would have blushed at the fantasies that fueled Rafe's dreams at night—Alex naked on his bed, her long legs bent outward, her musky woman scent all but drowning him as his mouth feasted on the tiny pink nub that guarded her entrance; Alex beneath him, her happy little cry as he thrust into her deep and hard for the first time… Lord, how many times had he awakened in a wet fever, wanting her so much that it was all he could do to keep from punching his fist through the wall?

If he had any sense he'd usher her out of here and forbid her to come back. Just being with her was like balancing on the edge of a razor. Whatever happened he couldn't let himself fall.

"Will you let me come to the aerodrome when you

take it up the first time?" she asked, stroking her brush over the surface of the rear elevator.

Rafe shook his head. "For one thing, your father will want to be there. For another, I can't be sure when I'll actually take off. I could spend hours, even days, circling the field, taking little hops while I do the final tuning of the engine and the wires. Even the smallest change in the warp of a wing or the angle of the rudder can make a difference in the air."

"So you've told me." She smiled bravely, refusing to voice the real reason he wouldn't have her on the ground at Hempstead. If something went wrong with the aeroplane and there was an accident, Rafe would not want her to see him die.

"Once I'm safely aloft I'll fly north and circle your house," he said. "If you're at home, you'll hear me, maybe see me, too, if you run outside fast enough."

"I'll hear you," she said, dipping her brush into the varnish. "I'll see you, too, and I'll wave. Then, before you know it, I'll be sitting behind you in the sky."

A week later the warehouse was empty. The finished aeroplane had been partly disassembled and trucked to the Hempstead aerodrome, along with Rafe's tools. Rafe had found a bachelor apartment in nearby Garden City and was using his motorbike to go back and forth. Alex rarely saw him now. It was as if Rafe had abandoned her for the real love of his life.

Buck reported at dinner that Rafe was still tinkering with his machine, taking brief flying hops across the field to test his refinements. He had yet to become fully airborne, and Buck was growing weary of waiting.

Alex took the news in discreet silence. She, too, was growing weary. Did he even remember his promise to take her flying? Did he even remember *her?*

Discouraged by her lack of interest, Allen Throckmorton had turned his attentions elsewhere. Maude was wringing her hands in despair, but Alex barely noticed his absence. She spent most of her spare time galloping her horse on the beach as she wrestled with the temptation to take the old green Cadillac and drive to Hempstead. Only the thought of being ignored or dismissed by Rafe kept her at home. She had her own share of pride, and she would not show her face at the airfield unless he wanted her there.

Today, as she saddled Cherokee, her leggy sorrel gelding, Alex grappled with reality. The nights were getting cooler and the maple leaves were already tinged with crimson. Summer was nearing its end. Had her time with Rafe reached its end as well?

From the moment he'd tumbled out of the sky and, almost literally, into her arms, Rafe had been the center of her world. She had loved him from the instant his jade-flecked eyes had locked with hers—loved him with an intensity that had consumed her like a constantly burning flame. There had been no past, no future, only the present—only Rafe and the magic that glittered around him like an aura.

As she tightened the cinch, a shadow caught her eye. The new stable hand, a surly young Irishman named

Mick, stood in the open doorway smoking a cigarette. Buck had hired him only last week. He showed up on time and seemed competent with the horses, but he had a way of skirting the rules that set Alex's teeth on edge. Like now. He knew he could be fired for smoking in the stable, so he stood mere inches outside the door, pushing the limits with open insolence.

Alex shot him a glare. He grinned and tipped the brim of his cap in a mocking salute. Then he dropped the cigarette butt into the dirt, ground it out with his heel and disappeared around the corner of the stable.

Putting him out of her mind, Alex swung into the saddle and turned onto the path that wound its way to the beach. Where the trees opened to dunes, she nudged Cherokee to a canter. They whiplashed down the slope, kicking up fountains of sand that blew away in their wake. On the hard-packed beach, the tall red horse broke into a pounding gallop that carried them along the water's edge, splashing through streaks of foam. Alex's hairpins had blown loose. She shook her head and let her hair tumble free to stream behind her. So much for Rafe Garrick. So much for her father, her mother and all the people who thought they had a God-given right to force her into a mold. If it were possible she would leave them all behind and just keep riding, to the very ends of the earth.

The wind, the murmuring waves and the thunder of Cherokee's hooves sang in her head, filling her ears. Lost in her own thoughts, Alex didn't hear the sound of the engine until the aeroplane was almost above her.

Rafe's machine was performing like a dream. The engine ran with a steady purr. Every surface—wings, elevators and rudder—responded flawlessly to his touch. The long days of testing, fine-tuning and retesting had been worth every tedious minute. Now, at last, he was airborne again.

He had circled the Bromley house twice, hoping Alex would hear him and come outside. When she'd failed to appear, he'd resolved to widen his third circle to include the beach, then head back to the aerodrome.

Rafe had just cleared the dunes when he saw her, dashing along the edge of the waves on her beautiful red horse. The sight of her took his breath away. Watching her, it was all he could do to keep his craft on a steady course.

Pushing the stick forward, he made a low, banking circle above her. By now Alex had seen him. She had pulled her mount to a halt and was standing up in the stirrups, waving frantically. Even from the air Rafe could see the ear-to-ear grin on her face.

Alex.

Heaven save him, she'd stolen a piece of his soul.

Without her at his side, the past weeks had been bleak and lonely. But he'd forced himself to stay away. The less he saw of her, the safer it would be for them both.

He had promised her one flight. As soon he could be sure the machine was stable enough for two people, he would keep that promise. After that he would bid her goodbye. Buck Bromley was his partner now, but Alex was off-limits. They might see each other at parties and other functions, but after that blistering encounter on the path, he couldn't let himself be alone with her. He ached with wanting her. But the only good thing he could do for her now was leave her alone.

Alex's days had become an ongoing drama with all the highs and lows of a Coney Island roller coaster. Rafe had tested, then retested his aeroplane with extra weight and pronounced it safe to carry a passenger. All that remained was for him to keep his promise.

Unfortunately, there were complications—frustrating, maddening complications over which Alex had no control. On his days off, Buck had taken to dropping by the aerodrome to watch the planes and hobnob with the pilots. Even when he was safely away, flight days were ruled by the weather. To minimize the risk to Alex, Rafe had insisted on waiting for a clear, quiet morning. So far the only perfect weather had occurred on days when Buck was around.

They kept in touch through furtive notes and rare, brief meetings, always in public places. But Alex could feel Rafe pulling away from her and she sensed the truth. When the promised flight was over, they would go their separate ways. Alex was braced for the loss. She had no power to hold him—and wouldn't have used it if she had. Rafe was a man who needed to be free. She would no more cage him than she would cage an albatross.

But she would never think of him without gratitude. Rafe had changed her life. He had shown her things that she'd never believed possible. He had given her a world of hopes and dreams that nothing could take away.

The streak of bad luck ended at last. On a morning when Buck was away on a business trip to Atlantic City, the sun rose on a day of pure sky and windless calm. Anticipating the weather, Alex was waiting at the end of the long graveled drive when he came by on his motorcycle.

He grinned, shaking his rumpled head as he caught sight of her. "No chance of getting past you on a day like this, is there, Miss Alexandra Bromley?"

"No chance at all. Papa's away, the weather's perfect and here I am. You're out of excuses, Mr. Garrick. Let's go flying!"

He surveyed her costume of knickerbockers, riding boots and a warm jacket. For the space of a breath he seemed to hesitate. Then he chuckled. "Well, you're dressed well enough. Let's go."

He straddled the motorbike and she climbed on behind him, cradling his hips between her knees. The intimate contact triggered a sensation so deliciously wicked that it brought a rush of color to her cheeks. Wrapping her arms around his waist, she held on tightly as he kicked the machine to a growling start and steered it down the path.

As they swung onto the graveled drive, Alex glimpsed a flicker of movement in an upstairs window of the distant house. Was Maude watching them go or had it been one of the servants? Either way, she was as good as caught. But as long as no one stopped her, what would it matter? Let her parents scold her, forbid her to go out, even lock her in her room. After today she wouldn't care.

By the time they reached the aerodrome, Alex's excitement had mounted to a near frenzy. Half a dozen aeroplanes were lined up outside a row of hangars. Most of them were small monoplanes with *Moisant School* stenciled on their sides. Rafe's biplane was tethered to a ground stake at the far end.

Alex waited as Rafe parked the motorcycle and went into a low, brown building to sign the register and fill a can of gasoline. As she stood watching the field, another monoplane, newer-looking than the ones on the ground, appeared in the sky, circled once and came in low, skimming the grass to make a perfect landing. Cutting the engine, the tall, slender pilot, dressed like Alex in knickerbockers and a warm coat, climbed down from the seat, secured the plane, then peeled off goggles and a close-fitting leather helmet.

Alex gasped as a wealth of red-gold hair tumbled free. The pilot was a woman, and a stunning beauty at that.

"Her name's Harriet Quimby," Rafe said, coming up behind Alex. "She's a writer for *Leslie's Magazine* and a damned good flyer. She just became the first woman in this country to get her pilot's license."

It was all Alex could do to keep from staring open-mouthed as Harriet Quimby gave them a friendly wave and strode out of sight behind the hangars. A woman pilot! Living, breathing proof that such a thing was possible!

Alex scarcely felt the ground under her feet as Rafe led her around the field to his aeroplane. A few student pilots were steering the little monoplanes over the grass. All of them appeared to be men.

"Up you go." Rafe buckled Alex into the rear seat, which was crammed between the engine and his own chair. Then he handed her the goggles and leather helmet she was to wear. Protection was important. In a craft going at the unbelievable speed of fifty miles an hour, any object drifting in the sky could become a dangerous missile.

Rafe donned his own helmet and goggles and climbed into the front seat. Two husky men in coveralls appeared out of nowhere. One of them unblocked the wheels while the other gave a powerful spin to the propeller, which was anchored by its shaft to the rear of the engine. As the motor roared to life, both men sprang to anchor the tail section while the propeller picked up enough speed for takeoff.

Alex hunched lower in her seat, overwhelmed by the noise and the rushing air that spattered her with castor oil from the engine. She felt an unexpected surge of terror but it was too late to lose her courage. The aeroplane was moving onto the field.

She clenched her teeth as the wheels jarred over the bumpy surface. Then suddenly the jarring ceased. Alex's stomach dropped as she realized that they had left the ground.

She took a deep breath as the plane glided upward. Below her, buildings, trees and roads were becoming smaller. Cars and wagons had taken on the appearance of toys. Little by little Alex began to relax. As she did so, the experience of flying began to seep through her senses.

Cool morning air swept into her face, carrying a

blend of perfumes that rose from the earth below—
pasture and forest, swamp and seawater, breakfast bacon,
manure and factory smoke. Behind her, muffled by her
leather helmet, the engine thrummed its steady song.

Below the wings, a flock of swallows darted and
swooped. Enchanted, Alex watched them. Strapped to
the wooden seat, she felt as vulnerable as a bird herself.
The thought that even a small mishap could send her
plummeting to her doom gave her a strange thrill. It was
as if she and Rafe were laughing in the very face of
death. Only in his arms had she felt more alive.

Rafe's helmeted head and broad shoulders loomed in
front of her. Alex wanted to speak to him, to share the
wonder she was feeling, but she knew he wouldn't be able
to hear above the engine. And she knew better than to
touch him. The pressure of her hand on his shoulder might
startle him or give him the idea that something was wrong.

Gazing out past the lower wing, she could see all the
way to the north shore of Long Island, the fabled Gold
Coast, where the grand estates stretched down to the
white rim of the Sound. She could see the sailboats that
flocked like butterflies around the yacht club and the
long stretches of paddock where blooded horses grazed
and frolicked in the morning sunlight. The autumn color
display had just begun. Flashes of gold and scarlet
mingled with the variegated green of the treetops, the
whole of it looking like an exotic Persian carpet.

Air whispered over the silken surface of the wings.
Alex had to hold her breath to hear it. She listened,
transfixed by everything she saw, heard and felt. She had

asked Rafe to take her flying one time, to give her a single perfect memory of the sky. But now she realized that once would never be enough. She wouldn't be satisfied until she could pilot her own aeroplane.

Today she'd seen a woman fly, and she knew it was possible. She had enough money for lessons, and she'd already learned a great deal by working on Rafe's machine. Her biggest obstacle would be her parents, especially her father. Somehow, she would have to find a way around them.

Lost in thought, Alex failed to see the large white bird until it struck the end of the wing. A shudder went through the aircraft and it began to pitch. Rafe struggled with the stick as Alex clung helplessly to her seat.

"I can't hold it!" he shouted above the drone of the engine. "Hang on! We're going down!"

Chapter Eight

It was a tribute to Rafe's skill that he was able to wrestle the aeroplane into a glide. Easing the stick forward, he searched for, and found, an open space in the trees. Alex swallowed a scream as they clipped a stand of towering elms to come in over a stretch of bumpy-looking pasture. She braced her knees against the back of Rafe's seat as the biplane touched down, bounced and touched down again. This time it rumbled over the rough hillocks of grass and coasted to a jarring stop, just short of an abandoned barn.

"Are you all right?" Rafe jumped to the ground and swung back toward her.

"I'm fine." Alex's blood was racing. The blend of terror, excitement and relief was as heady as champagne. She lifted her goggles and unfastened the chin strap on the leather helmet. "How's the aeroplane?"

"Seems to be in one piece." His cheerfulness sounded forced as he removed his own goggles and helmet. "Let's get you down and we'll take a look. Mind the wing."

Alex unbuckled the strap and eased out of her seat. She felt all right until she tried to stand. Then, surprisingly, she discovered that her legs would not support her.

Rafe caught her as she tumbled free of the aeroplane. His grip on her shoulders was fierce, almost painful. The flesh around his mouth was white. Only then did Alex realize how frightened he'd been. A tiny sob escaped her tightly pressed lips. She began to shake.

He clasped her hard against his chest. For a long time he simply held her, his heart pounding against her ear. Alex closed her eyes and lost herself in his strength. She had no memory of anyone ever holding her like this, as if she were a precious child. Only now did she realize what she'd missed.

She loved him—loved him with all her heart, body and soul. If she hadn't known it before, she knew it now.

"I didn't care about me," he muttered, finding his voice at last. "I didn't even care about the damned machine. I could've rebuilt it. But if anything had happened to you, I would never have forgiven myself."

"Hush." Her arms crept around his ribs, binding him to her. "I'm all right. You're all right. And you managed to get us safely to the ground." She sucked in a ragged breath. "The flight was astounding, Rafe. It was beyond anything I could ever have imagined. I—"

Her throat choked off the rest of her words. Dared she tell him what she wanted to say—that she loved him, that she'd been his from the moment she'd cradled his head in her arms to keep from drowning?

"What is it, Alex?" He was still holding her, his lips

brushing her forehead as he spoke. She could feel the tension in his body. What if he didn't love her in return? What if she told him and made a complete fool of herself?

Her courage failed her.

"I just wanted to thank you," she said lamely. "You didn't have to do this. You could've said no."

"Alex, saying no to you is like saying no to springtime. You're a force of nature." He sighed, his arms tightening around her. "With all the work you did on the machine, you deserved to get something you wanted. But, damn it, girl, when that bird hit the wing I was praying all the way down that you'd be all right. I felt like I was being punished for deceiving your father. I should never have taken you up, and I'll never do it again."

His words punched holes in her euphoria. She drew back with a little toss of her head. "Don't be superstitious, Rafe. I've made a lifetime career of deceiving my father, and God has yet to strike me down for it. Look at us. We're on the ground, both of us perfectly safe. The only one who got punished was that poor bird, and we'll never know what kind of avian sins he had on his conscience. Now let's pull ourselves together and see how much damage the creature did."

Rafe turned away with a half-voiced mutter and bent to inspect the tip of the wing. Bloodied white feathers showed the point of impact. The blow had been hard enough to splinter the wood and detach the wire that controlled the aileron. There was no sign of the bird, which would almost certainly have been killed.

"What kind of bird do you think it was?" Alex asked, looking over his shoulder.

"It would take something big to do this much damage. A goose, maybe, or a pelican. I tested the aeroplane, made sure the weather was calm, and look what happened. Goes to show you can't tempt fate."

"Can we fix it?" Alex brushed back a lock of hair that the rising wind had blown into her face. Clouds had begun to drift in from the Atlantic side of the island, murky and ominous above the far trees.

Rafe frowned at the sky. "Not bloody likely. All I've got with me is a screwdriver and a pocket-sized wrench. I'd have to hitch a ride back to the aerodrome and borrow some proper tools. And even then, in this wind…" He shook his head. "I might make it back with the aeroplane, but I wouldn't risk it. Not with you on board."

"So you're saying we'll have to hitch a ride together. Then you'll drop me off at home on your way back here with the motorcycle."

"It's that, or leave you here, and you've been gone too long as it is. Your mother will be looking for you. Have you got a better idea?"

Alex shook her head. What a dreary way to end the most glorious morning of her life. Rafe was getting testy and so was she. Before long they'd be snapping at each other. But how else could she bear to let him go? Maybe anger was the only thing that would give her the strength to walk away.

"Give me a minute to tie down. Then we'll get started." He rummaged under the seat and came up with a stout metal stake and a rope. Using his boot, he pushed the stake into the ground and tethered the plane to a ring at the top. By the time he'd finished, the clouds were moving in fast. A streak of lightning flashed above the trees.

Wind whipped Rafe's thick chestnut hair into tufts as he squinted at the sky. "I don't know if—"

His words were cut off by a blue-white flash and a thunderclap that sounded as if the earth had been split apart like a stump of firewood. Alex reeled and staggered against the plane. Grabbing her hand, Rafe plunged with her across the clearing toward the abandoned barn. By the time they reached the door, which sagged on one broken hinge, the clouds had opened up. Rain poured down in sheets, soaking them even before they could wrench the door open and stumble inside.

"What was it you said about God not striking you down?" Rafe shouted about the storm.

Still shaken, Alex forced a laugh. "Maybe it was a warning shot. I'll have to watch myself!"

The barn looked as if it hadn't been used in a decade or more. The interior was dim and silent, with fingers of gray light filtering through the cracks between the boards. Mellowed by age and freshened by rain, the earthy aromas of hay and manure lingered in the air. The earthen floor was littered with straw.

Rain drummed steadily on the shingled roof, leaking in a few spots but not too badly to be avoided. Alex huddled into her damp jacket, gazing up into the shadowy rafters where, suddenly, something moved.

She gasped as a wailing, ghostly shape floated down

toward her. With a little shriek she flung herself at Rafe, cowering against him as the thing cleared her head and drifted upward again on silent wings.

"It's all right." Rafe held her securely as she shivered against him. "It's just a barn owl. It won't hurt us. See?"

Alex followed his gaze to where a smallish owl with a pale, heart-shaped face stared down at them from a high rafter. She forced herself to laugh. "I think I've had enough birds for one day," she muttered.

"Your teeth are chattering," Rafe said. "Take off your wet coat. I'll warm you."

Rafe's flying coat was made of oiled sheepskin with the wool inside. He unbuttoned it down the front as Alex shed her quilted jacket and hung it over the side of a stall. Then he opened the coat and gathered her in.

She nestled into the heavenly warmth as his arms closed around her. His body felt so right, so comforting. Alex closed her eyes and breathed him in—the faintly spicy aroma of the soap he used, the clean, musky smell of his perspiration and the rich lanolin scent of the coat.

Heaven, how she loved him!

He exhaled, his tension easing a little as he cradled her against his cotton shirt. She slid her arms around his waist, holding him as if defying the world to make her let go. Alex had always taken pride in her ability to get what she wanted. But what she wanted most, she knew she couldn't have. Rafe Garrick wasn't a man for having.

He brushed a line of kisses down her temple. "Alex," he whispered. "Oh, damn it, girl…"

The contact between their bodies was warming them both. Alex could feel his arousal stirring against her, rising to a hard ridge against her belly. Her blood had begun to seethe, pumping molten heat into her loins. Need clenched in her like a hungry fist, spilling moisture between her thighs. She wanted him, wanted him now. Maybe Rafe could never be hers to keep, but one thing she knew in her heart. If she let him walk away without making love to her she would regret it for the rest of her life.

Hungering for the feel of him, she pulled at his shirt and singlet, loosening them from his belt. As her palms slid over the skin of his sleek, muscular back, she stretched up and kissed him, opening her mouth and giving him her tongue. He groaned and pulled her harder against him. "Alex, I'm warning you, if you don't stop…" he muttered as her lips nuzzled his. It was the feeblest of protests and the last one she heard.

Rain drummed around them, echoing their urgency as he cupped her buttocks in his hands and pulled her up hard against him. She ground her hips against the exquisite pressure, gasping at the sensations that shot through her body. For the space of a long breath he simply held her against him. Then he raised his hands to her blouse and began tugging at the buttons. When he fumbled with the tiny holes, her trembling fingers helped him, exposing her taut breasts beneath the silk camisole she wore.

Glancing around in the shadows, he moved toward a pile of clean straw in the far end of the barn. Spreading it out hastily to make a bed, he laid his open coat on top and lowered Alex onto the soft fleece. Stretching beneath him, she pulled his head down to her breasts. He kissed them through the thin silk, sucking the nipples in turn as they hardened to aching nubs in his mouth. A silvery heat shimmered downward through her belly and into her thighs. She whimpered as he worked the lacy straps off her shoulders. "So fine…" he murmured, stroking and nibbling one bare breast. "So beautiful…"

She arched against him, her blood blazing with the sweetest fire she'd ever known. Her searching hands worked their way beneath the waistband of his trousers and drawers to slide down his firm buttocks. He gasped as her hands cupped him, drawing his hardness in against her. Reaching down, he jerked open his belt buckle and fly. "Touch me, Alex," he rasped, moving her hand. "Don't be afraid."

Afraid? How many times had she dreamed of touching him? How many times had she lain wakeful and feverish at night, caressing herself and pretending it was his hand, his mouth, his body touching hers? Hesitant for only the barest instant, she closed her eager fingers around his swollen shaft. The feel of him was beyond anything her dreams could have imagined, like a thick iron spear cloaked in baby skin.

He drew a ragged breath as she stroked and explored him, her fingers moving lower to cup the intriguing weight of him. Alex had never experienced a naked, aroused man, but she'd seen her share of bulls and stallions. Rafe was not so different, but he was so much his own, so thrillingly male that the mere act of touching him left her breathless.

"You'll destroy me, woman," he muttered, lifting her hand away and burying his lips in her palm. His fingers unfastened her wool knickerbockers and the silken drawers beneath. With Alex's ready cooperation he eased them down over her boots. Clothed in little more than shadows and not the least ashamed, she gazed up at him.

"Take me, Rafe," she whispered, her heart pounding. "Whatever happens in my life, I want my first time to be with you."

Rafe exhaled slowly. His eyes glimmered with something akin to heartbreak. "I mustn't take you, my beautiful Alex. You'd regret it one day. But let me pleasure you. It's much the same and won't do you harm."

"Rafe—"

"Hush. Lie still." He bent and kissed her, nibbling at her lower lip and making small, darting thrusts with his tongue. She responded with a groan, weaving frenzied fingers into his hair. With a gentle hand he stroked her parted thighs, coming to rest on the soft nest of curls that guarded the entrance to her womanhood. She whimpered, arching against the light pressure of his hand and what it promised.

She was so wet that his fingers glided easily over her sensitive folds to find the tiny, hard nub at their center. His first touch triggered bursts of exquisite sensation that rippled through her body. She gasped, almost sobbing as she undulated against his hand.

"Shh, love…" He kissed her again, nibbling a path down her throat to her breasts. His mouth teased her nipples, nuzzling and sucking as his fingers worked their magic between her thighs. Wild with need, Alex teetered on the brink of total abandon, waiting for something she couldn't even name. Her fingers raked his hair. Her body ached with wanting him. His hands and mouth could give her exquisite pleasure but only one thing would give her peace.

His lips moved lower, trailing down the length of her belly until his head nested between her legs. A little cry escaped her lips as his mouth replaced his hand. The motion of his tongue was like nothing she'd ever imagined. The first few strokes roused her to a sensual frenzy. She gasped and writhed beneath him. "Take me, Rafe…please, for the love of heaven…"

Pausing, he raised his head to lean above her. In the faint gray light she saw the torment in his eyes, the anguish that spoke of needing her as much as she needed him.

"Please," she whispered.

Thunder crashed and rumbled in the sky, blending with the steady drone of the rain as she raised her knees and opened herself to him. She heard the rush of his breath, the small, masculine grunt as he filled her. He was inside her, home at last, where he'd belonged from the moment she'd pulled him out of the wrecked aeroplane. Bittersweet tears welled in her eyes. Instinctively she wrapped her knees around his hips, holding him as he pushed deeper into her unstretched body. The sensation was like the opening of a thousand flowers. "Yes," she whispered as he began a slow, pulsing glide, thrusting and withdrawing. "Oh, yes, it's like flying…"

He was lost in her now. She could sense it in his rasping breath, his closed eyes and slightly open mouth. She met each thrust, the sensation building, higher and deeper like the pounding of waves in a storm. She was on the edge now, and with a little cry she tumbled over, falling and spinning in a spiral of perfect ecstasy.

She felt the resistance as he tried to pull back in time. But Alex had long since passed the point of common sense. Her frenzied legs wrapped his hips, holding him deep as his body jerked inside her.

In the next instant she felt the hot, thick spill of his seed. He sagged above her, spent. What was done was done. Alex lay back and closed her eyes. For the first time in her life she felt whole.

The next day, Alex paid one last visit to the vacated warehouse. Rafe's things were gone, as she'd known they would be. The place had a musty silence about it as if he had never been here, never slept on the cot, never washed in the basin or shaved in the small, cracked mirror. The concrete floor of the warehouse had been swept clean. Only a few oil spots remained where the two of them had worked on the aeroplane together.

They had parted yesterday, when his motorcycle had dropped her off near the drive to the house. Alex had made no effort to change his mind. Even after their desperate lovemaking in the old barn, she'd understood that their time was over.

Since he'd be working with her father, they would

likely meet from time to time. It would be torture seeing him, knowing they couldn't be alone together, and wondering if he'd found another woman to share his bed.

Overcome, she sank onto an abandoned crate. She had promised herself that she wouldn't cry but now, as it struck home that their relationship had ended, it was all she could do to hold back the tears.

They had dressed in the stillness of the barn with the owl watching from the rafters. Rafe had avoided her eyes, his every move telling her that he viewed what had happened between them as a mistake. Alex had ached to go to him, to put her arms around him and tell him that she wasn't sorry. But even then she'd understood. Talking would only make matters worse.

By the time they were ready to leave the barn the storm had ended. Walking to the road, they'd caught a ride with a farmer hauling hay. He'd been a talkative man, filling the awkward silence until he let them off at the aerodrome. From there, Rafe had picked up his tools and his motorcycle and had driven Alex home.

There'd been a moment of awkwardness when she'd climbed off the bike and they'd stood face-to-face. "I never meant for this to happen, Alex," he'd murmured, gazing at her with bloodshot eyes. "Will you be all right?"

"Yes. Very much so." Alex had turned away and walked swiftly down the path, unable to say goodbye. The last she heard of him was the growl of his motorcycle starting up and fading away down the road.

Gathering her strength, she rose from the crate and

walked out of the warehouse. She hadn't looked back at him when they'd parted and she wouldn't look back now, Alex vowed. She would never regret loving the man. He had set her free and opened the door to a world of possibilities. Now it was up to her to walk through that door to a new life.

The first step would be to remove herself from the stifling Bromley household. Her mother would cry and her father would raise the roof. But there was only so much they could do to stop her. In a few months she would be twenty-one. At that time she would come into a modest trust fund from her Grandfather Burnsides. It wouldn't make her wealthy but it would give her the means to get her own apartment, do some traveling and take flying lessons.

But why wait? Why not run away now, before Buck had time to mount a counterattack? She had jewelry she could pawn for enough money to get by until her birthday. And like Harriet Quimby, she could certainly find a job to tide her over. After all, this wasn't medieval Europe. This was twentieth-century America, and a grown daughter could no longer be held hostage against her will.

She would do it tonight, Alex resolved. When the household was asleep she would write a short note to her mother, pack her essentials in a suitcase and walk the two-mile distance to the nearest railway station. The early-morning train would take her into the city.

It was a frightening prospect, but surely no worse than what hundreds of other young women had faced.

She was bright and healthy and resourceful. There was nothing she couldn't learn to do.

Lost in thought, she drove home, parked the old green Cadillac in the garage and trudged through the trees to the back of the house. White linen bedsheets hung from the clotheslines, snapping in the brisk sea air. Alex had always taken things like clean laundry and well-prepared meals for granted. Learning to manage on her own, especially without servants, was going to be a challenge. But she could accomplish anything once she set her mind to it. In any case, how hard could it be to wash out a couple of petticoats or cut up meat and onions for stew?

Young Katy, the freckle-faced laundry maid, was nowhere to be seen. Alex cut through the linen room and down the hallway that led to the back stairs. The route was designed for servants but Alex had made good use of it over the years. Now she mounted to the second floor, her mind churning with audacious plans.

When her inheritance came through she might go to Europe for a time and rent a little flat in Paris. By then, surely, she'd have her pilot's license. If not, she could find a good flying school in France, perhaps even buy her own aeroplane and take part in the big flying shows.

Maybe at one of them she'd meet Rafe again and be able to face him as an equal, not just a silly young girl with her head full of romantic dreams. She could almost imagine their conversation…

"A fine race, Mr. Garrick. Your time was almost as good as my own."

Alex had just reached the door to the carpeted upstairs hallway when her fantasy was shattered by Katy's hysterical scream.

"Help! Oh, Mary, Mother of God, somebody help!"

She flung open the door, stumbling over the heap of clean Turkish bath towels the girl had dropped. At the far end of the hallway, bathed in a streak of sunlight that turned her red hair to flame, Katy was crouched over something on the floor.

Looking up at the sound of the door, the girl saw her. "Oh, Miss Alexandra! Thank the blessed Lord you've come! It's your mother!"

Alex plunged down the hallway. Her throat choked on a cry as she spotted Maude crumpled on the carpet. She was curled on her side in a dead faint, her hair disheveled and a trail of spittle dotting her chin. The skirts of her pale mauve dressing gown lay limp around her legs like the petals of a fallen lily.

On the orders of Dr. Fleury, Maude was confined to her bed for the next four weeks. Her fainting spell had been diagnosed as a mild heart attack and she'd been placed on a regimen of digitalis, white hawthorn tincture and a supply of nitrite tablets to be kept on hand for emergency use.

"But it's the rest she needs most of all," the doctor had told Alex outside the bedroom door. "Her body's had a shock and it needs time to heal. Has she been under a strain lately?"

"No more than usual." Alex twisted a wad of her

skirt in a paroxysm of guilt. What if she'd carried out her plan and left home? Her mother could have died, and it would have been her fault.

"Sometimes it's the strain that doesn't show—the hurt and worry kept inside—that does the most damage." The doctor frowned beneath his bristly mustache. "Where's your father today, Alexandra? Has someone telephoned him?"

"I did. I telephoned his office at the plant right after I spoke with you. His secretary said he couldn't be disturbed for any reason. I had to leave a *message*. A message!" Alex bit back an outburst of rage. "He hasn't even called back."

"I see." Fleury sighed and shook his head. "How's that young pilot, Mr. Garrick, doing? I haven't seen him since he started walking on two legs again."

"He's closed the warehouse and taken an apartment in Garden City. Once his aeroplane was mended there was no keeping him."

"I take it you tried." He shot Alex a sly glance that triggered a flush of warmth in her cheeks.

"I confess I did," she admitted, knowing that the doctor, although he could pry secrets out of a stone, was never one to break a confidence. "He'll be working with Papa in the business, but Mr. Garrick wanted no part of our family. I can't say I blame him."

Dr. Fleury nodded absently, as if locking the tidbit away. "Your mother's going to need you, Alexandra. I'll send a nurse over to care for her physical needs, but Maude will be dependent on you for love and support."

Lord knows she can't count on any from Buck. Alex read the unspoken message in his eyes.

"I'll be there," she vowed. "I'll see that she rests and eats and doesn't have to deal with running the house."

"Do that—and more if you can. Try to make her happy." He checked his medical bag to make sure he'd left nothing behind. "I'll see myself out. You get back to your mother, dear girl. And telephone me if there's the least cause for worry."

Alex stood outside the bedroom door, collecting her emotions as the doctor's footsteps faded into silence. Her whole world had suddenly shifted on its axis. Her mother had always been there, so giving in her own quiet way, so undemanding of others around her. Now all that had changed. Maude was a mother who needed her daughter; and in the light of that need, Alex's grandiose plans were no more than fluff.

Lifting her chin, Alex placed her hand on the doorknob. She had lived her life as a spoiled, willful child. Now she would set aside her own wishes and do whatever needed to be done.

Maybe this was how it felt to grow up.

Chapter Nine

For the first few days, Maude spent much of her time sleeping. Fearful that she might have another attack, Alex hovered at her side, sometimes reading, sometimes pacing, sometimes napping on the cot she'd set up a few steps from her mother's bed.

It was an anxious time and a busy time. Only now did Alex realize how vital Maude had been to the smooth, silent running of the Bromley household. The servants peppered her with questions about everything under the sun, from the weekly menu and the correct amount of laundry starch to the stray dog raiding the trash bin and the gardener's boy caught breeches-down with one of the kitchen maids. Glancing into a mirror on the third day of her mother's illness, Alex was startled by the mussed and haggard stranger staring back at her.

Only Buck seemed untouched. Apart from brief once-daily visits to his wife's sickroom he kept to his usual routine, spending his days at the factory or in the city, where he often stayed well past midnight.

But at least he wasn't hypocritical enough to act worried. Alex was well aware of the marriage contract her Grandfather Burnsides had forced Buck to sign. Maude's death would set him free to marry some nubile young socialite and sire a dynasty of his own. Still, Alex would have liked her father better if he'd shown some concern.

In any case, Maude wasn't about to accommodate her husband by dying. On the fifth day she was sitting up in bed, eating everything put before her and demanding her spectacles.

"Heavens, Alexandra, you're a mess!" she fussed, peering at her daughter through the wire-framed lenses. "Go and get out of those rumpled clothes. Take a bath and wash your hair. My friends will be coming to visit. What will they think if they see you looking like that?"

Alex's sigh blended relief and resignation. Her mother was back and nothing had changed.

Sharp as she was, however, Maude was still physically weak. Dr. Fleury insisted that she stay in bed for the rest of the month and ease slowly back into her routine. From the bed she progressed to a wheelchair, which Alex dutifully pushed around the main floor and the terrace.

Although it wasn't heavy work, Alex found the effort draining. She ended each day in a state of exhaustion, and no amount of sleep seemed to be enough. Even Dr. Fleury remarked that she was looking peaked.

"When I asked you to be there for your mother, I didn't mean you should wear yourself out," he lectured her. "Maude's coming along fine. Let the servants take on some of your responsibilities, and you get some rest. If that doesn't bring some color back to your cheeks, give me a call, hear?"

Alex did her best to take his advice, but her whole body seemed to be in rebellion. She felt swollen and tender. Her nipples had darkened and her breasts were straining the seams of her camisole. When she realized that her monthly flow was late by more weeks than she cared to count, the dreaded suspicion began to grow. For a time, she took refuge in denial. Life wouldn't be ironic enough play that kind of joke. Not on her.

But three weeks later all denial came to an end.

By now Maude was nearing full recovery. The doctor had allowed her to take up her household and social duties on the condition that she rest an extra hour in the morning and take an afternoon nap. Maude used the morning time in bed to catch up on letter-writing and eat her breakfast on a tray. Often she invited Alex to join her. For the past few days, Alex had made excuses. In truth, she'd begun to feel so queasy in the mornings that she'd lost her appetite for breakfast. But on this particular day she'd been summoned. There was no way out.

Sitting beside her mother's bed, she lifted the pewter warming lid that covered her plate. Two fried eggs, swimming in grease, stared up at her, accompanied by thick slices of fatty bacon and a mound of fried potatoes cooked with onions. The greasy, smoky aroma rose to her nostrils, making her stomach roil.

Her mother was watching her. Alex lifted a morsel of the potatoes, pushed it into her mouth and forced herself to chew. When her throat balked at swallowing, she took a sip of orange juice to wash the potatoes down. It was no use. Her stomach clenched into spasms of nausea that sent her rushing out of the room.

Minutes later she returned, pale and damp and trembling.

Maude had put her breakfast tray aside and was sitting with her hands folded in her lap. Her eloquent eyes spoke of heartbreak—of twenty years spent watching a daughter grow up with spirit and promise, only to repeat her own damning mistake.

"I take it Allen Throckmorton isn't the father of your child, Alexandra," she said.

"No, Mama." Alex sank back onto the chair.

"I didn't think so." Maude sighed. "Does Rafe know?"

"Nobody knows except you."

"Me and a houseful of servants. They have eyes and ears, and they talk." She smoothed the coverlet over her knees. "Are you planning to have this baby?"

"Yes." Alex had sorted that much out, at least. There was no way she would destroy a child, especially a child fathered by the man she loved.

"You won't change your mind and go running off to one of those awful back-alley rooms where they'd likely kill you?"

Startled by her mother's frankness, Alex shook her head.

"Never. I didn't mean for this to happen, but I'm going to have my baby and raise it."

"So what are we going to do?"

Alex sighed. "I've thought about it. I could go to Europe for a year or two. Mary Beth Morgan's family has a villa in Tuscany where I might be able to stay. After a decent interval I could come home with the baby, concoct some story about a marriage gone wrong…"

"And what about Rafe? Shouldn't he have a part in all this? After all, he seduced you, an innocent young girl—"

"It wasn't his fault, Mama," Alex interrupted. "I was the one who seduced him. He didn't want to take my virtue. I gave it to him—shoved it in his face. The poor man didn't have a chance. So why should he have to bear the consequences? The last thing I want to do is trap him like—"

Like you trapped Papa. Alex bit off the words, leaving them unsaid, but the slight paling of Maude's face told her that she'd missed nothing.

"Nevertheless, I think he should be told. Rafe Garrick strikes me as a decent man. Surely he'll choose to do the right thing."

"The right thing? You mean marry me?" Alex was on her feet, quivering. "No! I won't have him! Not that way!"

"Do you love him, Alexandra?"

"Does it matter? It certainly won't matter to Papa. He'll be out for blood."

Maude's fingers twisted her thin gold wedding band. "It might be wise to go to Rafe before your father finds out…and, believe me, he *will* find out. The only question is, do you want Rafe to hear the news from you or from him?"

Nauseating panic welled in Alex's throat. She shook her head vehemently. "I can't go to him, Mama. The thought of seeing his face when he hears… No, I can't do it. I won't do it."

Maude sighed. "Very well, then. I will."

Rafe sat at the bare table wolfing down cold beans, warm beer and a pastrami on rye from the corner delicatessen. It was well into evening, but he'd only just arrived at his bachelor flat from the factory, where he'd been mapping out space to set up his production line. After running at full clip all day, without taking time for lunch, he was starved, tired and cranky.

His aeroplane had performed superbly at the last few air shows of the season. Orders for the model were already coming in. Buck was elated. Rafe was pleased, too. But he was learning that more time producing his planes would mean less freedom to fly them.

Outside the time-weathered brick house, now subdivided into flats, the first snow of November was falling. White flakes spattered against the dark windowpane, a sad reminder that winter was setting in. There would be air shows in California during the winter months, and Rafe was already making arrangements to be there. In his spare time, if he had any, he'd be sketching out design improvements and building new models.

It was going to be a long winter…working, traveling and trying not to think about Alex. Her memory had been a constant presence since he'd left her standing on the path, looking like a lost urchin in her rumpled knickerbockers. She had touched him then with her courage, her passion and her hunger to be loved. She haunted him now.

Did he regret making love to her? The question tore at him. The sweetness of her beautiful, giving body would stay with him forever, but he'd had no right to take her that way, without a modicum of honor or responsibility. He'd stolen her virginity, an act he could never undo. If he'd done her any lasting harm, Rafe would feel the guilt forever. He could only hope she'd forget him, move on and be happy.

As for him, he wanted her with a hunger that burned like a red-hot poker in his gut. But that was just something he'd have to live with. If he spent the rest of eternity in hell, he deserved it for what he'd done to her.

The sound of a motor car stopping in the street below caught his attention. Glancing out the window he saw the flicker of a headlamp through the falling snow. Who would be out driving at this hour, and in this weather? He hoped they hadn't come to see him. Tonight all he wanted was to finish eating, fall into bed and sink into oblivion.

Rafe was still brooding when he heard the sound of the car door closing and footsteps moving slowly up the creaky wooden stairs. Moments later there was a faint, polite knock on his door.

Rafe's pulse surged. But no, it wouldn't be Alex, he told himself. She wouldn't come here; and even if she did, she wouldn't be creeping up the stairs. She'd be running up, rapping energetically on the door…his Alex, who never did anything by half measures. And it wasn't her father. Buck would stomp up the stairs and pound on the planking with a demanding fist. This was someone else.

Cautiously Rafe opened the door.

Maude Bromley stood in the dim hallway, her wispy presence all but lost in the folds of a voluminous fur coat. Startled speechless, Rafe opened the door wide and ushered her inside. She crossed the threshold like a duchess visiting a peasant hovel. What in holy heaven was she doing here, and at this hour?

Then suddenly, before either of them spoke, he knew.

"Can I take your coat, Mrs. Bromley, or offer you a chair?" Rafe choked out the words.

She shook her head. "It's cold in here. And I doubt that I'll be staying long enough to sit down. I told Felix to keep the motor running."

He stared down into her face—a careworn face that must have been pretty once. "It's Alex, isn't it? Is she all right?"

Maude nodded slowly. "Yes, my daughter is quite all right. But it seems you're going to be a father, Mr. Garrick."

Even though he'd known it from the moment she'd stepped through the door, Rafe felt as if the earth had opened under his feet. His legs threatened to give way beneath him, but he couldn't sit. Not while Maude was standing.

"Alexandra didn't want to tell you," Maude said. "Even after I pointed out that you'd rather hear the news from her than from her father, she refused to face you. So I came in her place."

"Buck doesn't know?"

"Not yet. But he'll find out. And when he does, you'll want to be prepared. That, or be out of the country." A ghost of a smile tugged at Maude's thin lips.

"I understand." Rafe was sweating in the small, cold room. "You say Alex wouldn't see me?"

"She said she didn't want you to feel trapped. The girl has a cockeyed plan for having the child in Europe and raising it on her own."

The radiator hissed and clattered in the silence, sending out more noise than heat. Snow beat a light tattoo on the windowpane.

Rafe exhaled, his emotions churning. "Believe it or not, I care very deeply for your daughter," he said. "I didn't mean for things to happen the way they did, but we can't go back in time. If Alex will have me, I'd be more than willing to marry her."

Maude studied him with her head cocked to one side, a pose that reminded him uncannily of Alex. "So, if you care for her, why didn't you ask her while you had the chance? Why did you turn your back on her?"

Rafe's gesture encompassed the cramped apartment, the bare walls and sparse furnishings, the piled-up boxes he hadn't gotten around to unpacking. He could afford a bigger place now. But why bother when he only came home to sleep? "Look around you. What kind of life could

I offer a girl who's accustomed to the best? I'm not a fortune hunter, and I won't be kept like a bloody pet dog."

"I see." Maude's eyes narrowed. "You're a proud man, Rafe Garrick. But I don't care a fig for your precious pride. The only things that matter to me are my daughter's happiness and the welfare of my future grandchild. Do I make myself clear?"

"Perfectly. The same things matter to me."

"Do they?" Maude pulled her fur coat tighter around her shoulders, took a step away from him and turned toward the door. "I can see you've a great deal to think about. I'll leave you to ponder your decision. You have two days before I tell Alexandra's father. I trust that will be enough time to set your course. Good evening to you, Mr. Garrick. Please don't trouble yourself with seeing me to my car. Felix will be watching for me, and frankly I'd rather he didn't know whom I came to visit."

Rafe held the door for her and she passed through without a glance in his direction. He watched her until she'd reached the end of the hallway and started down the stairs. He'd always viewed Maude Bromley as a meek woman who endured her husband's ways without a murmur. But as he'd just learned, when it came to standing up for her only child the lady could be a tigress. Not all of Alex's steel had come from her father.

Alex.

Good Lord, she was carrying his child, his baby, in that lovely, girlish body of hers. Their passionate interlude in the old barn had created a life. Overwhelmed, he sank onto a chair. He felt higher than a god and lower than a snake. How could he have walked out and left her to deal with this? How could he ever make it up to her?

But he already knew the answer to that question. Maude had made it clear, in so many words, exactly what was expected of him. He would go to Buck and ask for Alex's hand. Then he would do whatever it took to persuade her to marry him.

Alexandra Bromley was a thoroughbred—beautiful, fiery, intelligent and courageous. Rafe couldn't imagine a woman he would rather have by his side or in his bed. He would do all he could to live up to her expectations and make her happy. But marriage would tie him to the Bromleys for life.

He had viewed the partnership as a step on his way to the top. Now Buck would be not only his partner but his father-in-law. Even if the chance came, Rafe could hardly leave the company and strike out on his own in direct competition. Not unless he left Alex as well.

He would fling his ambition into the new venture and make it thrive. Both he and Buck would profit from his hard work. But for reasons that had nothing to do with his beautiful Alex, Rafe felt as earthbound as a caged eagle. He would never be a free man again.

Alex sat alone in the darkened parlor, huddled on a green velvet ottoman. Her eyes gazed pensively into the fireplace where orange flames licked at the smoldering logs.

Across the hall, in her father's study, Rafe and Buck had been closeted with the family lawyer for nearly an

hour. They were going over the marriage contract that
Buck had drawn up for Rafe to sign. It was her parents'
arrangement all over again, so nightmarishly similar to
the original that the very idea of it had driven Maude
upstairs with a splitting headache. Alex's Grandfather
Burnsides had created the document to protect his
family from a too-ambitious son-in-law. Buck had
chafed under it for the past twenty-one years. Alex had
little doubt that his frustration had fueled the fires of his
infidelity.

Heaven save her, what if the same thing were to
happen with Rafe? How would she ever bear the hurt?

Growing more agitated by the minute, she rose
and began to pace the Persian carpet. She'd had no
chance to speak privately to Rafe about this debacle.
From the moment Buck had learned that Alex was
pregnant and that Rafe was willing to marry her,
Alex's father had begun making demands. First and
foremost, he'd insisted that Rafe appear at the house
and meet with the lawyer before being allowed to see
Alex again.

So here she was, meekly waiting while they haggled
over her like a blasted piece of property! Had anybody
thought to ask *her* what she wanted? Did anybody care?

Alex felt sick to her stomach, and it wasn't because
of the baby. This replay of her parents' disaster was unthinkable. In twenty years, she and Rafe would be Buck
and Maude, living separate lives under the same roof,
each of them doing their best to ignore the other, both
of them desperately unhappy.

Heaven help her, she'd wanted Rafe. She'd wanted his love. But not like this. Never like this.

A door opened across the hall, the sound of it scattering her thoughts. The lawyer, a priggish little man in a leather overcoat, came down the hall carrying his briefcase. Without so much as a glance into the open parlor, he let himself out the front door and closed it behind him.

As Alex waited, the leaden tick of the great clock in the foyer was like blood dripping slowly from a wound. With each second her resolve hardened. Why should she let herself be sold like a prize heifer at a cattle auction? Why should she let a trio of *men* bargain away her fate behind closed doors? She had a brain and a heart. She was entitled to use them.

By the time the study doors opened again and Buck walked out, followed by Rafe, she was seething.

The two men entered the parlor together. Buck's expression was stony. Rafe's was unreadable.

"Well, I suppose congratulations are in order." Buck opened a cabinet, removed a cut crystal decanter and poured brandy into two small glasses. "Granted, the circumstances aren't quite what any of us would have chosen. But I believe in making the best of what can't be helped." He handed one of the glasses to Rafe. "To your happiness!"

Alex saw Rafe hesitate slightly. Before he could raise his glass, she stepped between the two men. "Aren't you forgetting something, Papa?"

Buck looked down at her. One dark eyebrow slithered upward. "Is something wrong, Alex?"

"Is something wrong? Good heavens, Papa, everything's wrong!" she snapped. "Nobody's asked me what I think or what I want. I haven't received anything resembling a proposal of marriage. In fact, I'm not sure I want to get married at all!"

"You *what?*" Buck's color had darkened to deep plum above his white collar, the sure sign of a coming explosion.

"You heard me. Rafe hasn't proposed and I haven't accepted. As far as I'm concerned, there isn't going to be any marriage. This is a farce, and I refuse to play any part in it!"

Alex stole a glance at Rafe. His expression was so stoic that he might have been standing before a firing squad. Blast the man, why didn't he say something?

Buck's eyes narrowed. "The time to refuse was before you opened your legs, missy. Now that there's a baby on the way, it's a little late for you to be so high and mighty. We're acting in your best interest. The least you can do is show some gratitude."

"Gratitude!" Alex was beside herself now. "Whatever for? You're out to ruin my life and Rafe's as well! For your information, Papa, I don't want him! He doesn't want me! I can raise my child by myself, and I will!"

Buck raised his fist. "Why, you little—"

"That's enough." Rafe stepped between the two combatants, his eyes glaring into Buck's. "If you'll excuse us, I'd like to speak to Alex alone. I have some things to say to her, and it's best that she hear them in private."

Buck turned away, grumbling under his breath. "Fine.

Maybe you'll have better luck. But watch the little wild-cat. She's got claws." He downed the brandy in his glass and stalked out the door, closing it behind him.

Rafe set his own untouched glass on a side table. "Has your father ever struck you, Alex?"

She sank onto the ottoman, feeling shaky. "No. The fist was only a gesture. You needn't worry on that account."

He lowered himself onto the settee, making no effort to touch her. "Well, we've made a fine mess of things, haven't we?"

Alex stared down at her hands. "I never meant to drag you into this, Rafe. If my parents hadn't interfered, I could have managed on my own. Women do, you know."

He leaned toward her. "Good Lord, Alex, do you think that's what I'd want you to do? Manage on your own? Raise our child without me?"

She met his eyes, her fury verging on tears. "Do you think this is what *I* wanted? You being forced to marry me, signing your dreams over to Papa? The same thing happened with my parents, Rafe. My mother was in love with my father. When she found out I was on the way and he offered to marry her, my Grandfather Burnsides forced him to sign a contract just like the one Papa drew up for you. It destroyed any chance of happiness they might've had. Look at them! You've seen their marriage—if you could even call it a mar-riage. Do you think I want that for you and me, or for our child?"

"Alex—"

He reached toward her but she turned aside. "Let me

save you, Rafe," she pleaded. "If I refuse to marry you, Papa can't hold you to the contract. You'll be free."

"Damn it, listen to me!" He captured her hands, his grip almost painful as he whipped her back to face him. "I didn't sign a bloody thing. When your father and that little weasel of a lawyer shoved the papers in front of me, I shoved them right back, told them I didn't give a damn about your fortune or inheriting the company or anything else, except you. I said we were getting married if I had to kidnap you at gunpoint and haul your butt naked over the county line."

She stared up at him in disbelief. "*That* took an hour?"

His mouth twitched in a wry smile. "Well, there was a bit of shoving in both directions. But I finally convinced them to see things my way." His hands softened, holding her gently by the shoulders. "I love you, Alex. I think I fell in love with you the moment you pulled me out of the water and I looked up into those amazing violet eyes. Our circumstances aren't perfect, I know. But the last time I saw you, there was no chance of our being together. Now everything's changed. We have that chance."

"But at what cost, Rafe? Maybe you think you can live with this arrangement, but I know better. You're a proud, independent man. In time you'll grow to resent me, then to despise me."

He exhaled slowly. "Alex, do you love me?"

"I'm afraid to love you. What if I turn out like my mother, and you turn out like Papa? You are very like him, you know. Strong, ambitious and willing to fight for what you want. That's why he respects you, in spite of everything."

Rafe growled impatiently. "Why do you have to make everything so bloody complicated? It all boils down to one thing!"

Still clasping her hands, he moved forward off the settee and dropped to his knees on the carpet. "Marry me, Alexandra Bromley. Take me with all my miserable, annoying faults and throw in a few of your own. Make mistakes with me. Laugh and cry and learn the hard way with me. I can't promise you sunshine and roses. I can't promise you a bloody thing except that I'll love you and love our children and hold all of you in the night when you have bad dreams. If that's not enough then I'm sorry, because it's the best I can do. So what's your answer, Alex? Will you have me?"

Chapter Ten

Alex didn't realize she was weeping until she tried to speak. Rafe was right. Life and love didn't come with guarantees. People made mistakes. If they were wise, they forgave each other and moved on. As for happiness, it wasn't an entitlement but a gift, like a butterfly settling on her hand. Fear and distrust would only build barriers to keep it away.

At this moment the only man she'd ever loved was on his knees asking for her hand. What kind of fool would she be to turn her back and let him walk out of her life? She had to risk her heart, even though it meant giving him the power to shatter it.

"Alex?" He was looking up at her, waiting. Alex knew she had to give him her answer now. If she said no, Rafe's pride would never allow him to ask her again.

Her lips moved, but the words were blocked by the tightness in her throat. She could only lift his hand, press it to her face and bury a kiss in his palm.

"Is that a yes?"

She nodded, cradling his hand against her cheek. "Hold me, Rafe," she whispered, finding her voice. "Hold us both."

Rising from his knees, he gathered her in his arms and pulled her onto the settee. She nestled against him, her head cradled against the hollow of his throat. His nearness made her feel safe and protected, and yet so frightened that part of her wanted to tear herself away and bolt from the room.

"You're trembling," he said, kissing the spot where her hair came to a little peak at the center of her forehead.

"Yes, I know."

"Are you afraid of me, Alex?"

"Not you. Life."

He sighed, his arms tightening around her. "It's bound to be a bumpy ride, love. How could it be otherwise, with you and me? We're like paired swords, perfectly matched but capable of doing some damage when we cross."

"I didn't know you could be so poetic," she murmured, nibbling kisses along the firm line of his jaw.

"I can be a lot of things, including an addle-brained son of a baboon, as you so aptly put it the day we met. But no matter what happens I'll always love you, Alex. Never forget that."

She nibbled his earlobe. "I liked the part about you hauling my butt naked over the county line. Why don't we just run away and get married tonight? No fuss. No dealing with my parents. Just you and me."

He shook his head. "One of us needs to be sensible,

and I can see it's not going to be you." He eased away from her, rising to his feet. "Come on, we'd better go and tell your father before he breaks down that door."

"And my mother. Maybe it will ease her headache." Alex uncurled herself from the settee. If only their lives could be simple, with just the two of them making their way in the world. Then they might have a real chance to be happy. But she knew better. With Buck trying to pull strings, every day would be a new battle.

Opening the door, Rafe turned toward her and offered his arm. "Are you ready to face the lions, Mrs. Garrick?"

"As ready as I'll ever be." She forced her bravest smile, laid her hand on his arm and walked with him through the open doorway.

They were married ten days later by a justice of the peace in the county courthouse at Minneola. Rafe wore a plain dark business suit. Alex wore a simple princess-style gown of peach-colored silk embroidered with seed pearls. In keeping with the holiday season, she carried a bouquet of winter roses and white holly. The only witnesses were Buck and Maude, Dr. Fleury, and Rafe's friend, Jack Waverly.

Maude had argued for a larger, more traditional church wedding. "I've looked forward for twenty years to seeing my little girl walk down the aisle in a white gown and veil," she'd pleaded. "What will my friends think when they hear about this hush-hush ceremony of yours?"

"The same thing they'll think when my belly starts

poking out," Alex had answered with a weary sigh. "People aren't stupid, Mama, so let's not make a spectacle. All that matters is that Rafe and I will be married."

And so they were. Alex trembled as Rafe slipped the plain gold band on her finger. Then she was in his arms, and they were man and wife.

After the ceremony the entire wedding party drove into the city for a lavish wedding supper at Delmonico's. By the time it ended, leaving Rafe and Alex to retire to their honeymoon suite at the Waldorf, Alex was exhausted. Rafe supported her with his arm as she sagged against him in the elevator. Finally, after all this craziness, they would have some time alone.

Their honeymoon would be brief. After the holidays Rafe, along with his aeroplane and a pair of mechanics, would be leaving by train for the California air shows. If all went well, he would attempt the return trip by air, taking a southern route in the hope of becoming the first flyer to cross the continent from west to east—a feat that could only be accomplished in short hops and might take as long as six weeks. Success would mean free publicity and recognition for the new Garrick and Bromley aircraft line.

Alex, meanwhile, would remain with her parents to rest and to supervise the refurbishing of the large house Rafe had bought for them in the fashionable outskirts of Garden City.

Rafe had mixed feelings about the trip. Opening up the West Coast market was vital to the growth of the new company, but he could be gone for more than three months. Being parted from Alex so soon after their wedding would be a strain on them both.

But he wouldn't think about that now. Alex was his bride and the next two weeks were theirs to share. Even now he could scarcely believe she was his, to love and cherish and protect for the rest of their lives. The thought of it thrilled and terrified him. What did he know about being a good husband, let alone a good father? Did he have any business risking his life in the sky now that he had a wife and a baby on the way?

As a flier, Rafe was the soul of prudence. Before every flight he checked his aeroplane and the weather conditions, and he knew better than to push himself or his machine beyond safe limits. But accidents happened. He had seen two of his friends killed and another crippled for life in such accidents. He himself had very nearly died when he'd crashed into the Sound on the afternoon of the Bromleys' lawn party. Next time he might not be so lucky.

But what would he do if he stopped flying? How would he support his family? Who would he be as a man?

The elevator stopped with a little bump. Alex stirred against his shoulder. Her face looked up at him with a tired little smile.

"Almost there." His arm tightened around her. "Can you make it, Mrs. Garrick?"

"I can." She flashed him an impish grin. "Maybe I'll even carry you over the threshold!"

"Ha! We'll see about that!" Rafe scooped her up in his arms and strode down the long hallway to the door of their room. Their bags had been delivered earlier, so it only remained for him to maneuver the key out of his pocket and open the door. She clung to him as he carried her into the bridal suite and set her feet on the thick cream carpet.

He couldn't help gaping as he took in the room. It was lavish beyond belief, all done in shades of white, gold, rose and ivory. Satin brocade fabric covered the walls and ceiling. Velvet as thick and rich as ermine draped the immense, canopied bed and framed the high windows that looked out over the glittering landscape of downtown Manhattan. Such luxury would be nothing new to his bride. But Rafe had never spent a night in such a grand place.

Alex glanced upward at the ornate gold-and-crystal chandelier that hung from the peak of the tented ceiling. "Oh, dear," she fussed. "This won't do at all!"

"What?" Rafe glanced at her in alarm.

"No barn owls! Rafe, dear, can't we get room service to bring one up here, just for us?"

Rafe caught the twinkle in her eye and burst out laughing. "You outrageous little minx, come here!" He caught her in his arms, kissed her soundly and waltzed her across the room to the bed. They collapsed together into the luxurious velvet nest.

He pinned her beneath him, carefully bracing his weight above her so that their bodies barely touched. Even in that position, Rafe felt his arousal stirring. He wanted to be inside her, wanted it so much that his whole body ached.

"I won't break, you know," she whispered. "Neither will the baby. It's tiny and well-protected. The doctor said we could enjoy our honeymoon and not worry."

Despite her reassurances, Rafe didn't want to risk crushing her. Wrapping her in his arms, he rolled them both onto their sides, so that they lay across the bed, face-to-face. "You're sure you're not too tired? It's been a long day for you."

She gave him a low woman-growl and nipped his earlobe. "I'll only be tired if I have to wrestle you down and tie you up to have my way with you!"

"Smart mouth." He kissed her deeply and passionately, knowing her bravado was mostly an act. They were both scared going into this marriage—scared that they weren't up to the challenges of making it work. He was desperate not to disappoint her, and he suspected that Alex felt the same way toward him.

"I love you, my little spitfire," he muttered between kisses. "And I want you so damned much I can taste it. So what do you say we get ready for bed?"

"I've a lovely nightgown in my bag. Mama picked it out. Long sleeves, lots of lace and a high collar with tiny little buttons…" Her eyes sparkled mischievously.

"How would your mother like to see it after I rip it off you?" he snarled in mock ferocity. "Forget the nightgown, woman. I'll take you as nature made you!"

Rafe turned off the lights, leaving the windows uncovered to let in the glow from the full moon and the city below. He wanted to see her, to watch the expression that flickered across her face as he made love to her with slow, gentle tenderness, the way he should have done the first time.

He undressed in the semidarkness, hanging his suit, shirt and tie over the back of a chair. When he turned around he saw that Alex had shed her clothes in a careless heap on the rug, turned down the bed and lay gazing up at him, shamelessly naked, with her glorious hair spilling over the rose satin pillow.

The sight of her took Rafe's breath away. Moonlight played on her golden skin, revealing long, elegant limbs, swollen breasts and a tapering waist. Only the slight roundness below her perfect little shell of a navel hinted that a child was growing in her womb. His child. The awareness weakened Rafe's knees. He found himself wanting to press his face against her belly and kiss the small mound of flesh that their love had caused to be.

She held out her arms and he eased into bed beside her. The satin sheets were chilly against his skin, but her body was silkily warm. He gathered her close, his naked arousal hard and ready against her belly. "The last time we made love, you were wearing boots and wet knickerbockers wadded down around your ankles. The straw was poking us, and I was half-afraid some farmer would see the aeroplane and come to investigate," he murmured against her shoulder. "I like this much better."

"Mmm, so do I." She slid her hands over his back, kneading his muscles like a contented kitten. "Show me how to make you happy, Rafe. Show me how to be a good lover and a good wife to you. I want to more than anything, but I don't know how…"

Her words ended on a moan as his mouth found her swollen, sensitive nipple and began a slow, gentle laving with his tongue. Her breasts were larger than he remembered, the skin taut, the aureoles as dark as raisins. The feel and taste of her in his mouth sent bursts of heat rocketing to his loins. He was ready to take her now, to thrust into that sweet, wet darkness and slake his lust with a few pounding strokes. But no, tonight would be for her, to thrill her, to pleasure her, to give her the love she so desperately needed. Today Alex had placed her life and her future in his hands. This would be his gift to her, the only one he had to give.

"Just be my Alex," he whispered, answering her. "Be yourself and let me love you."

His hand slid down her belly to rest on the small, firm rise that hadn't been there the last time he'd made love to her. For a moment he let it linger there in a loving caress. Then his fingers eased lower to the damp nest at the joining of her thighs. She gasped as he found his way between the slick folds and began to stroke her, taking his time as his mouth sucked her nipple. Her fingers tangled in his hair, pressing his head against her breast. He could feel her trembling as her breath deepened, feel the jerking pulse of her climax against his hand.

"Oh…" she groaned. "That was so…so…"

"We're just getting started, Mrs. Garrick." He shifted upward and kissed her, his erection coming to rest between her thighs. She moved against him, so sensitive now that the slightest pressure sent spasms rippling through her body. His kisses trailed down her throat to her breasts and lower still, brushing her navel.

"I want you, Rafe," she whispered. "Now…inside me, where you belong."

He hesitated, still reluctant to risk hurting her. Then he eased away from her and rolled onto his back. "Come here, Alex. I happen to know you're a fine horsewoman. I've seen you ride. Can you mount a different kind of steed?"

He wasn't sure she'd understand but her grin flashed in the darkness as she shifted above him, her knees straddling his hips. He guided her as she lowered herself onto his rigid shaft. "Oh!" she gasped, settling into place with his full length inside her. Instinctively she leaned forward and began to move. Her hair fell around him like a curtain. Her beautiful, swollen breasts hung above him, as rich and heavy as ripe fruit. He cupped them in his hands, filling his eyes with the sight of her—hair loose and wild, eyes closed, lips parted, little nuances of sensation flickering across her exquisite face. Her sweet flesh enfolded him, sheathing him in satiny warmth. He thrust upward with her motion, deepening the penetration, holding back to prolong her pleasure. She shuddered, clenching around him as the spasms took her again and again, each more intense than the last, until at last he could wait no longer. When the next peak took her, the two of them shattered together and lay quivering in each other's arms.

Rafe cradled her as she drifted off to sleep with her body spooned against his. Here in the night, at least, there were no barriers between them, no Buck Bromleys to manipulate their lives. If they could preserve this small refuge for themselves, keep it safe and warm and private, there might be a chance for them to be happy. He would guard what they'd found, Rafe vowed. He would keep Alex and their children safe, protected from the ugliness and the dangers of the outside world. He might have to be away from her physically, but he would always be there emotionally. He would never give her any reason to doubt his love.

He lay awake, still holding her as the moon rose out of sight and the lights of New York faded into dawn.

Two weeks later, after an awkward Christmas holiday with Buck and Maude, Rafe boarded the train for Los Angeles.

Alex went with her father to see him off. She and Rafe had said their real goodbyes last night in the privacy of their guesthouse bedroom. But she wanted to feel his arms around her one last time. Months would pass before they could be together again. And if the worst were to happen…but no, Alex couldn't let herself dwell on that possibility. If she did, she would be constantly frantic.

The more she learned about her husband's profession, the more she realized how dangerous it was. Aeroplanes crashed and their pilots died. It happened so often that it was almost commonplace. Nightmare images had begun to haunt Alex's dreams—Rafe's plane breaking apart in the air or spiraling to a fiery explosion on the ground. She hadn't told Rafe about her fears. To give them voice would be to make them even more real. But every moment they spent apart would be fraught with worry.

Why did Rafe have to go away now? she brooded as they stood on the crowded platform. He would miss her twenty-first birthday celebration. He would miss the chance to help her pick out new color schemes and furnishings for the guesthouse. He would miss the entire second trimester of her pregnancy. And she would miss him every moment of the day. Why couldn't he be here when she needed him so much?

If anything went wrong, she would never forgive him for going on this trip.

The conductor was shouting, "All aboard!" Rafe shook hands with Buck. His aeroplane had been dismantled, crated and bolted onto a flatcar. The two sharp young mechanics he'd hired were already in their seats, eager to start their adventure.

At the second call, Rafe gathered Alex into his arms and held her close. "Take care of yourself," he whispered.

"You, too," Alex said, fighting tears. "Come back to me."

He released her, and in the next instant he was gone, swinging onto the steps as the train chugged into motion and picked up speed. She stood watching as it glided out of the station and disappeared into the blur of falling snow. Even though she knew Rafe wouldn't see her, she waved.

Swathed in a thick woolen coat, Alex walked the trampled path through the beech grove to the stable. The morning was bright but cold, with sunlight glittering on the crusted snow. A flock of crows winged overhead to settle on the roof of the old carriage house where Rafe's aeroplane had been stored.

By now he'd been gone nearly six weeks—each day an eternity of waiting and wondering. When he could, Rafe telephoned, but the long-distance connections were so bad that Alex could barely hear his voice. His letters were more satisfying, even though they were infrequent and took as long as two weeks to arrive.

She read them again and again, her eyes caressing each close-spaced line.

Alex had moved back into her girlhood room while workmen remodeled their new home, sanding and varnishing the woodwork, enlarging the windows and adding a door between the master bedroom and the small chamber next door that would become a nursery. Now that she was more wife than daughter, it seemed strange, living with her parents. But at least they no longer treated her like a child. She was a married woman, entitled to an extra measure of privacy and freedom—a freedom she relished.

Ahead, through the trees, she could see the low, peaked roof of the stable with its small cupola on top. She walked out almost daily to visit Cherokee. Today she might have enjoyed saddling up for a winter gallop along the beach, but the doctor had forbidden her to ride or even to lift the saddle. She would have to content herself with stroking her beloved sorrel and feeding him an apple from the kitchen.

Alex lengthened her stride. By now her middle had begun to thicken. The morning sickness was gone. She felt strong and energetic. If only Rafe were here, everything would be fine. But she was wretched without him, and the days could not pass swiftly enough to suit her.

The stable hand had finished his duties and was nowhere to be seen. The stable was quiet with the four horses—Cherokee, the two matched bays and Buck's gray hunter—munching their feed. Cherokee raised his handsome head as Alex approached, nickering for his treat.

As she reached up to stroke him, Alex felt the now-familiar flutter below her navel. Her baby—and Rafe's baby—was swimming in its secret sea. Would it be a little boy with her eyes? A little girl with Rafe's thick chestnut hair and keen intellect? Even now, the love she felt for her unborn child was astonishing. In the not-too-distant past, she'd denigrated women who surrendered their lives to birthing and raising children. But that was before she'd experienced the power of that love. Now, at last, she understood.

Cherokee's nose butted her insistently. Alex fished the Jonathan apple out of her pocket and held it on the flat of her hand. The sorrel's velvety lips brushed her palm. His big flat teeth crushed the apple into pulp and juice.

A sense of peace stole over Alex as she stroked the gelding's russet forehead. All seemed right with the world this morning. Even Rafe, she sensed, was safe and well.

The letter she'd received from him yesterday crackled in her pocket. She'd already read it three times, but this calm, bright morning struck her as a good time to read it again. Settling onto a mounting block near the stable's sunny entrance, she unfolded the double sheet of cheap hotel paper and began to read.

My Little Spitfire,

Alex smiled at the pet name he'd given her. She had yet to think of one for him. Nothing seemed to fit the spectacular man he was.

Someday I want to take you to San Francisco. It's beautiful here, with the green land jutting out into the bay and the fog drifting over the rocky islands. The city is raw and alive, with so many fine new buildings that you have to look hard to see the ruins of the 1906 earthquake. Yesterday I took a motorcycle up the coast and saw redwood trees towering into the sky. Standing with those giants all around me was like being in a cathedral. I found myself wishing I could have married you in such a place.

The air shows are going well, the aeroplane performing without a hitch. Your father will be pleased when he receives the dozen new orders I've taken for flying machines. In my spare time, what little there is of it, I've been sketching out more designs for a monoplane. They're popular in Europe, and there's a growing demand for them here. Since the single wing has less drag, they tend to be more maneuverable in the air, although in my opinion you can't beat a biplane for stability.

But I don't want to bore you with technicalities. I'll just close by saying how much I miss you and wish I could hold you in my arms tonight. I'll be counting the days until I can see you, all plump and rosy with your beautiful belly poking way out to there…

Alex refolded the letter, a wistful smile on her face. Rafe's letters were always cheerful. He never complained about the long hours, the drab hotel rooms and tasteless food or the tedium of living out of a suitcase. She knew he was trying to keep her spirits up. For that, she loved him all the more.

Rising, she tucked the letter into the pocket of her coat, and turned back to give Cherokee a farewell pat.

That was when she saw it—a sight that made her temper explode like a keg of gunpowder.

Lying on the straw-littered floor of the stable was the burned-out stub of a cigarette.

Mick, the stable hand, did his work well enough, but Alex had distrusted him on sight. Now she knew why.

For anyone who worked around horses, smoking in the stable was an unthinkable sin. A match or butt, carelessly tossed, could ignite the straw, turning the place into a blazing inferno within seconds. The very idea that this young lout would endanger Cherokee and the other horses by breaking such a vital rule was enough to send Alex into a rage.

Picking up the cigarette butt, she snatched a riding whip from a rack near the door and stormed outside. She was going to find Mick, wherever he'd slunk off to. And when she did, he would wish he'd never been born!

Chapter Eleven

The short search it took to find the stable hand did nothing to cool Alex's temper. Fury welled in her afresh as she spotted Mick behind the house. He was leaning against the clothesline pole, smoking as he chatted with Katy, the red-haired laundry maid.

Bristling, Alex strode up the path toward them. "Go into the house, Katy," she snapped. "Now."

The girl flashed her a startled glance and bolted up the back steps, leaving the two of them alone. Mick continued to lean against the pole, blowing puffs of smoke out through his nostrils.

"Somethin' wrong, ma'am?" he asked.

"Yes, something's wrong!" Alex spat out the words as she thrust the cigarette butt in his face. "I found this in the stable. I believe it's your brand."

He shrugged. "So?"

"Smoking in a stable? Don't you know what could happen?"

Again, he shrugged. "It was snowing out. I needed a fag. Horses didn't care."

He put the cigarette to his lips, then removed it and blew a stream of smoke toward her. The riding whip cracked down hard on his wrist. He yelped as the cigarette fell to the trampled snow. He stared at Alex, clutching his arm to his ribs.

"Watch it, lady, you damn near broke my hand," he whined.

Alex shook the whip in his face. "Next time I'll break something else. You're fired. Get your things and get off the property now. If I see you around here again I'll have you arrested for trespassing."

He stood his ground. "Mr. Bromley owes me wages."

"I'll mention that to my father when I tell him what you did. Now get out of here. I won't have you near our horses again!"

He hesitated, glaring at her with an expression of pure hatred. Alex's flesh crawled with sudden fear. Mick was not a big fellow, but he was tough and wiry. If he set out to hurt her, even with the riding whip, she'd be no match for him.

Moving with slow insolence, he eased away from the pole, spat on the ground and stalked around the house. Alex's legs quivered beneath her as she watched him go.

Dealing with such a man again could be dangerous. She would ask Mr. Ames, the groundskeeper, a husky man who was loyal to the family, to keep an eye on Mick and make sure he was gone. Then tonight at dinner she would let Buck know what had happened.

Feeling drained, she mounted the back stairs to the second floor. If only Rafe were here. She missed his powerful body and comforting arms. She missed the sense of safety she always felt with him—never more than now.

Buck scolded her that night when he heard what had happened. "I agree that the bastard deserved to be fired," he said. "But you should never have taken him on alone, Alex. There's no telling what he might have done. Why didn't you wait for me to deal with him, or at least call someone to back you up?"

"Oh, you're right." Alex played with her mashed potatoes, feeling like a child called on the carpet. "I was so angry, it didn't occur to me that he might be dangerous. The idea that he could have set the stable on fire—"

"Well, never mind, what's done is done." Buck sliced into his filet mignon and speared a generous hunk of meat with his fork. "But don't take any chances with your safety, girl. I don't want you wandering out alone until we know the fellow's no threat. You've got a child to protect now."

"I know. Believe me, I'd never do anything to put my baby at risk." But she had, Alex chastised herself. If Mick had attacked her physically she could have fallen or been pushed against something with enough force to trigger a miscarriage. In the future she would be more careful.

Too agitated to sleep that night, Alex spent two hours writing a letter to Rafe. Since he was on the road, sending any kind of mail to him was a problem. More often than not her letters missed him and came back to Long Island unopened. But sometimes she simply needed to pour out her heart. Tonight she described her wonder at the baby growing and moving inside her. She told him about her disturbing day and how much she'd wished for his protecting arms around her. And she spent most of her time on a lengthy paragraph telling him how much she loved him.

It was after ten o'clock when she slipped the letter into the drawer of her writing desk, turned off the lamp and climbed wearily into bed. She lay awake for what seemed like hours before drifting into slumber.

Her dreams were fitful and frightening. Flames were roaring from the stable. She could smell the smoke and hear the screams of the trapped horses. She was running frantically toward the fire. Her legs thrashed, carrying her at the awful slow-motion pace that only comes in nightmares. The horses were dying and she couldn't move fast enough to reach them.

Something startled her awake. Her eyes were looking at a flickering reddish light through the far window.

Flying across the bedroom she jerked the window open. Through the trees she could see the hellish glow of the burning stable and hear, faintly, the clamor of shouting men and shrieking horses.

Somehow she got her boots on her bare feet and found her coat. Throwing it on over her robe she raced down the back stairs and onto the path that wound through the beech grove. The fire would have been

Mick's doing, of course. When she remembered the hatred in those brutish eyes she knew there could be no other cause. God in heaven, why hadn't she realized he was capable of this?

Lungs heaving, she burst clear of the trees. The stable was an inferno, beyond saving. In the hideous glow she could see her father moving in and out of the smoke. She caught glimpses of Felix, Ames and some of the kitchen staff.

The horses! Her heart convulsed. Then she spotted Buck's big gray hunter and the two bays safely tethered in the trees beyond the stable. But where was Cherokee?

Then she saw him.

Felix and Ames were dragging her horse around the corner of the stable on double lead ropes. Cherokee was screaming, rearing and plunging in a frenzy of terror. Buck was walking toward the horse. Firelight glinted on something in his hand—a pistol.

"No!" Alex sprinted toward him. "No, Papa!"

Buck glanced over his shoulder and saw her. "Get back, Alex!" he shouted. "The horse was burned. He's blinded and in a lot of pain. We've got to put him down."

"No!" She darted past him and plunged toward her beloved animal. "Cherokee! No!"

The red gelding reared. Alex caught a glimpse of his beautiful head, horribly burned, before his hooves came down, striking her to the ground.

The last thing she remembered was the sound of a gunshot.

* * *

Rafe was awakened from a sound sleep by a pounding on his door. "Mr. Garrick! Can you hear me?" It was the voice of the hotel night clerk.

Rafe staggered out of bed and unlocked the door. "What is it?" he asked groggily.

"You have a long-distance telephone call at the desk. A Mr. Bromley. He says it's urgent."

The word *urgent* snapped Rafe fully awake. There was only one reason Buck would be calling at this hour. Something had happened to Alex.

"I'll be right there. Tell him I'm coming." Rafe fumbled for his shoes. Still in his pajamas, he charged down the stairs to the empty lobby and seized the telephone off the reception desk. The California night was warm but he felt cold and clammy all over.

"Buck?" The connection buzzed and crackled. He would have to shout to be heard. But right now he didn't care if he woke the whole damned hotel. He raised his voice.

"Buck! Can you hear me? What is it?"

"Alex…accident…" Buck's voice filtered through the static.

"Talk louder! Is she all right?"

"She will be." Buck was shouting now. "But she lost the baby."

Something sharp and painful clenched in Rafe's gut. "Tell her I'm coming!" he yelled into the phone. "Next train out of here!"

"Nothing you can do!" Buck shouted back. "You don't need to—"

"No. I'm coming." Rafe hung up the phone. If Buck thought he was going to stay here and peddle aeroplanes when Alex needed him, he was crazy. Bloody hell, why had he left her in the first place? He had yet to learn what had happened. Whatever it was, if he'd been there he might have protected her.

Returning to his room, he turned on the light, dressed and began checking train schedules from the list in his bag. He would leave the two mechanics to see to the aeroplane. If need be, they could crate it up and bring it home to Long Island. He would let them know later. Right now he couldn't be bothered to make that decision.

Alex would be devastated. She'd been happy and excited about the baby. So had he, once he'd gotten used to the idea. Heaven willing they would have more children; but this first child of their love, this wondrous little person he would never have the joy of knowing, was gone forever.

Red-eyed and weary, Rafe climbed out of the taxi, paid the driver and shouldered his duffel bag. He'd spent the past five days and four nights sitting up on trains and agonizing over Alex. He ached to see her, to feel her in his arms as they held and comforted each other. Tomorrow he planned to speak with Buck about these long separations. She was going to need him, and he wanted to be here for her.

At the front door he hesitated, then pressed the latch. He was family now, but it still felt strange to enter the grand Bromley house without raising the massive lion-headed knocker and waiting for the butler to let him in.

As he stepped into the foyer he saw Maude coming down the stairs. She looked older than he remembered, with a sag about her shoulders that hadn't been there the night she'd walked like royalty into his drab little room.

"Thank goodness you're here!" She hurried down to meet him. "You'll want to see Alexandra, of course, but I was hoping to speak with you first and spare her having to tell you…" She looked him up and down. "You must be worn out. Would you like something to eat? A sandwich? Some coffee?"

Rafe shook his head. "I just want to find Alex. How is she?"

Maude shook her head. "Physically she's as well as could be expected. But she's taken this hard, Rafe. She blames herself for not having been more careful. And the loss of her horse…merciful heaven, how she loved that animal. That's made things even worse."

"Tell me what happened," Rafe said.

Staggering emotions swept over him as Maude's story unfolded. Rage, horror, pity, grief… Rafe's hand gripped the newel post on the banister, his knuckles whitening as he listened.

"What about the bastard who set the fire? If he's still out there, so help me—"

"No, he's in jail," Maude said. "The police found enough evidence to keep him there for a long time, especially since he's been linked to other fires. Buck's furious with himself for having hired the man without checking his references. And I'm partly to blame as well. I didn't even wake up until they carried Alexandra back into the house. If I'd heard her leaving I might have been able to stop her."

"It seems we're all at fault in some way." Rafe turned and mounted the first few steps. "If I'd been here, I'd have been with her. I could have kept her safe."

Leaden-hearted, he climbed the stairs. His Alex had been through hell and he'd been on the other side of the continent, out of reach. No more, he vowed. The next time he left for any length of time, he would take her with him. He never wanted to be parted from her again.

The door to her bedroom was slightly ajar. Rafe opened it softly, slipped inside and closed it behind him.

The room was dim, the shades drawn over the lace-curtained windows. The air smelled cloyingly of hot-house flowers and disinfectant. Alex lay on her back beneath the white canopy of her rosewood bed, her slender body barely making a rise beneath the quilted satin coverlet. At first Rafe thought she was asleep. Then he saw that her eyes were open. Silent tears trickled down her temples to soak into the damp tangle of her hair.

"Alex." He bent over her. She stared up at him, her gaze empty. Without a word, Rafe reached between the sheets and scooped her up in his arms. Her limp white nightgown drooped around her like a shroud. But she'd lost so much weight. There was nothing to her.

"I'm here, love," he murmured, cradling her against

his chest. "You've been through a bad time, but the worst is over. You're going to be all right."

Her arm crept around his neck. "I lost our baby, Rafe. It was a boy—Dr. Fleury told me that, but he wouldn't let me see him. And Cherokee's gone. Papa had to sh-shoot him. It was my fault, all my fault…that awful man…"

"Hush. It's not your fault. Bad things happen, Alex. Nobody blames you." He kissed her colorless forehead. In his line of vision was a shelf with a large silver trophy cup on it. Above the shelf a framed photograph hung on the wall. It showed a pretty teenager jumping a gate on a magnificent russet horse. The girl was Alex. The horse was Cherokee.

"There's another thing," she whispered. "Dr. Fleury says, because of the way I was trampled, there's a chance I might not be able to have more babies. I made him promise not to tell Mama and Papa. They'd be devastated. But I can't keep it from you. You have to know, in case you want to l-leave…" Her voice and body quivered as she spoke. "I keep asking myself, why am I alive? I don't deserve to be."

"Stop it!" Genuinely frightened, he gave her a none-too-gentle shake. "You can't talk like that! We'll get through this! Lord knows, people have survived worse!"

She shook her head. "I've been thinking about the way things are, Rafe. Why should you stay married to me now that the baby's gone? You could walk away and be free."

"Stop talking nonsense. How long's it been since you had a decent meal?"

Alex didn't reply. Looking past her, Rafe noticed the

untouched tray on the bedside table. A wisp of steam rose from a bowl of chicken soup.

Settling her back in the bed, he arranged the pillows behind her and placed the tray on her lap. "No more talking. You need to get your strength back," he said firmly. "Now, are you going to eat this or do I have to spoon it into your mouth?"

She gazed up at him, her violet eyes welling with tears. Rafe sighed as he stroked a knuckle along the soft curve of her cheek.

"Come back to me, Alex," he pleaded gently. "I need you. I need my wife."

Her hand moved. Slowly and shakily she picked up the spoon, dipped it into the soup and raised it to her lips. Rafe watched her eat, feeling the effort in every swallow. She was a strong woman, his Alex. She would recover from this blow. But this nightmare episode had made him realize how vulnerable she was. He had very nearly lost her. He would never leave her unprotected again.

Spring had come early to Long Island this year. Clumps of daffodil and grape hyacinth dotted the grounds of the Bromley estate. Seagulls dipped and soared above the Sound. The sunlit air was so warm that it was pleasant to be outdoors with a light jacket.

Alex had spent the morning visiting her mother. Now she sat in a wicker chair on the terrace of her parents' house, sipping hot tea and nibbling a fresh scone Maude had brought from the kitchen.

"You really should eat more, Alexandra," Maude chided. "Look at you! You're as thin as a rail!"

"I do eat, Mama. I stuff myself at every meal." It was a lie. Since the miscarriage, her body had lost all desire for food. When she looked in her mirror, the stranger gazing back at her reminded her of a half-starved wolf. The worst part was, she didn't care. Not about food, not about clothes, not about furnishing the newly remodeled home she and Rafe had moved into six weeks ago.

Even her desire for her husband was at low ebb. Rafe had been kind and tender, and she loved him deeply. But there were times when even love wasn't enough. Something was wrong with her. She'd tried pretending everything was fine. It hadn't helped.

"Would you like to drive into town this afternoon?" her mother asked brightly. "I hear Buckingham's has some new china patterns. Maybe you'll see something you like."

"Oh, Mama, the old guesthouse dishes will do us fine. It's not as if we planned to do a lot of entertaining." *Especially not with Rafe working sixteen-hour days on the new monoplane design,* she added silently. It was good to have Rafe at home, but this new project had swallowed him up. He was so busy that most days he left for the factory at dawn and didn't get home until well after dark.

"But at least you'll need monogrammed linens," Maude fussed. "There's that new store in Minneola. Minton's Emporium? It might be worth looking."

Alex sighed. She'd always considered monograms a useless bit of vanity. "Oh, all right. But only if you promise to drive."

"What? Oh, no, Alexandra! Maybe on the back roads, but not in town!"

Alex's one accomplishment in the past few weeks had been teaching her mother to drive Buck's old green Cadillac. At first Maude had protested vehemently, but Alex had convinced her that knowing how to drive might be useful in an emergency. Now, with Alex coaching, Maude could crank and start the car. She'd even found the courage to chug along country lanes at twenty-five miles an hour, her white hands clutching the wheel as if she were driving a runaway locomotive.

"I'll drive to the main road and home again," Maude said. "But you'll have to take it the rest of the way. My heart—"

"Oh, all right." Alex stretched lazily. These days she was getting around on Rafe's motorcycle, which she'd commandeered after he'd bought a new Packard to drive to work. Rafe had offered her a car, but she enjoyed the simple freedom of the bike, as well as the scandalized glances she drew when she rode it. "Really, Mama, driving to town's easy once you get used to it. Next time, all right?"

"We'll see." Maude rose from her chair. "Give me a few minutes to change. We can have lunch in that cute little tea shop Elvira Townsend was telling me about." She eyed Alex's divided pongee skirt, middy blouse and short, quilted coat. "I do wish you'd worn something nicer. But I suppose when you ride that awful machine…" She left the sentence unfinished.

Alex stood watching as her mother disappeared into the house. Dr. Fleury had checked Maude's heart and pronounced it healthy enough for normal activity. Still, Maude used it as an excuse to avoid whatever she didn't want to do.

But what of it? Lately Alex had caught herself using her own tragedy in the same fashion.

A mutter of realization escaped her lips. What she'd feared and fought against all along was coming to pass. She was evolving into her mother.

Here she was, like Maude, passing time with empty amusements while her husband buried himself in work, then turning away at night because she was too dispirited to care about pleasing him, let alone pleasing herself. Rafe was a compellingly attractive man. She'd seen the way women flocked around him. How long would it take him to lose patience and seek affection elsewhere, just as Buck had?

Alex had never understood her parents' marriage. Now she was well on her way to reliving it.

She gathered the tea things onto a tray, fighting the impulse to fling the dainty heirloom cups against the brick wall. What was wrong with her? It was as if she had a caged animal trapped inside her and she didn't know how to set it free.

She was walking back toward the French doors when she heard the distant drone of an aircraft engine. Looking up, she saw a dot above the horizon. As it flew closer she recognized one of the Bleriot monoplanes from the Moisant Flying School. The pilot appeared to be practicing turns, banking the wings, dipping and circling like a silver bird in sky of infinite blue.

Alex's heart crept into her throat as she watched it...so beautiful, so free. Her eyes misted as she remembered her lost dream of flying. Was it too late to get that dream back?

She followed the little craft with her eyes, imagining her hand on the stick, her feet on the rudder bar, her body one with the soaring wings. Only when the monoplane had swung back toward the airfield and vanished behind the trees did she turn around and go into the house. Her pulse was racing, pounding so hard that she felt dizzy.

She would do it—she had to do it.

Tonight she would talk to Rafe. Surely he'd understand and support her decision. If he loved her, how could he deny her something so vital to her happiness?

For the first time since the loss of her baby, Alex felt alive inside.

It was after nine o'clock when she heard Rafe's Packard coming up the drive. The cook had gone home for the night, but Alex had kept his favorite dinner of roast beef and baked potatoes warming in the oven. She bustled around the kitchen to get everything on the table.

Minutes later Rafe walked through the door, shrugged out of his leather jacket and laid it over the back of a chair. Alex loved seeing him in the rumpled khakis he insisted on wearing to work. He reminded her of the nineteenth-century explorers who'd trekked the exotic regions of the globe. All he lacked was a walking stick, a map and a pith helmet.

Tonight her explorer looked exhausted. His blood-shot eyes were ringed by pits of shadow, and there was a smudge on his left cheek that he hadn't bothered to wipe away. Alex's heart contracted. She'd been so wrapped up in her own misery that she'd failed to see what was happening to her husband. Why hadn't she realized how worn down he was?

She gave him a hug, which he barely returned. "You look all in," she said. "How's the monoplane coming along?"

"Fine." He sank into his place at the table, looking at the food as if it were made out of papier-mâché. "It's just that—" He shrugged. "Never mind. I don't want to trouble you with business."

Alex sat, reached across the table and laid a hand on his arm. "Tell me, Rafe," she insisted. "If something's bothering you, I want to know about it."

He took a sip of the wine she'd poured, then put the glass down as if it had no taste. "Let's just say your father and I had words."

"Is that so bad? Papa's the sort of man who has words with everyone."

Rafe shook his head. "Your father wants me to design a new heavy-duty biplane to carry weapons. Guns, bombs…" His shoulders sagged. "He believes that war is coming in Europe, and that sooner or later America will be caught up in it. He wants to be in position to make a huge profit. I've always held that the best use of aircraft in a war is for reconnaissance. But Buck wants to turn flying machines into killing machines. He doesn't give a damn about the innocent people under his bloody bombs—women, children…"

His fist balled on the white tablecloth. "The hell of it is, he's probably right. The way things are going in Europe, there could be a war soon. And if we don't start putting weapons on aeroplanes, somebody else will." He sighed. "I just don't want it to be me, Alex."

"You're full of surprises. I didn't know I'd married a pacifist."

"I don't know that I am. I can't say I believe in peace at any price. But your father's plan has triggered some soul-searching and some painful memories."

Alex rose, walked around the table and began massaging his shoulders. His muscles were tight knots of frustration.

"My grandfather lived with us in England," he said. "As a younger man, he fought in the Crimea. He came home blind, with a scarred face and a missing leg. It was the only way I ever knew him. All he ever talked about was the war, maybe because it was the last thing he saw. As a boy I used to sit with him while he filled my head with stories—villages blown apart by cannon fire, limbs and heads flying, men impaled on bayonets... The images he created in my mind were so vivid I can still see them." Rafe shook his head. "One night—don't ask me how—my grandfather got his hands on a pistol. We heard a shot and came running to find him dead. After that my parents sold the house and we came to America."

"Oh, Rafe!" She laid her cheek against the top of his head. "What an awful thing for a child. I'm so sorry."

"For as long as I've cared about flying, I've had this vision of the aeroplane as an object of freedom and beauty," he said. "Your father only sees it as a way to make money. He can't understand why I'd refuse to turn it into a weapon."

"So, did you refuse?"

"Yes, on no uncertain terms. But he'll do what he pleases, even if it means hiring another engineer to design the warplane. I could walk away right now. But then I'd lose any hope of changing his mind. Essentially, I'd be right back where I was when we met."

Alex sensed what he hadn't said. If he left Buck it would take time to find a new backer for his designs. And he had a wife to support—a wife whose money he was too proud to touch. Rafe had gotten himself into this trap for her sake.

"For what it's worth, I agree with you," she said, "and I expect Mama would, too. But Papa wouldn't listen to either of us. I feel so helpless."

"Then sit down and let's eat." He waited for her to take her chair, then picked up his fork and took a dispirited bite of the roast. "We've got some time. He won't be pushing to start on the new models until the end of the flying season. For now I'm going to focus on getting the monoplane ready for the summer air shows. The ones we've scheduled are in the East, so I won't be far from home. You could even come along sometimes. Would you like that?"

Alex's pulse jumped. It wasn't the best time, she knew, but Rafe had just given her the perfect opening.

"I do want to come along," she said. "But not just to watch. I want to fly, Rafe. I want to share that with you."

Shock was stamped all over his face. "Alex—"

"No, *listen.*" She leaned toward him across the table. "I can take lessons and get my license this spring. By summer I'll be ready to fly in the shows. I've got the time, I've got the money. I can do this!"

Rafe's jaw tightened. He shook his head. "No, Alex. It's out of the question."

"Why not?" Her fist clenched on the table. "Give me one good reason!"

"You're a woman. And a wife. My wife."

"I don't see that being married has anything to do with this!" Alex retorted. "And Harriet Quimby's a woman. If she can be a pilot, why can't I?"

"You don't understand. It's too dangerous. In an aeroplane there's no such thing as a small mistake. If something goes wrong, chances are you'll pay with your life. Harriet knows that. She takes that chance every time she goes up."

"*So do you!* You think I don't worry about you?"

He sighed and laid a hand over her fist. "Alex, I've been flying almost as long as the bloody Wright brothers. And I don't take risks. I'm very careful, especially now. That wouldn't be the case with you, and we both know it." His fingers tightened over hers. "Damn it, woman, I don't want to lose you! I don't want to lose the years we could have together."

He released her hand. "I'm sorry, but the answer's no. Find some less dangerous way to amuse yourself, maybe a new horse—"

"No. Not a new horse. Never again." Alex picked at

her food, knowing that further argument would be useless. Amuse herself, indeed! How could she make him understand? She wanted to fly. She *needed* to fly.

And by heaven, fly she would!

Chapter Twelve

Alex gripped the lever as her plane fishtailed across the field. The thirty-horsepower Gnome engine droned like a giant bumblebee, spraying castor oil onto her goggles and onto the grimy mechanic's coveralls she wore.

The Moisant training craft, designed for students, would rise only a few feet off the ground. The challenge of the exercise, known as grass clipping, was to steer the machine in a straight line. It was harder than she'd expected. Only after she'd mastered the skill would she be qualified to take short hops of twenty feet or so in an intermediate plane.

Two weeks ago, while Rafe was at work, she'd ridden the motorcycle to the aerodrome and enrolled in the Moisant School of Aviation. Her timing had been good. The next round of classes was set to start in a few days.

She had paid the $750 instruction fee plus the $250 breakage deposit in cash. The five-week course included two weeks of ground school and flight simulation, followed by three weeks of various practice runs with time off for bad weather.

After the first two weeks of ground school the daily lessons were brief. Alex would show up on the field at dawn, pull the stained coveralls over her knicker-bockers and wait her turn to climb into the little three-wheeled monoplane. If there was no wind, she would be lucky to get five or ten minutes of skimming across the field. Learning was a painstakingly slow procedure, but it made for safe, competent fliers.

Alex's mechanical experience and her burning desire to fly had made her a star student. But she could barely control her impatience. She crossed off each day on a mental calendar, living for the moment when she would soar into the sky for the first time.

Ahead of her, on the far side of the mile-wide field, the burly mechanic stood waiting to swing the trainer around for the return trip. The same man had assisted Rafe the day he'd taken her flying. At first she'd been concerned that he might recognize her. Now, masked as she was by helmet, goggles and grease, she knew her secret was safe.

Alex wasn't worried about running into her husband here. Since he'd put in hangars and an airstrip near the factory, Rafe no longer flew from the busy field at Hempstead Plains. As an added precaution, however, Alex had left her wedding ring home and registered under her maiden name. Rafe was well-known around the aerodrome. She didn't want word getting back to him that his wife was learning to fly.

She hated deceiving him. But even deception was better than watching their marriage decay. Rafe had fallen in love with a fearless, passionate woman who'd earned the right to be treated as his equal. Somehow she had to find that woman again.

Rafe's predawn work schedule made it easy for Alex to get to her flying lessons, and she was always waiting when he came home. But sooner or later Rafe would learn that she'd defied his wishes. He'd be hurt and angry and would likely force her to stop flying. Then what? Would she defy him again, this time at the price of her marriage?

Guilt and.worry weighed on her. But the flying lessons had given her back her appetite for life. How could she abandon them, like a butterfly crawling back into its chrysalis to fold its wings and die? It was unthinkable.

After days of agonizing, Alex had made her decision. She would keep her secret until she earned her pilot's license. With that accomplishment in hand, she might be able to change Rafe's mind about letting her fly with him. It would mean weeks of lying to the man she loved. There would be times when she'd hate herself for it. But she couldn't risk losing what she'd found. It was too important.

She wiped her goggles clean while the mechanic turned the plane. Then she headed back across the field to where the instructor and the other students waited. This time the run was flawless. Soon she would be in the sky.

"Excellent, mademoiselle." The instructor, a natty little Frenchman, gave her an approving nod as she climbed out of the seat. "Tomorrow with the Blériot, yes?"

Alex left the field walking on air. She'd removed her goggles and helmet and was headed for the locker room when she passed an elegant figure in a purple silk flying suit. Harriet Quimby had just become the first woman to fly across the English Channel. The feat had made her an international star. Sunlight glinted on her titian hair as she flashed Alex a radiant smile.

"How's it going?" she asked.

Alex found her tongue. "Better than usual today. Sometimes it's frustrating. I just want to get off the ground."

Harriet laughed. "You will. And when you do, you'll know that all that grass clipping was worth it!"

Bedazzled, Alex watched her idol stride toward the field. She'd had a good run, her teacher had praised her and the fabulous Harriet Quimby had just spoken to her as an equal. How could the day get any better?

Rising late, the spring moon hung like a silver teardrop above the trees. The night was warm, the air vibrant with cricket songs. From beyond the six-foot hedge that framed the yard, a pair of owls serenaded each other in the darkness.

Rafe sat with Alex on the porch swing, his arm lying across her shoulders. She nestled against his side, her hair a fragrant tickle against his throat. He'd left work early tonight and they'd driven into Garden City for a pleasant dinner. Walking in from the car, they'd crossed the wide porch and ended up on the swing. After a frenetically busy week, it was heaven, he thought, just to sit, relax, cuddle a bit and anticipate the night to come.

Tilting her head, she nibbled playfully at his earlobe. She was back, his Alex. After long weeks of despondency she was his lively, glowing little hellion once more, challenging him at every turn. She'd also become a tigress between the sheets, something he planned to take full advantage of when they went inside the house…or maybe sooner, he thought, as he took a mental measure of the porch swing.

Rafe sighed. It was tempting as hell to enjoy the change in Alex without questioning what lay behind it. But he knew better. Alex was often gone when he telephoned the house during the day. He'd noticed fresh mud spatters on the motorcycle and oil stains under her fingernails. Without any visible reason, she seemed happy to the point of giddiness.

Under similar circumstances, a man might suspect his wife of having an affair. But he knew his Alex. She wasn't seeing another man. The little vixen was flying, damn it! Flying against his express orders!

An affair might be easier to deal with. He could find the man, beat him to a bloody pulp and threaten him with worse if he ever came near her again. But flying? Rafe knew all too well how it felt when something got into your blood and you had to have it. It was like a drug. You couldn't look at the sky without wanting to be up there.

Should he stop her? Could he?

She shifted against him, pulling his hand down to cup her breast. Her ripe warmth seeped into his palm. His thumb brushed her taut nipple through the fabric of her bodice. He could feel his arousal stirring, straining the seam of his trousers. No, the swing wouldn't do tonight. He wanted her in bed, spread naked beneath him, or maybe leaning above him, her breasts skimming his face as she drove him deeper and deeper into her wet, silken darkness.

Rafe swore silently. What in bloody hell was he going to do? Alex seemed so happy. He wanted to keep her that way. But whenever he imagined her in the air the memory of every horrific crash he'd ever witnessed came back to haunt him. He saw the shattered wreckage, the twisted bodies, the blood... How could he risk losing her that way?

She raised his free hands to her lips and brushed a nibbling trail across his knuckles. "You're so quiet tonight," she murmured. "What are you thinking?"

Should he tell her? Should he bring everything out in the open now so she could lie through her pretty teeth and deny it?

Rafe exhaled raggedly. They'd had a good evening with more to come. He didn't want to spoil it. But one thing was clear. Whatever the outcome, the lies between them had to stop. He would stop them tomorrow, he vowed. He would do it the only way he could—with the truth.

"Rafe?" Her violet eyes reflected miniature moons in the darkness. "What is it?"

He kissed the tip of her nose. "I was just thinking that this bench is too hard and too narrow for what I'd like to do to you right now."

"Oh?" She blinked innocently. "And what, precisely, is that, Mr. Garrick?"

Rafe leaned forward and whispered in her ear, using language calculated to make a streetwalker blush.

"Oh, my goodness!" She wiggled away from him and tugged him to his feet. "In that case, what are we waiting for?"

Not too high, now, mademoiselle. Three or four meters at first, no more. Like a baby learning to walk. Alex forced herself to remember the instructor's words as the Blériot monoplane kangaroo-hopped across the field. It was all she could do to keep from pulling the stick all the way back, causing the craft to shoot upward like a bird. She'd seen one student do that. The aeroplane and the young man had both survived the crash, but the little Frenchman had been livid.

Alex had no desire to make the same mistake. Still, every time the wheels left the ground her pulse rocketed. Soon she'd be making higher leaps in the plane, then taking off and landing on the field. Once she'd mastered turning maneuvers in the air, she'd be ready to try for her pilot's license.

Reluctantly, she steered back to the line of waiting students and climbed out of her seat. The instructor gave her a nod of approval. She was finished for the day.

She winced as she lifted a leg to step out of her coveralls. Last night's loving with Rafe had been even more passionate than usual. Afterward, as they'd drifted off in each other's arms, she'd been sorely tempted to tell him about her flying lessons. She loved him so much, and she hated the idea of keeping secrets from him. Still, she'd held her tongue. What would he do if he learned the truth?

Could he force her to stop flying? Would he? The questions had gnawed at her for weeks. He could hardly take her prisoner and lock her in the house. But Rafe was an influential man. He could contact the Moisant School and demand that they cease giving her lessons. As her husband, he'd be considered well within his rights.

And then what? Faced with the choice of submitting or leaving him, what would she do?

Preoccupied, she washed her hands and face, fluffed her hair and headed for the lot where she'd left the motorcycle. There was more than just flying at stake here. The real question was, did Rafe love her enough to care about her happiness? Would he give her the freedom to pursue her dreams, or would he demand that she be his subservient little wife for the rest of her days?

Lost in thought, Alex didn't notice the tall man waiting next to the motorcycle until he spoke.

"Hello, Alex."

Alex's heart seemed to drop into the pit of her stomach. Her first impulse was to turn away and pretend she hadn't seen him. But this was no time for cowardice. It was time to face the truth…and Rafe.

She walked toward him until they stood almost toe to toe. His eyes flashed cold fire. Alex forced herself not to flinch.

"How long have you known?" she asked him.

"Only since I got here this morning and saw the bike. But I've suspected for a while. You've been happy, and I knew it had nothing to do with me."

"Oh, Rafe!" At that moment all she wanted was to fling herself into his arms, beg forgiveness and promise never to disobey him again. But she couldn't back down now. There was too much at stake.

He took her arm, steering her toward his car. "Why didn't you tell me?" he demanded.

"You know why. If you'd known, you'd have tried to stop me."

"So you lied."

"Yes, I lied." She swung around to face him again, blocking his path to the Packard. "Put yourself in my place, Rafe. What if somebody ordered you to stop flying? What would you do?"

"That would depend on who was giving the orders."

"What if it was me? What if I were to say that I couldn't bear the thought of losing you in a crash and I ordered you to stop. What would you do?"

Turning away from the car, he led her onto a path that meandered away from the crowded parking lot.

"In the first place, I'm your husband," he said. "You'd have no right to give me orders of any kind."

Alex swallowed a gasp. "You sound like my father talking to my mother."

"I'm only trying to talk sense into you. And I'm doing it for your own good."

"Then answer my question. What if I were to beg you

to stop flying, beg you out of love for me? Surely I'd be within my rights to do that."

He paused in mid-stride. "I can't imagine your asking such a thing. You know what flying means to me."

"Then understand this, Rafe, it means as much to me."

His grip tightened on her arm. "You're my wife. I can stop you with a word."

"I know," she said softly. "But would you? What if I threatened to leave?"

In the stillness, Alex could hear the distant cry of a kittiwake. The rising sun touched Rafe's chestnut hair, brushing it with a halo of flame. She felt as if she'd just stepped over an invisible line, as if their whole marriage had come down to this frozen moment, with the two of them standing at an impasse.

His hand dropped from her arm. "Would you do it, Alex?" he asked in a taut whisper. "Would you really leave me?"

Somewhere behind them a monoplane roared down the field and rose into the sky. Alex waited for the sound to fade. She was trembling.

"I'm hoping it won't come to that. I love you, Rafe, but I won't be denied my dream. And I won't be controlled like a piece of property."

A muscle twitched in Rafe's jaw. "Do you think that's what I'm trying to do? Control you? Damn it, I've watched people die in aeroplane crashes—good friends, good pilots! I'm trying to save your life, you little fool!"

"And what kind of life would you be saving me for? What if the doctor's right, and I can't have more children? How would I spend all those empty years? Dressing up and going to teas? Raising delphiniums? Planning dinner menus? Maybe Mama could teach me to do needlepoint!"

She could see the frustration boiling up in him. A man with less self-control than Rafe would likely have slapped her. "This is getting us nowhere," he said. "I'm going to work. We'll talk tonight. Can you promise me that you'll be home?"

"Yes. I'll be home, ready to talk." Alex felt as if her knees were giving way beneath her. She fought the impulse to fling her arms around him and give him a desperate kiss. Rafe wouldn't want that. Not now.

He turned and walked to his car without looking back. Alex battled tears as he drove away. What if this impasse couldn't be resolved? Would losing him be worse than turning into an imitation of her mother? Could she stand it if he never held her in his arms again, never kissed her, never made love to her?

Somehow she found her way to the motorcycle. Straddling the seat, she started it up and headed for home.

Rafe willed himself not to speed as he drove the winding back road to the factory. His gut was churning with helpless rage, but that didn't give him the right to cause an accident.

Damn the woman! Why couldn't he get through to her? Didn't she understand that he was trying to save her life?

He remembered the day she'd run Buck's car off the

road. If the car had been an aeroplane she would likely have died. Alex was impulsive and reckless. He adored those traits in her. But impulsive, reckless fliers tended to have short lives. They ignored precautions. They took chances and pushed past safe limits. Sooner or later their luck ran out.

He would lose her if he let her fly.

He would lose her if he didn't.

Rafe knew how it felt to crave the sky. Up there, above the earth was a freedom like no other. A man—or a woman, he supposed—couldn't get enough of it. The urge to fly was a fever in the blood. If Alex had caught that fever, heaven help her. Force her to stop flying and one of two things would happen. Either she would die inside, or she would leave him to follow her dream.

He loved Alex more than life; more, even than he loved the sky.

What was he going to do?

Alex huddled on the front porch steps, her knees pressed to her chest. Her hands bunched and twisted the fabric of her skirt in an agony of waiting. Her eyes peered into the darkness, searching for the familiar headlamps that would tell her Rafe was coming home.

The waning moon slipped apologetically over the neighbor's big spruce trees. A spiritless wind teased at her hair. Crickets droned in the black shadows of the hedge, the sound grating on her raw nerves.

Rafe was late. Even later than usual.

As the parlor clock struck ten, she rose to her feet and

began a restless pacing of the long porch. What if something had happened to him? What if he'd died tonight in some awful accident? She would always remember that the last words they'd exchanged had been spoken in anger.

A few days ago he'd mentioned that the first new monoplane was almost ready for testing. What if he'd taken it up and something had gone wrong? But no, Alex reminded herself. If the plane had crashed, someone would have let her know.

So where was he? Why in heaven's name hadn't he telephoned?

Sinking onto the steps again, she pressed her face to her knees. How had it ever come to this? She loved him so much. Why hadn't she told him, shouted it after him as he stalked away from her this morning. What if she never saw him again?

Raising her head, she caught the gleam of approaching headlamps on the road. Would it be Rafe, coming home at last? Would it be the police, bringing terrible news, or only some traveler passing in the night?

She rose again, scarcely daring to breathe as the auto swung onto the drive. Now she recognized Rafe's Packard and saw the outline of his rumpled figure at the wheel.

She hadn't planned it, but Alex found herself flying down the walk to meet him as he climbed wearily out of the car. Moon shadows deepened the tired lines around his eyes.

She was out of breath by the time she reached him. "I've been worried sick! Where on earth have you been?"

"Working. Thinking." He closed the car door, then

reached out and pulled her close. Alex's arms enfolded him hungrily. Was anything, even the freedom to fly, worth sacrificing Rafe's love? At this moment, with his heart drumming against her ear, she came very close to throwing her dream away. What did it matter as long as they were together? Couldn't she be content with that?

His throat moved against her hair. When he spoke she could hear the strain in his voice. "I've made my decision, love. If flying is the only thing that will make you happy, I won't stand in your way."

"Oh, Rafe—" Her arms tightened around him.

"Listen to me, damn it. I won't pretend it's going to be easy. Every minute you're in the air will be torture for me. Just promise you'll be careful, and that you'll let me keep an eye on you. Otherwise I won't be able to stand it. You hear?"

Alex felt her heart swell and burst. She'd told herself she loved Rafe. But her love seemed a pitiful thing compared to his. She'd told herself he was like her father; but Buck would never have given a woman this kind of freedom. That Rafe loved her enough to risk losing her—the thought was overpowering, more than her selfish little soul could contain.

"Alex?" He worked his thumb under her chin and raised her face to the light. "Oh, Lord, girl, don't cry. You can always change your mind."

"What did I do to deserve you, Rafe?" she whispered. "I've been a spoiled, self-centered brat my whole life. Then life turned around and gave me you. I don't understand it."

"Does anybody understand these things?" He kissed her damp, salty cheeks. "I was a rootless loner before I crashed into your arms. Maybe that makes us even. There's only one thing I know for sure."

"What?"

"Just this. If life gives you a gift, don't waste it. Use it up. Drain it to the last drop. And right now all I want is to make wild, passionate love to you, Mrs. Garrick. So what do you say we go inside?"

Catching her waist, he swept her up the porch and into the house. They were headed for their upstairs bedroom, but in their eagerness, they didn't get far. Tearing at each other's clothes they tumbled together onto a thick sheepskin rug in front of the unlit fireplace.

Their coupling was bittersweet and laced with a savage desperation. He thrust into her with rock-hard urgency, his kisses bruising her swollen lips. She clung to him as if they were falling through space, her hands clawing at his back, her legs clasping his hips, forcing him ever deeper inside her. She cried out as he carried her mercilessly over the brink again, then again…

They made love as if it might be for the last time.

Spent at last, they found their way to the bedroom and collapsed naked between the sheets. Alex was just drifting into slumber when a troubling thought crossed her mind.

"Oh, no," she whispered. "Papa. He'll be apoplectic when he hears about my flying."

"Hush." He kissed her firmly. "I'll deal with your father. He'll be angrier with me than with you. I'm the one who's supposed to be keeping you out of trouble."

"And Mama…oh, dear, she'll be frantic. I just know she'll threaten me with another heart attack."

He sighed. "I'm afraid you'll have to handle her, love. I can go head to head with Buck, but I'm no match for your mother. When it comes to protecting you, she's a lot tougher than she looks."

"Oh, Rafe, I'm sorry for this." She buried her face against his chest, tasting the salt on his skin. "I feel so selfish!"

"It's not too late to change your mind." His lips brushed her tangled hair. "But I won't stop you, Alex. I won't take away your freedom."

"Thank you." Her arms tightened around him. "I love you for that. You don't know how much."

She lay awake, holding him while he sank into exhausted sleep. His skin was cool and smelled of their lovemaking. She drew him into her senses, matching the cadence of her breath to his. She loved him so much. How could she risk losing him? How could she risk his losing her?

Lying here beside her husband, Alex felt ready to give up anything for him. But she knew that tomorrow the sky would call to her, and the urge to fly would be too strong to resist. She could only bless Rafe for understanding.

She would do as he'd asked and make every effort to be careful. She owed him that much. And in the meantime she would cherish every day they had together…aware, as he was, that it might be their last.

Chapter Thirteen

Rafe was at his drafting table, reviewing blueprints, when Buck burst into his office. Rafe steeled his nerves for the confrontation. He'd been expecting this visit and he knew it was going to be ugly.

"I can't believe this!" Buck's face was the color of boiled lobster. "You married my daughter! It was your duty to protect her! And now she's risking her life in those damn fool aeroplanes! Why in hell's name didn't you stop her?"

Rafe gazed at him calmly. "Have you ever been able to stop Alex from doing anything?"

Buck ignored the question. "You're her husband! You could've forbidden her! And if that didn't work, you could've locked her up or even beat some sense into her! I'd rather see her black and blue than see her dead! She's my only child. Anything happens to her, and it's the end of my line! You should be filling her belly with babies, not letting her risk her fool neck in the sky!"

"Sit down, Buck." Rafe indicated the chair next to his desk. "I have something to say, and you need to listen."

Buck glowered from beneath bristling eyebrows. "Whatever lamebrained excuse you've got, I'll hear it on my feet."

"All right. There's something Alex hasn't told you. Maybe it's time you heard it." Rafe cleared the tightness from his throat. "That accident with the horse did a lot of damage, maybe more than we know. Dr. Fleury told her she might not be able to have more children."

Buck sank onto the chair, looking as if he'd been kicked in the stomach. His face appeared to have aged ten years. "You're sure?"

"There's no way to be sure. But it hasn't happened yet, and it's not from lack of trying. Alex has been through a hard time. Harder, I think, than a man can imagine. For the past few months she's been so despondent that I've worried about her mind. I forbade her to fly at first. She did it anyway, of course. What can I say? It's brought her back. I've never seen her so happy."

"So now she's flying with your approval?" Buck demanded.

"Yes."

"Don't you worry that she'll crash?"

"I worry all the time. But I love her too much to stop her."

The air hissed out between Buck's teeth. "Damn you to hell, if she'd married that fine Throckmorton boy, we wouldn't be having this conversation." He rose and stood, glaring at Rafe from across the desk. "I'm warning you here and now, Garrick. If anything happens to my daughter because you let her fly, I'm coming after you with a gun—and so help me, I'll shoot your guts out!"

With his threat quivering in the air, Buck stalked out of Rafe's office and slammed the door behind him. An instant later he opened it again and stood looming in the doorway.

"Another thing," he snarled. "I want your plans for that warplane on my desk by the end of June. No ifs, ands or buts!"

The door slammed again and he was gone.

Rafe stood at the edge of the field, his eyes fixed on the sky. His heart crept into his throat as he watched the Blériot monoplane trace long, looping figure-eights in the air.

Behind him stood the instructor from the Moisant School and two officials from the Aero Club of America. Students lounged around the perimeter of the field. Every eye was on Alex as she tested for her pilot's license—takeoff and landing, two distance flights with turns over a marked area and an altitude ascent of at least fifty meters.

So far his little spitfire had done magnificently. The woman was a damned good pilot—maybe too good. Overconfidence was a dangerous thing in a flier.

Alex had invited her parents to watch the test. Both of them had declined. Maude had pleaded her heart condition. Buck was still furious at Rafe for not having put a stop to his bride's dangerous hobby. Their work relationship had grown cold and formal. Their personal relationship had all but dissolved. Only the fact that their business was thriving kept a lid on Buck's hostility.

The issue of the warplane lay between them like a gauntlet. Rafe hadn't drawn so much as a pencil line and he didn't plan to. Buck could bloody well find someone else to design his killing machine. Sooner or later, he probably would.

Right now Rafe didn't care. His eyes and thoughts were fixed on a white speck in the sky. Alex had taken the little Blériot to a height of more than a hundred and fifty feet. Now the plane descended in an easy spiral. Its motor stopped the instant the skids touched the grass. Coasting, the craft came to a halt within inches of the white landing marker. The watchers burst into cheers.

Alex climbed out of the seat. Her goggles, her helmet and her face were coated with oil from the engine. Grinning, she ripped off the goggles and helmet, flung them skyward and hurled herself into Rafe's arms.

He hugged her, heedless of the greasy mess. Seeing her like this, so utterly happy, had been worth the worry, Rafe told himself. Now if only he could persuade her to stop…but no, he knew better. His Alex was drunk on wind and sky and speed, an intoxication as heady as first love.

The instructor pumped her hand. The officials from the aero club followed, assuring her that she would receive her official pilot's license within two weeks. Then her fellow students, all male, closed in. Laughing and joking, they clapped her shoulders, telling her she'd put them all to shame. Rafe let his wife have her triumph. She'd earned it.

It took Rafe another twenty minutes to get her out of the greasy coveralls and into the car. As he cranked the motor, Alex let her head fall back against the seat and closed her eyes.

"Are you all right?" Rafe asked, climbing into the driver's seat.

Alex nodded, laughing. "It's like a dream. I've never felt so happy in my entire life!" Reaching out, she laid a hand on his knee. "Thank you, Rafe. Thank you for not standing in my way."

Rafe exhaled, letting the worry and tension flow out of him. Maybe now that she'd finished her lessons, she'd ease off on the flying and find safer pursuits. "So what would you like to do for the rest of the day, Mrs. Garrick?"

"Don't you have to go to work?"

He pulled out of the parking lot and onto the road. "I've arranged to take the day off. I'm all yours."

She pondered a moment. "Let's go home and clean up. Then we can go out for lunch to celebrate. After that, I want to see the new monoplane that's been taking so much of your time. It might be just the thing for me."

"For you?" He shot her a startled glance, his heart sinking.

"Why not? Now that I'm no longer a student, I'm going to need my own aeroplane. And since I learned to fly in a monoplane, that's what I'd prefer."

"But your own plane? Hold on a minute, lady, we need to talk about this."

She smiled sweetly. "Harriet Quimby has her own Blériot. I could certainly afford one of those. But you wouldn't want me buying from the competition, would you?"

Rafe took time to weigh his answer. The new monoplane was a revolutionary design, fashioned for speed and maneuverability. The single model Rafe's team had built from his blueprints had surpassed even his expectations. It was capable of dazzling speed and could turn like a falcon in the air. But its limits remained untested. In the hands of a neophyte pilot, especially one with a reckless nature… Bloody hell, the very thought of Alex in that plane was enough to make him break out in a cold sweat.

"The monoplane's a handful," he said. "Besides, we only have one aeroplane. It won't be in production until we've done more testing. Meanwhile, since it's familiar, a Blériot might not be a bad idea. You could always sell it later."

"Maybe." She gazed pensively at the road. "But if I'm going to fly in the air shows with you, it shouldn't be in some other company's machine."

Rafe sighed. He'd forgotten about her plan to fly with him in the air shows. More worry. But as long as she was going to fly anyway, it might not be a bad idea. At least he'd be there to keep an eye on her.

He gave her a slow nod. "In that case, my love, I suggest you learn to fly the biplane. The new monoplane isn't ready, and neither are you."

"Ha! My mother could fly your old biplane."

Rafe chuckled. "Cocky little thing, aren't you? Learn to fly it yourself before you say that. I'll even teach you. What do you say?"

She sighed and squeezed his knee. "All right. But you have to promise."

"I promise. Just let me know when you're ready."

"Tomorrow?"

"Fine. Tomorrow morning before work if the weather's good. The biplane's like a well-broken horse. You'll be flying it in no time."

She laughed. "It's more like a rocking chair. You could sell it to little old ladies."

Rafe breathed a wordless prayer. With the improvements his team had added, the biplane was as stable as any aircraft could be. Its safety was its strongest selling point. As long as she watched the weather and didn't take foolish chances, Alex should be fine in it. Even so, knowing his Alex…

Her fingers crept up his knee, triggering an erotic tingle. He flashed her a wink. "You're a sight, Mrs. Garrick. You're going to need a good bath before you're fit to go anywhere. I'd be happy to wash your back."

"Oh? And what else would you be happy to wash?"

"Try me and find out. You might be surprised." Rafe grinned as he swung the Packard toward home. The day was young and their celebration was just beginning.

Alex stretched like a lazy cat beneath the tangled sheets. "You know, we really ought to get up and get some clothes on. It's nearly eleven."

"What for? I could spend the whole day right here." Rafe pulled her down and nuzzled her bare breast. After the early-morning flight test, they'd arrived home and gone from bath to bed. There they'd stayed, alternately loving and napping, for the past three hours.

Alex raised up on one elbow, her damp hair tumbling in her eyes. "You promised me lunch. And then you promised to show me the monoplane."

"Oh, yes, the monoplane." Rafe sighed. "Did anyone ever tell you that you have the tenacity of a rat terrier?"

"Never!" Alex bent and kissed him. He looked so handsome, so deliciously rumpled, that the sight of him made her throat ache. She loved him so much, and they were so happy right now. Was she a fool to keep pushing the limits?

"All right, if you insist, let's get up." He gave her bare bottom a playful slap. Alex squealed and bounded out of bed.

Forty-five minutes later they were on their way to Toddy's Diner, an unpretentious Garden City restaurant they both liked. After a meal of fresh clams, fried potatoes and baked beans, washed down with ice-cold beer, they took the back road to the factory. Alex felt pleasantly stuffed and completely happy. This was just possibly the best day of her life, and since her father had gone to the city, she knew he wouldn't be around to spoil it.

The factory sprawled on a tract of open land north of Minneola, about eight miles inland from the Bromley estate. Alex had been there many times but not since her marriage. She was amazed at the changes she saw. Rafe had added a row of hangars and a long airstrip on the back of the property. There was also a vast warehouse with space for several aeroplanes to be built at the same time. Rafe walked her through the building, where perhaps a dozen men were working on six biplanes in varying stages of completion. He introduced her to each of them by name—not as Buck Bromley's daughter, but simply as his wife, which pleased her. It was clear to Alex that they all thought highly of their boss.

"If we get enough orders coming in at once, we'll set up an assembly line," Rafe said. "For now, each plane's built separately. The engine parts are machined inside the main factory. Everything else is done right here."

"So where's the new monoplane?"

"You and your one-track mind." He laughed. "Come on outside."

He led her across the grassy lot to the line of six hangars that flanked the runway. Most of the doors were open. In the first hangar she recognized the biplane she and Rafe had rebuilt together. Its silk-covered wings were still in fine condition, but Alex could see the small repair where the bird had struck on that day when her life had changed forever.

It had been eight months since that first flight, Alex realized. If her baby had lived, she'd be great with child and waiting to become a mother. Weeks from now, she'd be holding Rafe's little son in her arms and feeding him at her breast. But she couldn't let herself think of that now. Her life had taken a different course and she was making the best of it.

"This way." Rafe tugged her toward a closed hangar and slid back the door. Alex stared openmouthed.

Rafe's monoplane was like nothing she'd ever seen, or even imagined. Longer than the Blériot, with a single, canted wing mounted on struts above the body, it was as sleek and elegant as a shark. Dark gray silk, varnished to a silvery sheen, covered not only the wing but every inch of the frame. The propeller and rotary engine gleamed with polish. Behind them, two seat compartments lay below the wing.

Alex moved forward to touch the plane's satiny side. "Oh, Rafe, it's like some kind of beautiful animal," she whispered. "I always knew you were an extraordinary man, but to create something like this…" She held out her free hand. He took it and squeezed her fingers.

"So you like our new baby, do you, ma'am?" The voice behind her carried an Irish lilt. Alex turned to see a wiry young man about her own height, with carrot-colored hair and a homely, freckled face, standing in the open doorway.

Rafe grinned. "Alex, this is Tom Flinders, our test pilot. He'll be flying the monoplane in the shows."

"Not you?" Alex asked, surprised.

Rafe shook his head. "I've made my share of flights in it. But I've discovered it's better for business if I stay on the ground and answer questions. Besides, Tom here has cast-iron nerves. That's what it takes to put this machine through its paces."

"Would you like to see what she can do, ma'am?" Flinders asked. "I was about to take her out for a spin."

"Oh, yes!" Alex restrained herself from jumping up and down. As Rafe's wife, it behooved her to show some decorum.

"No fancy stuff, now, Tom," Rafe cautioned. "The lady just got her pilot's license. I don't want you putting any ideas into her head."

"I hear you, sir!" Flinders shot Alex a conspiratorial wink as he and Rafe wheeled the spectacular craft out of the hangar. Whether Rafe liked it or not, Alex knew he would give her a show.

She stood back while Flinders set the chocks in front of the wheels and climbed into the control seat. Rafe gave the propeller a hard spin. When the engine caught, he yanked the chocks aside. The silvery monoplane roared down the runway.

The plane rose and made a low circle of the field. Then it banked and shot into the sky. Up and up it climbed, at a speed and angle Alex would never have believed possible. She gripped Rafe's hand as it all but disappeared into the blue, then descended in a long, ripping dive that would have torn the wings off any other aircraft. Flinders zoomed over the field, banked a turn, barrel-rolled, circled twice and came down to a perfect landing.

Alex began to breathe again as the monoplane coasted to a stop. She ran forward as the young man climbed out and jumped to the ground. "That was amazing!" she exclaimed. "I've never seen flying like that!"

"The credit goes to the machine, ma'am," Flinders replied with a grin. "In case you don't know it, you're married to a genius."

Alex glanced up at Rafe, expecting to see him looking pleased. His jaw was clenched, his mouth white around the edges. "Fly like that again, Tom, and I'll ground you for six bloody months!" he growled. "I want you alive, and I want that aeroplane in one piece! Understood?"

"Understood." Flinders turned away and busied himself with putting the plane back in the hangar. One of the workmen jogged over to help him. Rafe took Alex's arm and led her away.

"How could you talk to him that way?" she demanded once they were out of earshot. "He was only trying to please me."

"How pleased would you have been if he'd crashed and died? Tom's a great pilot but he's too cocksure for his own good. Taking him down a few pegs today could save his life tomorrow. Maybe he'll think twice next time he wants to impress a pretty woman."

"He's a nice young man," Alex said. "I like him."

"So do I. And he's a good pilot. I want to keep him alive." Rafe slipped his arm around her shoulder as they walked to the car. "Sooner or later, if you go to enough air shows, you're bound to see a crash. It's not a thing you'll forget, Alex, especially if it's someone you know. If I'm hard on Tom, and hard on *you,* it's because I don't want any accidents. Don't forget that when you think I'm being an ogre."

"And such an adorable ogre, at that." Alex leaned up to kiss his cheek. "Let's go home. Later we can take the motorcycle and some wine and watch the sunset from the beach."

"Sounds like a fine way to end the day." Rafe cranked the starter and they sprang into the Packard.

"And tomorrow you'll give me a lesson on the biplane?"

"First thing in the morning if it's a calm day. Then you can take the car home and pick me up after work. How's that?"

"Lovely." She settled her head on his shoulder for the ride home. What a spectacular man she'd married—handsome, loving and gifted. She'd known all along that he had talent, but only today, seeing the silver monoplane in flight, had she glimpsed his true genius. Rafe Garrick was just possibly the most brilliant aircraft designer in the world.

When she closed her eyes, she could still see it, the heartbreakingly beautiful craft shooting into the blue. Then that dizzying dive and that barrel roll. In her wildest dreams she'd never have imagined an aeroplane doing such maneuvers. How would it feel, being at the controls of such a machine? She could almost imagine the thrill of it….

Heaven help her, she had fallen in love with Rafe's creation. And no matter how passionately he might argue against it, there was one thing Alex knew.

She was determined to become one of its pilots.

Under a blooming dawn sky, with the air as still as glass, Alex took her first lesson in the biplane. Rafe sat in the passenger seat to help if needed, but after a few pointers, flying the craft became pure pleasure. Its boxy wings lifted so gently that it seemed to float.

"Once you get the knack of it, you'll need some practice in a light wind," Rafe shouted above the sound of the engine. "When you're flying in an air show, you can't wait for calm weather."

Alex nodded, her attention fixed on the airstrip below. She was dressed in her usual helmet and goggles, knickerbockers and one of Rafe's flight jackets. Anyone watching would have guessed her to be a slender young man. Maybe it was time she designed her own flying suit, she mused. Harriet Quimby's one-piece, hooded purple silk costume which, by means of a few fasteners, converted from knickerbockers to a narrow skirt, was as elegant as it was unique. But she could hardly design.

Pulling her focus back to the landing, she glided onto the field, cut the engine and coasted to a stop. Tom Flinders was waiting by the hangar. He grinned up at her.

"Right smart flying, ma'am," he said. "From the looks of it, you'll be piloting our monoplane in no time."

"Don't be putting ideas into her head, Tom," Rafe growled. "My wife will *not* be flying that plane!"

"Got that, sir." Flinders nodded contritely. This time he didn't wink.

"Well now," Alex said sweetly. "Since I won't be piloting the monoplane, the least I deserve is a ride. Don't you agree, gentlemen? After all, it does have two seats."

Flinders took a step backward. "Leave me out of this. I want to keep my job!"

Alex turned to her husband. "Am I asking so much,

Rafe? Just a short flight. No showy maneuvers. Please, I want to understand how it feels to fly in that beautiful machine."

She sensed his hesitation. Rafe knew her too well. One flight would never be enough. She would want another, then another, and before long she'd be begging him to let her pilot the craft. But for now, hers was a reasonable request. With his employee looking on, there was no gracious way to refuse.

"All right. You'll be flying with me. Let's wheel her out, Tom."

Minutes later, Alex was strapped into the front seat of the silver monoplane. Looking down toward her feet, she could see the inner framework, light and strong and perfect. Every inch of wood was varnished, every connection firmly bolted.

Tom Flinders spun the propeller. The engine coughed and roared to life. Alex's pulse thundered as the silver craft sang down the runway. Her breath stopped as it left the ground and soared into the sky. Although she was seated right behind the powerful engine, there was no oil spattering her goggles. Had Rafe devised some sort of screen, or were the engine parts so exquisitely fitted that no oil leaked out?

Alex forgot the question as the monoplane angled upward and began to climb. The landscape shrank away beneath them. She could see the factory and the roads and nearly all of Minneola. She could see the courthouse where she and Rafe had been married. She could see the aerodrome at Hempstead Plains, with aircraft scattered on the field like so many winged insects.

The plane banked, turned and leveled off toward the north. How high were they? A thousand feet? More? She only knew that she'd never flown at this altitude— nor at this speed. At least fifty-five or sixty miles an hour, she guessed. Rafe was just behind her, at the controls, but there was no way to ask him. The drone of the engine was too loud for conversation.

For a few minutes they flew above the jagged north coastline with its sheltered coves and sprawling estates. Flocks of seabirds rose like clouds from the water. Trawlers, stringing out their lines, chugged along the deep channels.

All too soon Rafe swung the craft for home. There would be no stomach-dropping dives, no barrel rolls, Alex knew. Her husband would get her back to earth without risk. What a shame.

It crossed her mind that Tom Flinders might take her up for a more adventurous flight when Rafe wasn't around. But no, even if she could charm him into it, she wouldn't risk the young man's job. And she was through lying to Rafe. They'd built too much trust for that.

The wheels touched the ground. Rafe cut the engine and rolled to a stop outside the hangar.

"Your eyes are dancing," he said as she raised her goggles. "I know that look. And the answer, my little spitfire, is no. You're not flying this aeroplane, so put it out of your mind."

"But Rafe, it was so wonderful." She wriggled free

of her harness and let him help her out of her seat. "Promise me you'll take me up again, at least."

"We'll see." He frowned in mock severity. "It depends on how well you behave. Come on, I'll walk you to the car."

His hand lay lightly on the small of her back as they walked to the side of the field, where he'd left the Packard. "Our first air show of the season's a month off," he said. "Can you be ready to fly the biplane?"

"What a silly question, Rafe Garrick!" She flung her arms around his neck. "Of course I'll be ready! I'll fly every day, if that's what it takes!"

"It will take just that. I want you to be completely confident. Tom can set up pylons to mark the course you'll be flying and give you some pointers if I'm not around. Unless there's a nor'easter blowing, you'll be out here practicing every morning. Understand?"

"Aye, aye, sir!" She gave him a quick kiss, then climbed into the driver's seat and waited while Rafe turned the crank. It was going to be a busy day. First she'd need to go home and change out of her knickerbockers. Then, as long as she had the car, she'd pay a long-delayed visit to her mother. After that it would be off to the dressmaker's to choose the fabric and design for her flying costume.

Gold, or maybe green…yes, a deep emerald-green, definitely!

Chapter Fourteen

Philadelphia, July 1912

The crowd cheered as Alex swung the biplane around the sixth pylon, banking sharply to cut another second off her time. In yesterday's race she'd come in third, behind the legendary Glenn Curtiss and an unknown Frenchman in a Blériot. Third place was her best so far, but it wasn't good enough. This time she wanted to win.

Finishing her course, she landed the plane at the end of the field and coasted to a stop. Rafe was there to meet her as she jumped to the ground, yanked off her goggles and turned to look at the giant scoreboard. Her spirits sank as her time was posted. She was in fifth place with no chance of finishing in the money.

Rafe caught her waist and drew her close. "You may not have been the fastest, but I can guarantee you were the prettiest. Emerald-green is definitely your color."

She gave his stomach a none-too-playful poke with

her fist. In a sport where women and men competed as equals, she was determined to prove herself with a winning time. So far it hadn't happened. "Tomorrow," she vowed. "Tomorrow I'll do it. You'll see."

Turning her toward him, he lifted her chin with his thumb. His jade-flecked eyes probed hers. "I'm not asking you to win, Alex. All I'm asking is that you show off the biplane and land in one piece. You're racing against seasoned fliers. Keep trying to beat their times and you're going to get hurt. Be careful. I mean it."

He released her. Alex pulled back the hood of her green satin jacket, letting her hair fall free. Oh, she knew what he expected of her. Rafe wanted people to see a woman piloting his biplane. It would help convince them that the machine was safe and easy to fly. Orders would come pouring in.

Blast him! She loved the man, but why couldn't he understand what mattered to *her?* She wanted to be more than a pretty ornament. She wanted to be judged on her own merits, to earn her own stars, like Harriet Quimby.

She finger-combed her hair and pinned it up in a loose knot. "Harriet's flying an exhibition in a few minutes," she said. "Do you want to come and watch?"

"Go on. I'll put the aeroplane away."

"Thanks." She strode toward the stands without looking back. Rafe watched her as she paused to peel off her quilted jacket. The white cotton shirt underneath clung damply to her skin. The satin knickerbockers she wore with knee-high boots outlined her shapely little rump.

Two young mechanics checking their machines ogled

her as she passed. One of them dropped his wrench. Rafe battled the urge to flatten them both with his fists. No man could be blamed for looking at Alex, especially the way she was dressed. He could suggest she slip on a linen duster after her flights. But then she'd accuse him of trying to control her. He didn't need another useless argument with his beautiful, stubborn wife.

Opening the hangar doors, Rafe wheeled the biplane inside. Alex had seemed so happy while she was learning to fly. But the air shows had brought out the hidden Buck Bromley in her. Flying the biplane wasn't enough. She had to compete. She had to go for the win, even if it meant risking her neck in every race.

He'd tried to steer her toward tamer events, such as the precision takeoffs and landings or the "bomb" drop, which involved dropping a weighted bag onto a target. She'd swiftly mastered these and become bored with them. Only racing seemed to feed her what she craved— that, and the notion of flying the new monoplane. She'd asked him again last night. His refusal had left her so angry and withdrawn that they'd slept on opposite sides of the bed.

Where were they going, he and his little spitfire? He loved her with his whole heart, but they seemed more at odds every day. She was determined to live on the edge of danger. He was equally determined to keep her safe. If he drew lines, she stepped over them. If he made rules, she challenged them. The tension was pulling them apart.

For the second time in their marriage, Rafe was afraid of losing her.

* * *

Alex shaded her eyes with her hands as Harriet Quimby put her Blériot monoplane through its paces. Harriet, who flew with the Moisant exhibition team, always put on a breathtaking performance, flying intricate patterns, then spiraling high to zoom downward in a long dive. As she watched, Alex imagined doing the same maneuvers in Rafe's new monoplane, now christened The Garrick-Bromley Falcon. The Blériot was a fine machine, but at the Falcon's controls her own turns would be sharper and cleaner, her climb higher, her dive a blinding blur of speed.

She'd heard only that morning that a flier in California had performed the first complete loop in a Blériot. Surely the Falcon was capable of the same feat. She pictured herself in the pilot's seat, pulling back on the stick as the silver monoplane shot upward, curved backward in a graceful somersault and zoomed into its tearing dive. What a thrill that would be—the first woman pilot to loop!

Of course she wouldn't try it at first. But with enough practice, anything was possible. All she had to do was talk Rafe into letting her fly the Falcon. Right now that seemed the most daunting challenge of all.

Last night his refusal had thrown up a wall between them. Somehow she needed to break through that wall. She loved her husband passionately. But she would not suffer his treating her like a helpless female. In the air she was the equal of any man, and she deserved the chance to prove it.

How could she get past Rafe's stubborn, old-fashioned attitude toward women? There had be some way to change his mind. She would think about it while she watched the flights and waited for Tom Flinders to show off the Falcon.

Nothing could have prepared Alex for life on the circuit of summer air shows. It was the most exhilarating, and exhausting, time of her life. Meets could be held wherever there was room to fly, storage for the planes and an area for the spectators, who flocked in by the thousands. Grandstands were built at existing airfields. Some meets were even held at racetracks, such as Belmont Park outside New York. A big air meet could last as long as a week, with up to ten aeroplanes in the air at once, and dozens more waiting on the ground.

And the aeroplanes! Alex couldn't get enough of them. There were boxy American biplanes, built by pioneers like Glenn Curtiss, Henri Farman and the Wright brothers. The European machines included Blériots, of course, as well as a long, elegant craft called the Antoinette and the tiny Demoiselle, so small that its pilot had to weigh less than a hundred and twenty pounds.

But nothing could touch Rafe's Falcon. Not in beauty, not in maneuverability and not in speed. Because he had no backup plane, and because the craft had yet to be thoroughly tested, Rafe had chosen not to risk it in competition. But when the Falcon roared over the stands in one of its twice-daily exhibition flights, a hush fell over the crowd. People gazed upward as if aware that they were seeing something extraordinary—a masterpiece of engineering and design.

Alex felt that and something more—a deep, gut-gnawing hunger. She wanted to be up there, streaking across the sky with the power of lightning at her fingertips. Maybe then she would be satisfied.

"I watched your race today." Tom Flinders had wandered over to stand beside her. "Nice flying. You get better every time."

"Better? Oh, good heavens, Tom, I came in fifth today!"

"Out of seventeen fliers. That's pretty good—"

"If you say 'for a woman' I'm going to punch you!"

Tom chuckled. He was aware of her frustrations. "Watch the angle on that left turn," he said. "Today you came around a little steep. Much more and you could flip over and crash. Trust me, you don't want that to happen."

"Have you ever crashed?" she asked him.

The wind ruffled his carrot-hued hair as he squinted upward. "A couple of times. Nothing big, or I wouldn't be standing here. I had one bad landing where I ran a wheel into a ditch and smashed a wing. And another time, on the ground, the wind blew me into another aeroplane. But I've been lucky. Too many good pilots die in crashes. One little mistake, or a turn of bad luck…"

His voice trailed off as two planes narrowly missed each other in the air. A collective gasp went up from the crowd.

"Damned bloodsuckers." Tom glanced toward the stands. "That's what brings them in, you know. Not the fine machines. Not the great flying. They want to see some poor devil die in a crash so they can talk about it over drinks at their fancy parties. Every time I go up, I remember that, and I remind myself not to give them what they want."

"What's it like flying the Falcon, Tom? Is it wonderful?"

"Wonderful?" He shook his head. "Truth be told, it scares the blazes out of me. With that much power and speed in your hands there's no such thing as a small mistake. A lapse you could correct in most aeroplanes would kill you in the Falcon. I know you want to fly it. Take my advice, and put the notion out of your head."

"Why? Because I'm a woman?"

"Being a woman's got nothing to do with it. It takes experience and a steady hand to pilot a machine like the Falcon. You've only had your license a couple of months. Buy yourself a nice Blériot. Fly it every day for a year. Then maybe you'll be ready." His homely young face scowled at her, brown eyes level with her own. "You've a good life with a fine man who loves you. That's worth more than all the aeroplanes in the world. Don't throw it away for a few minutes of glory."

Alex watched a lone biplane circling in the sky. "Do you have a sweetheart, Tom?" she asked.

He nodded. "A gem of a lass back in Brooklyn. Meg's her name. She's been after me lately to quit this crazy business and get married. Her da' would give me a good job."

"Then maybe you should take your own advice."

He grinned. "Maybe I will."

Alex watched him make his way through the crowd, headed for the hangars. Every word Tom had said made sense. She'd be wise to get more experience in a monoplane before attempting to fly the Falcon. Maybe she could find a Blériot for sale at one of the shows. That way she could start practicing right away. Surely Rafe wouldn't object to that. He'd even suggested it once.

As for the rest…yes, Tom was right about that, too. Rafe loved her. They had a glamorous life that many people would envy. She should thank her lucky stars and be content with that.

So why wasn't she content? What was she missing?

"Excuse me, ma'am." The voice came from behind her left shoulder. Alex turned to see a young girl holding up a program and a pen. She looked about fourteen, with blue eyes and long brown pigtails. Her skirt and middy blouse were clean but well-worn, as if they might be hand-me-downs.

"Please, could you sign my program?" she asked.

"Of course." Flattered, Alex scrawled her signature on the cover of the program. She'd signed autographs before. It always gave her a lift.

"When I grow up, I want to be a pilot like you," the girl said. "My pa says that girls can't fly airplanes, but I know different. Someday I'll show him, and my brothers, too."

Returning the pen and program, Alex laid a hand on her thin shoulder. "We girls can do anything we put our minds to," she said. "Whatever your dream is, don't let anybody talk you out of it. Hear?"

"I hear." The blue eyes sparkled. "My name's Jenny Fitzpatrick. When I get old enough to study flying, I'll write you a letter. Maybe you can help me find a place to learn."

"If you're going to write me a letter, you'll need an address," Alex said. "Give me the program and I'll write it for you." She printed the company address below her name. "Here you are. Don't lose it."

The girl grinned, showing slightly crooked teeth. "I won't! I'll keep it in my secret box! You'll hear from me, I promise!"

Clutching the program, she darted off back toward the grandstand. Alex gazed after her, surprised by a surge of warm emotion. It had never occurred to her that she could inspire young women, just as Harriet Quimby had inspired her. Maybe that was just as important as winning races—not that she intended to stop trying.

Jenny Fitzpatrick. Alex tucked the name into her own secret box, the one in her memory. She'd lost the race, but a bright-eyed girl with a dream had just rescued her day.

Life in the air shows had three facets. There was the tense, competitive, danger-filled milieu of the shows themselves. Then there was what Alex had come to think of as gray time—the tedium of long train trips and hotel rooms that all looked the same; loading and unloading; waiting for the weather to clear; waiting for the aeroplanes to be reassembled; waiting for the crowds to arrive. Boredom. Headaches. Flaring tempers. Aching feet.

Finally, there was the glittering world of receptions and parties. These were staged by air show promoters, city fathers and businessmen with one common aim—to promote every aspect of the growing aviation business. The fliers were the bait to lure wealthy investors and those who had the political clout to clear the way for expansion.

Alex had enjoyed these affairs at first. Now, like Rafe, she viewed them as a necessary part of the business. At the end of a long day, she'd gladly have chosen room service and a hot bath over dressing up in evening clothes and charming the locals. But it needed to be done.

Tonight's event had been set up in the ballroom of Philadelphia's most elegant hotel. The buffet table was lavish, the champagne abundant, the ten-piece orchestra adequate, if not quite first-rate. A full-scale model of the original Wright brothers' aeroplane, rendered in chicken wire and flowers, hung suspended from the ceiling.

Alex had worn her most flattering gown, ruffled silk organza in a deep periwinkle blue that brought out her eyes. As always, she was on the arm of the handsomest man in the room. Admiring glances followed them as they moved around the floor. Rafe worked the crowd, shaking hands and answering questions. Alex floated along beside him, her face fixed in a gracious smile.

Bloody hell, as Rafe would say, her feet were killing her! And she felt one of her headaches coming on. All she wanted to do was go back to their hotel room, crawl into bed and close her eyes. She'd been so tired lately, and so emotional. She really needed to get more rest.

And more sensible food, Alex reminded herself. Breakfast that morning had been coffee and a sticky cheese Danish, bolted down in the taxi between the hotel and the airfield. She hadn't eaten a bite since then, and her stomach was growling with hunger. But the smoked salmon, caviar and goose liver pâté on the buffet table smelled so revolting that she had no desire to go near them.

A slender figure moved toward them through the crowd. Even when she wore flying clothes, Harriet Quimby was elegant. Tonight, dressed in pale sea-green lace, she was a goddess—a Botticelli Venus rising from the foam. Alex sighed. It was a pity the woman was so nice. Otherwise it might be cathartic to hate her.

"There you are! I've been looking for you!" She greeted them graciously, complimenting Alex on her gown and her flying. Then, turning to Rafe, she went straight to the point. "I do believe I've fallen in love with that new monoplane of yours——the Falcon, is that what it's called? How soon can I buy one?"

Alex felt something coil and knot in the pit of her stomach. She forced herself to keep smiling.

"Not in time for this season, I'm afraid," Rafe said. "We need to do more testing and make a few adjustments. If all goes well, we'll start production in August."

"Do you have many orders?"

"Enough. But it's going to be an expensive machine. The price alone will put a limit on the number we sell."

Harriet laughed. "I don't care if I have to steal the crown jewels to buy it! I want one. And if you'll put me at the front of the line, I can give it some exposure for you. I'd like to be the first woman to fly your beautiful aeroplane."

Alex realized that her fingers were digging like talons into the sleeve of Rafe's dinner jacket. She forced her grip to relax. Short of making a spectacle of herself, there was nothing she could do.

"That could be arranged," Rafe said. "I'm going to require anyone who buys the Falcon to come to the factory for a few days of training first. But I can have Tom take you up as a passenger tomorrow. How does that sound?"

"That would be lovely." Harriet sighed. "Unfortunately, I won't be here tomorrow. The Moisant team will be leaving for Boston first thing in the morning. We'll be doing flights over the harbor as part of the Boston Aviation Meet." She glanced at Alex. "Is that your next stop, too?"

"We'll be staying here until the end of the show, then going to Richmond," Alex said. "If our paths don't cross again, we'll see you back on Long Island."

"Most certainly." She clasped both their hands. "It's been such a pleasure…" The rest of her words were lost in the music as she glided away to greet someone else.

The first woman to fly the Falcon.

Given a loaded pistol at that moment, Alex would have been hard-pressed to decide—should she shoot the woman she idolized, or would it give her more pleasure to gun down her own husband?

Alex managed to hold her tongue until she and Rafe were back in their room. At that point it was speak up or explode.

"Do you think I'm being childish, Rafe?"

"That's a loaded question if I ever heard one. Do you think you are?" He stripped off his jacket and began to unbutton his collar.

"No," she said. "I've begged and pleaded that I be allowed to fly the Falcon. You've always refused. Until tonight I thought it was because I was a woman. Then I stood there and watched you fall all over yourself to give that honor to Harriet! Right in front of me! How could you?"

"Would you rather I'd done it behind your back?" He laid his shirt over a chair and crossed the room to where she stood. "Harriet's an experienced flier. With a few pointers from Tom, she should have no trouble handling the Falcon. And her flying it in the shows will give me the kind of advertising money can't buy." He laid his hands on her shoulders. "Now, my little spitfire, does that make sense to you?"

"Only in my head. Not in my heart." She sagged against his chest, breathing in the clean, sensual aroma of his skin. She loved him so much. Why couldn't she just let go of her own ambitions and be the woman he wanted her to be?

"I know what you must be thinking," she said. "As your wife, I should accept it and be happy for you. But I've never been that kind of wife. I don't know that I could be, or even that I'd want to. I have my own dreams, my own needs, and I'm too selfish to give them up. It's a poor bargain you've made, Rafe. I wouldn't blame you if you left me."

"Hush." He cupped her face in his hands and began kissing her softly on her cheeks, on her eyes, on her mouth. "Don't you know that I love you, you little fool?" he murmured. "I don't want to change you. I just want to keep you safe. Lord, girl, don't you know that it would kill me to lose you?"

She closed her eyes, wanting to drown in his kisses. When his hands moved downward to slip the gown off her shoulders, she ached to let him, to surrender completely and lose herself in the sweet frenzy of loving him.

But that would resolve nothing, Alex knew. It would only melt away the tension between them, leaving the hurt to fester like a deep-driven thorn. He had wounded her. Until that wound was healed, making love with Rafe would be acting out a lie.

She went rigid in his arms.

"What?" He stopped kissing her.

"I'm sorry. It's been a long day, and I'm extremely tired. I just need to rest."

"Fine." He released her and turned away to finish undressing. "Go on to bed. I'll sit up and read for a while."

Alex felt the chill in the room as she slipped out of her clothes. Rafe was a proud man. He would not risk being turned away again. The chill, she sensed, would last for many nights to come.

By the last day of the Philadelphia air show, Alex was raw with exhaustion. She'd continued to race but her performance had fallen off. Today she'd finished a dismal eleventh, but she was too tired to care. She looked forward to a few days of gray time, when she could rest and leave the work of crating the aeroplanes to Rafe, Tom and the two mechanics.

Rafe had been kind but distant. The last few evenings

he'd found reasons to stay out of their room until long past her bedtime. Alex had no solid reason to believe he was cheating. But Rafe attracted women like a lamp attracts moths. After growing up with her father's behavior, it was hard not to be suspicious.

Where was this standoff going to lead? She loved Rafe, but there was no way she was going to play the submissive little wife to win him back. And Rafe had his own pride. He would never beg her forgiveness for something he didn't believe to be wrong.

She stood by the hangar, gazing forlornly at the overcast sky. Maybe a change of scene would be good for them both. But they wouldn't be getting a break from the air shows until after Richmond. And in between, there would be the long days of gray time.

Right now all time seemed gray.

A light breeze ruffled her hair. Her own part in the show was done, the biplane shed of its wings and ready for crating. All that remained was for Tom Flinders to make the final flight of the show in the Falcon.

With less than thirty minutes until flight time, the silver monoplane was fueled and waiting in front of its open hangar. Tom's leather flight jacket, helmet and goggles hung on a hook inside the door. So far there was no sign of Tom. Alex hadn't seen him since noon, when he'd mentioned that he was going into town to pick up a souvenir for his girl. But Tom was the soul of dependability. Any minute now he'd show up, grinning and a little out of breath, apologizing for the last-minute rush.

In the adjoining hangar, she could hear the two mechanics working on the biplane. Rafe would be in the stands, she knew. He usually positioned himself near the expensive seats when his aeroplanes were flying. It was the best time to answer questions and line up potential buyers. Maybe Tom was with him and had lost track of the time.

Alex was about to go and look for Tom when a skinny youth in a messenger cap came dashing up on a bicycle. Spotting Alex, he braked in front of her.

"Message for Mr. Rafe Garrick. Know where I can find him?"

"I'm Mrs. Garrick," Alex said. "I can give it to him."

"Sign here." He thrust a grubby clipboard in front of her. Alex scrawled her initials and reached into her khaki knickerbockers for a tip. The lad handed her a folded note, pocketed the change she gave him and pedaled away.

Since the note wasn't sealed, Alex assumed it wasn't private. Unfolding the single sheet of paper, she began to read.

Dear Mr. Garrick:
I regret to inform you that your pilot, Mr. Tom Flinders, was struck by a motorcycle this afternoon. He was taken to the emergency room with a badly dislocated shoulder. Rest assured his injuries aren't serious, and he is to be released shortly. But he was most anxious to let you know that he will be unable to fly your aeroplane today.

He has asked me to write this note and to make
sure you receive it.
Yours truly,
Frances Lehman,
Nursing Assistant

Alex stared at the handwritten message. Maybe it
wasn't too late for Rafe to fly in Tom's place. Acting on
first impulse, she started off to find her husband. After
a dozen steps, she stopped as if she'd just run into a wall.

Could she do it?

Of course she could. She was familiar with the Falcon's controls. The stick and rudder bar were no different from the ones in the Blériot she'd flown as a student.
Tom and Rafe had both warned her that the new plane's
power made it tricky to handle. But how hard could it
be to take off, circle the field a couple of times, maybe
climb a few hundred feet and do an easy dive if she felt
confident, then land? She'd done all those maneuvers
in the Blériot.

Rafe would be furious with her. But things were already rough between them. How angry could he possibly get, especially when he wouldn't find out until
after she'd landed?

No, she couldn't do it! She loved Rafe! How could
she betray his trust?

Tom's gear, hanging by the door, caught her attention. She and Tom were close to the same size. Dressed
in his jacket, helmet and goggles she'd look enough
like him to fool the mechanics into helping her move the

plane and spin the propeller to start the engine. From a distance, she might even fool Rafe. All she needed to do was keep her mouth shut.

No—what was she thinking? Of course she wouldn't do it! The very idea was madness!

The first woman to fly the Falcon...

Decision made, Alex crumpled the note and shoved it into her pocket.

Chapter Fifteen

Rafe walked out of the announcer's booth, stunned by the news that had just come over the wire. What a senseless, god-awful tragedy! And the way it had happened, in front of thousands of people… He shuddered, struggling to blot the image from his mind.

Purple silk, rippling on the wind…

The air meet officials had decided not to inform the crowd. People would find out soon enough. The story would be in all the papers, complete with photographs.

Alex would take it especially hard. It would probably be best to tell her in private, back at the hotel. Thank heaven she wouldn't be flying for a few days. After what he'd just heard, Rafe couldn't stand the thought of sending her back into the sky. Maybe he should just cancel the next few shows and take her home. She needed a rest. He did, too. Those late nights he'd spent shooting billiards in the hotel lounge were catching up with him. Maybe tonight he could just go to bed and hold Alex in his arms. She would need holding after she learned what had happened today.

Take her home. That would be the thing to do. For him, it would mean dealing with Buck and his crazy war plans at close range. But it would do Alex a world of good. Physically and emotionally, she was getting so frayed around the edges that he'd begun to worry about her health.

He glanced at his watch. It was almost time for Tom's last flight in the Falcon. Then they could crate up their machines and move on. Rafe had done some good business here, but it was hard to think of that now. For the first time in his life, he felt sick of flying.

The watchers in the stands were already stirring, some trickling out to get a head start on the crowded exodus. Others were likely waiting to see the Falcon, which was scheduled to take off any minute.

But what was this? Rafe sighted a familiar head of curly orange hair bobbing up through the stands toward him. Tom's face was bruised and skinned. One eye looked like a swollen plum. A fresh white sling supported his left arm.

"Tom, what the devil—?" Rafe plunged between rows of seats to reach him.

"You didn't get my note?" Tom gazed up in dismay as Rafe shook his head. "Blast! I watched the nurse write it and paid the messenger myself!"

"Never mind. What happened?"

"Tangled with a motorbike in town. Dislocated my shoulder and got hauled off to the hospital. Had to argue my way out of the place to get back here. I'm all in one piece, thank the Lord, but I can't fly the Falcon. I was hoping you might do it yourself if you got my message in time."

"Don't worry, I can still give it a run," Rafe said. "Tell the announcer it'll be a few minutes la—"

He choked on the last word as the roar of the sixty-horsepower Garrick-Bromley engine, the most powerful in the show, thundered across the stands like a breaking wave. In the next instant, the silver monoplane flashed down the runway and shot into the sky.

"Holy Mother of God," breathed Tom.

"Bloody hell!" Rafe watched with his heart in his throat. Even if Tom hadn't been standing beside him, he would have known it was Alex in the Falcon. She was climbing fast, too fast. If she didn't level off she would never be able to bank and turn back toward the grandstand. She would stall or lose control, and it would all be over.

"Pray to your Irish saints, Tom," he muttered. "Pray with all your heart. It'll take a miracle to get her and that damned plane down in one piece!"

Silently, as he hadn't done in years, Rafe prayed, too.

Alex's pulse exploded as the Falcon climbed upward. The roar of the engine deafened her ears. The wind blasted her face.

Her nerves screamed terror. But fear wouldn't bring anyone to her rescue. There was nobody here to hold her hand or tell her what to do. She was on her own, faced with one vital choice—control this machine or die.

Scarcely daring to breathe, she brought the lever

forward by millimeters. The Falcon's controls were as sensitive as antennae on a butterfly. Too much force would cause the plane to plummet into a vertical dive and crash before she could pull it up.

By slow degrees the Falcon leveled out. Alex gulped air into her breathless lungs. Tom had been right. She didn't have the experience to fly this aeroplane. But by heaven she was about to learn. Rafe would be watching from the ground. Today she would show him what his little wife could do.

She'd already flown too far beyond the airfield. Now she would have to turn around and go back. Her feet trembled on the rudder bar as she banked into a wide turn. "Easy…" she whispered to herself. "Easy, now. You can do this…."

She was getting the feel of the machine now. The Falcon's streamlined body cut through the air like a knife—a sweet sensation that lay beyond the edge of fear. Guiding its flight demanded total concentration. With her hands and feet on the controls she could not so much as twitch. Even a sneeze might send her into an uncontrolled dive.

Ahead she could see the grandstand and the airfield. The runway was empty of traffic. It might be prudent to lower the flaps now and ease in for a landing. But she was just beginning to get comfortable with the craft. Another pass or two and she'd have it mastered. Rafe would be furious when he discovered she'd been piloting his aeroplane. Only after she'd proved her competence would she be ready to face him.

Moving the lever gently forward, she roared over the grandstand, fifty feet above the heads of the crowd. Then she swooped high, banked and came back in the other direction.

The first woman to pilot the Falcon.

She had just snatched that plum from the elegant fingers of Harriet Quimby. Harriet might be annoyed, but the woman had garnered more than her share of aviation firsts. As Rafe's wife, Alex felt she was entitled to this one.

Jubilant now, she made another pass over the grandstand, coming in even lower this time to give the watchers a thrill. In the next instant she was clear. All she had to do was pull up and climb, bank again and glide in for the landing.

A hundred yards ahead, a cluster of tall pylons stood where they'd been moved after the morning races. Alex froze as she realized she was headed straight for them.

Pull up! Pull up! her brain screamed. Her arm yanked back on the stick but not fast enough. As the Falcon roared upward its undercarriage clipped the pylons and tore loose, pitching the monoplane forward. It plowed into the ground at a flat angle, screeching over the grass on its unprotected belly. Alex lurched against her harness, slamming her forehead against the cockpit's reinforced edge. By the time the wounded craft hit a drainage ditch, rolled sideways and came to rest on one shattered wing, her world had imploded into blackness.

Rafe was already running, pounding across the grass to the far side of the grandstand. *That little fool! That*

*precious, crazy little fool! Please, God, let her be alive...
please...*

He could see where the Falcon had come to a stop.
It was lying on its side with one wing thrusting straight
up, the other crushed beneath the fuselage. The plane's
angle hid his view of the cockpit, but he could see no
sign of anyone moving. *Please, God, I'll do anything.
Let her be alive....*

From the fringe of his awareness came the howl of
a siren. The ambulance crew, standing by, would finally
have something to do. But Rafe had a head start on
them. He would reach the wreckage first.

His chest was bursting by the time he rounded the
wreck. He could see Alex now. She was dangling out
of the cockpit like a broken doll, suspended by her
harness. There was a gash on her forehead and a trickle
of blood at the corner of her mouth. Her goggles were
askew. One lens was cracked and smeared with blood
from the cut on her head. She did not appear to be
moving.

Memories flashed through Rafe's mind as he flung
himself down beside her. Alex...her violet eyes shining
through a fog of pain...her happy face grinning at him
over a greasy engine...her hair flying in the wind as she
galloped her horse along the beach...

When he slipped off the goggles he saw that her eyes
were closed. Her lashes lay wet and still, as if they'd
been painted onto her ivory cheeks. God, he couldn't
lose her. She was the only thing on earth that truly mattered to him.

His fingers ripped open the buckled chinstrap and groped the hollow along the side of her throat. Yes, it was there, the faint but steady throb of a pulse. "She's alive!" he yelled to the stretcher crew racing across the grass. "She's alive!" he shouted to Tom who lagged behind, slowed by his injuries.

Alex whimpered as he unbuckled her harness and eased her out of the cockpit. Her hands lay limp on the grass like two dead white birds. The only visible injuries were the gash on her forehead and the blood on her mouth; but she could have serious head injuries or internal bleeding. Rafe knew he wouldn't take an easy breath until she'd been examined by a doctor.

What the hell had she been thinking? But Rafe already knew the answer to that question. Alex had been wild to fly the Falcon. Tom's accident had given her the chance she needed. The little sneak had probably signed for the message and kept it to herself. If she'd landed safely he might have been tempted to shake the living daylights out of her. As it was…

Lord, he could have lost her. He could still lose her.

"Listen to me, Alex." He clasped her cold hands. "Whatever you've done, know that I love you. If you can hear me, never forget that. I love you, my little spitfire, and we're going to get through this together."

The medics reached them, moving in close to check her vital signs. With Rafe's help they eased her gently onto the stretcher. He sat beside her in the back of the ambulance as they raced to the hospital, gripping her hands and gazing down at her blood-smeared face. First Harriet, now this. So help him, if Alex survived this disaster, he was never going to let her fly again!

Alex opened her eyes to a white room with a blinding electric bulb wired into the ceiling. Reflexively she jerked her head to one side. The pain was so sharp that she yelped.

"Hello, little spitfire, how are you feeling?" Rafe was leaning over her now, blocking the light that glinted like a halo on his rumpled hair.

"Hurts…" she muttered, thick-tongued. "My head… all over." Her eyes took in the bleached curtains drawn around the bed. The air smelled of disinfectant. "Am I in the hospital?"

Rafe nodded. His eyes were bloodshot. His face looked a decade older than the last time she'd seen him. "Do you remember what happened?"

"I was flying…wasn't I?" Alex groped for the memory, her fingers exploring the gauze bandage that wrapped her head.

"You got too big for your britches and crashed the Falcon into some pylons." Rafe was making an effort to sound lighthearted but a twitching muscle in his jaw betrayed his tension.

Now Alex remembered pocketing the note, donning Tom's gear and taking off in the Falcon. What had she done? To Rafe's trust? To him? To her marriage?

"I'm sorry," she whispered, fumbling for his hand and not finding it. "Your beautiful aeroplane—oh, Rafe…"

"Forget the damned aeroplane. The factory can make another one. We can make a hundred, a bloody thousand! But you—you damn near died today, or crippled yourself for life! Do you have any idea how lucky you are?"

He rose to his feet, glaring down as if he were about to deal her some devastating blow. Then, as if changing his mind, he turned away. "I'll go find the doctor. He'll be glad to know you're awake."

Without looking back he strode out of the room and disappeared down the hall.

Alex lay there staring at the open doorway as if she could will him to reappear. She deserved the worst he could give her. She'd committed a dishonest and reckless act, deceived her husband and destroyed his finest work. If Rafe had shouted at her, even cursed her, it would have been easier to bear than this stony restraint of his.

Cautiously she moved her toes, her legs, her arms, her hands. There was feeling and movement in every part of her body. Given time, the soreness and bruising would heal and she would be whole once more.

But what about her splintered marriage? Would Rafe forgive her, or had she passed the point of forgiveness?

Alex had been a rule-breaker all of her life. Maybe this time she'd gone too far.

Maybe this time she would lose him.

The next morning Alex was released from the hospital. Aside from bruised ribs and shoulders, a cut lip and a bandaged forehead, she was in reasonably good condition. The doctor agreed with Rafe that she would rest more comfortably in their hotel room.

Rafe, who'd spent the night in a chair at her bedside, signed the paperwork and hailed a taxi. His eyes were bloodshot, his hair uncombed, his cheeks dark with the stubble of his unshaven beard. He'd spoken only a few words to her that morning. Was he still angry, she wondered, or just exhausted?

"You look even worse than I do," she commented as they settled themselves in the backseat of the cab.

"Do I?" He rubbed his chin absently, as if he'd given no thought to his appearance. "If you want, we can go in through the back and take the service elevator. That way we won't need to parade through the lobby."

"I'd appreciate that." Alex was dressed in the clean calico morning gown and slippers Tom had fetched from the hotel last night. From the shoulders up she was a mess of bandages, bruises and disheveled hair. "I appreciate everything you've done for me, Rafe. You didn't have to stay last night, but it was a comfort to have you there."

"You're my wife." He gazed out the side window. "I'm cancelling our shows for the next six weeks. It'll take that long to replace the Falcon. That should give you some time to recover before I leave again."

"Before *we* leave, you mean. I do plan on going with you."

He turned back to face her, his eyes like burned-out coals. "No, Alex, you're not coming with me. Not even if you promise not to fly. I can't trust you around aeroplanes, and I can't be worrying about your safety all the time. You're grounded—for good."

She sucked in air, pain stabbing through her sore ribs. "You can't do that! You can't stop me from flying!"

"As your husband, I can and I will."

She sagged in her seat, knowing he was right. One word from him and she'd be barred from the aerodrome at Hempstead Plains. And she wouldn't have a prayer of using the aeroplanes or the airstrip at the factory. He could enlist her parents to keep an eye on her while he was gone or even stay home and watch her himself. She would be a virtual prisoner.

Her stomach roiled. She clenched her jaws, fighting the urge to be sick. This couldn't be happening.

Alex was still reeling when the taxi pulled up to the rear entrance of the hotel. They rode the service elevator in silence, accompanied by a grim-looking janitor with a cleaning cart. Alex held her tongue, steadying herself on his arm as they made their way down the long, carpeted hallway to their room. Only after they were inside, with the door locked behind them, did she turn on him.

"How dare you, Rafe Garrick? I'm your wife, not your slave or your dog! I should be able fly if I want to!"

His eyes were cold slits. "You just got out of the hospital. Get into that bed. Then we'll talk."

The room shimmered before Alex's eyes. She would have chosen to defy Rafe on her feet, but this time he was right. She belonged in bed. Accepting the nightgown he thrust at her she turned away from him to unbutton the front of the simple morning dress. There was a time when she'd have taken pleasure in letting him watch her disrobe. But things had changed.

The buttons were small, her fingers unsteady. She fumbled in frustration, wasting time. Her breath caught as she felt his hands on her shoulders. Turning her around he lifted her hands gently away from the buttons.

"Take it easy. I'll do it."

Alex stood frozen as he opened the front of her dress, willing herself not to feel the brush of his fingers on her skin. Underneath she was wearing nothing but her muslin shift. Her darkly swollen nipples stood out through the gauzy fabric. He was making an effort not to look down.

"There." He stepped away as the dress slid off her shoulders. Alex pulled the loose cotton nightgown over her head and shoulders. Emerging, she saw that Rafe had turned down the bed. She crawled between the sheets like a wounded animal. Her initial fury had drained away leaving a residue of gritty determination.

"All right, let's talk." She settled back onto the pillows.

"Fine." He sank onto a chair, looking as if he'd spent the night in hell. "I found Tom's message in your pocket when I bagged your clothes in the hospital. You could have brought it to me. Instead you chose to commit a deceitful, dangerous and plain stupid act that damn near got you killed. If you can think of one good reason why I should let you keep flying, I'd like to hear it."

Alex sat up straighter against the pillows. "I'm sorry for what I did, Rafe. But I had my reasons. If you'd taught me how to fly the Falcon, this never would have happened. I took a chance because I knew it was the only chance I was going to get. You would never have let me fly your precious plane—and I wanted to show you that I could. You can't imagine how much I wanted to show you."

His expression darkened. "So you're saying it's my fault? That I'm responsible for what you did? That's hogwash, Alex. Next you'll be blaming your father or your mother for raising you to be a spoiled, willful brat. What happened was your doing, and I'm still waiting for you to take responsibility."

"All right, I will." She spat the words at him. "I wanted to be first. Is there anything wrong with that? Harriet Quimby was the first woman in America to earn a pilot's license. She was the first woman to fly the English Channel. When she said she wanted to be the first woman to fly the Falcon, and you agreed to let her, it was like slapping my face. I was so hurt, Rafe. I tried to tell you, but you just brushed me off."

Alex paused, fingering the cut on her lip. "So what are you going to say to her? Are you going to tell Harriet that I flew the Falcon, or do you plan to hush it up and keep that bit to yourself?"

Rafe rose to loom over the bed. The expression on his face was one Alex never wanted to see again.

"Harriet was killed yesterday. Her Blériot lurched in the air. She was thrown out and fell fifteen hundred feet into Boston Harbor." He swallowed the roughness in his voice. "By the time you pocketed that note and climbed into the Falcon she was already dead."

In the silence, a low animal sound rose from Alex's throat. She did not speak, could not. There were no words. Shocked beyond tears, she turned away from Rafe and curled onto her side like a child.

She could hear his ragged breathing as he stood next to the bed. At last he reached down, tugged the coverlet over her shoulders and walked out of the room. The door closed behind him with a soft click.

Alex slept fitfully for the rest of the day and for most of the night that followed. In her wakeful moments she was aware of Rafe's presence—his quiet footsteps crossing the floor, the sound of water running in the bathroom, the opening of drawers and the subtle clink of his belt buckle as he dressed and undressed. In the night he lay on his side of the bed, so cold and remote that she dared not reach out to him, even for comfort.

When she came fully awake the next morning, the only sound in the room was the slow ticking of the bedside clock. She sat up amid the tangled nest of sheets and blankets, aware that she felt clearheaded for the first time since the crash.

"Rafe?" she called out, then waited for an answer. None came. That was when she saw the note, scrawled on hotel stationery and anchored beneath an empty coffee mug on the nightstand.

Gone to airfield to pack and load Falcon. Back before dinner. Stay put. Rest.

Alex crumpled the note and tossed it into the waste-paper basket. Was his curtness a sign of his feelings toward her, or had he simply been in a hurry to leave?

Moving cautiously, she stretched her stiffened limbs, lowered her feet to the floor and stood. She felt light-headed and vaguely nauseous, but she could attribute that to hunger. Using the house telephone, she ordered oatmeal, buttered toast with marmalade and green tea with milk. Then she tottered into the bathroom and peered at her reflection in the mirror above the basin.

She looked as ghastly as she'd expected. But at least her lip was healing. With care, she might even be able to peel the bandage off her head. Then she could wash her hair.

Reaching up, she found the knot that anchored the gauze and picked it undone. The wrapping fell away from her hair but was stuck to the place where her forehead had bled. Soaking a washcloth, she pressed it to the dried spot and sank onto the edge of the toilet seat to wait.

The events of the past two days crashed in on her with gut-wrenching clarity. What a childish thing she'd done, taking off in an aeroplane she didn't know how to control. What if she'd crashed into the grandstand, taking innocent lives with her? No wonder Rafe was so determined to stop her from flying. In his place, with a loved one at risk, she would have done the same thing.

"You've a good life with a fine man who loves you. That's worth more than all the aeroplanes in the world. Don't throw it away for a few minutes of glory."

Tom's words came back to haunt her now. Such sound advice. Why hadn't she taken it? Now it was too late. Rafe would never forgive her for the things she'd said and done.

Yesterday, when he'd confronted her, she'd tried to blame him for her selfish actions. But his scathing response had been right on target. She had no one to blame but herself.

And then there was Harriet. Alex had tried to prove herself a worthy equal to the gallant aviatrix; but she had failed every test. And while she was moping around the hangars, feeling sorry for herself, Harriet Quimby had been plummeting through that awful void to her death.

Even now, when Alex closed her eyes, she could see the dot of purple against the clouds, the empty Blériot rushing toward the water. Sweet God, it wasn't fair. Why couldn't she have died instead of Harriet?

A wave of dizziness swept over her. Her stomach clenched, sending a nauseous surge into her throat. Surrendering, she flung open the toilet lid and slumped over the bowl, retching bitter bile. The damp bandage loosened and dropped to the floor.

By the time the spasms stopped, Alex felt better. But she was in sore need of a bath. Turning on the faucets, she took a moment to study the gash on her forehead. The jagged red line had scabbed over. Not pretty, but at least it wouldn't keep her from getting clean.

The warm water felt heavenly. She sank deep, her hair floating around her face. *What next?* she wondered. Her life and her marriage were at a crossroads. What would she do if she had to choose between her husband and her love of flying?

But then she might not have that choice to make. After what she'd done, there was a fair chance Rafe would no longer want her.

Finding the soap, Alex lathered it between her hands. Her body lay under the clear surface of the water—breasts swollen and tender, puckered nipples as dark as raisins. She could make out a faint brownish line that started at her sternum and ran down the center of her belly to lose itself in her pubic hair. Strange, she hadn't noticed that since—

Alex's eyes shot wide open. No, it couldn't be. After what Dr. Fleury had told her, it just wasn't possible.

Or was it? She couldn't remember the last time she'd had her flow, but between her nausea, her moodiness, her need for rest and the changes in her body, there could be little doubt.

When she'd taken her wild flight in the Falcon, she'd endangered not one life, but two.

Trembling, Alex finished her bath and toweled off. When should she tell Rafe? Not yet, she decided. She needed time to get used to the idea herself. And with things so rocky between them, this news would only add to the strain. If the marriage was really over, it might be easier not to tell him at all.

Right now, just one decision was clear. Life had given her a second chance—a chance too precious to risk. She would not be flying anytime soon.

By the time the bellman delivered her breakfast, Alex

was dressed in a comfortable skirt and blouse, with her clean hair twisted into a loose knot. Her stomach was still in a state of rebellion but she forced herself to eat the bland food she'd ordered. Good nourishment had suddenly become all-important.

She looked forward to being home again. Maybe she and Rafe could work out their differences in the weeks ahead. She would make every effort to meet him halfway. But if he thought she was going to play the submissive little wife—

A brisk knock on the door scattered her thoughts. Alex opened it to find a messenger boy in a Western Union cap standing on the threshold. "Telegram for Mr. Rafe Garrick," he said, extending a yellow envelope and a clipboard.

Alex signed for the message and tipped the lad. As the door closed behind him, she stood staring down at the sealed envelope. The last time she'd read a message meant for Rafe it had gotten her into no end of trouble. But Rafe's note had said he'd be gone all day. What if the news was important, even urgent?

She hesitated. Then she noticed the sender's name in the envelope window. The telegram was from her mother.

Alex's fingers shook as she tore along the edge of the flap. Her legs weakened as she read the message. She sank into a chair and read it again.

BUCK WAS SHOT LAST NIGHT. CONDITION POOR. BRING ALEXANDRA HOME NOW. URGENT.

How like Maude it was, sending the message to Rafe so that he could break the news more gently to his wife. But that wasn't how things had worked out.

URGENT…URGENT… The word flashed like a semaphore in Alex's brain. Buck had always been so strong, so charged with life and vigor. Now he was wounded, maybe dying. Alex knew she had to get home before it was too late. Her mother would need her. And there was so much she wanted to tell her father, especially now.

She struggled to think clearly. By the time she got word to Rafe the day could be half gone and so could the trains. She'd be better off packing a small valise and leaving for the train station now. Rafe could finish his business here and follow later with the rest of their things.

Questions shrilled in her head as she scrawled a note at the end of the telegram. Who would have shot Buck? Or maybe an easier question might be, who *wouldn't* have shot him? Could it have been a robber? A business rival? A disgruntled worker? A jealous husband? And how badly hurt was he? Would he be conscious? Would he even be alive by the time she reached him?

Those questions would torment her all the way back to Long Island.

Chapter Sixteen

Rafe strode across the hotel lobby and punched the button to summon the elevator. It had been a long day, but the two biplanes and the wrecked Falcon were finally crated, loaded and awaiting shipment to the factory on Long Island. Now he could get back to his unfinished business with Alex.

One hand massaged his tense neck muscles as he rode up to the ninth floor. He'd been hard on her. Maybe too hard. But her brush with death had pushed him to the breaking point. When she'd sprung to her own defense instead of apologizing, he'd snapped. He'd said things no man should say to the woman he loved. Then he'd used Harriet's horrific death as a club to deal the coup de grâce. Once he'd delivered the news, he'd walked out and left her shattered.

For that alone, he'd deserved a horsewhipping. He needed to tell her so.

Maybe now that she'd had a chance to rest they could

have a quiet dinner and a long talk. He wanted an end to this standoff between them. He wanted to finish the night with his wife in his arms.

Unlocking the door, he walked into the room.

The room was empty, the bed made up.

"Alex?"

There was no sign of her anywhere. Her party gowns still hung in the armoire, along with her flight jacket and boots, but her small suitcase and some of her clothes were missing, as were her combs, brushes and other toiletries.

Desperation gnawed at him, eating deeper by the second. Had it really come to this? Was the woman so determined to run her own life that she would leave him?

Rafe stared out the window where dark clouds loomed above the jagged Philadelphia skyline. This was the last thing he'd wanted. He had to find Alex and make things right before she did something crazy.

Maybe the desk clerk had seen her leave. He glanced around for the telephone. Only then did he catch sight of the telegram that lay open on the nightstand. Snatching it up, he read the message and Alex's hastily scrawled note at the bottom.

Gone home. Come as soon as you can.

Rafe sank onto the bed, staring at the telegram and feeling like a jackass. Alex must have been frantic. If she'd sent word, he would have left Tom in charge of the aeroplanes and rushed to take her home. As it was, she hadn't even contacted him. After the way he'd behaved, he couldn't say he blamed her.

But it was too late to change the past. The important thing now was that he be there when she needed him. Checking the railroad table in his bag, Rafe discovered that the last train north left in less than an hour. Rushing now, he flung the suitcases onto the bed and began stuffing them with clothes.

Come as soon as you can.

Alex's words slammed him to a halt. Never mind. He could pay the bloody hotel staff to pack and ship the bags. Right now he couldn't risk missing that train.

Toward the end of a stifling day, Alex reached her parents' home. Dragging her valise, she stumbled out of the cab and paid the driver. She'd been away from Long Island for just a few weeks. It felt more like years.

The sun lay like an angry red welt above the lethargic waters of the Sound. A solitary gull flapped above the dunes. The house appeared lifeless, as if the rampant energy that Buck Bromley lent to his surroundings had drained away. No one came outside to greet Alex or take her bag as she toiled up the steps. Maude hadn't mentioned where she and Buck would be, but the place seemed too quiet for either of them to be here.

Cummings, the aging butler, met her in the foyer. "Miss Alexandra." He greeted her gently and took her bag. Alex was no longer a "Miss," but this was no time to remind him.

"Where's my father, Cummings?"

"At the hospital in Minneola. Your mother's there with him. She left you the key to the Pierce-Arrow. Have you eaten?"

"No, but I'm all right. Can you tell me what happened? How badly off is he?"

Something rippled beneath the surface of the butler's dignified mien, but he'd been with the Bromleys for twenty years and had learned not to involve himself in their personal matters. "Your mother would be the one to answer those questions, miss. Would you like me to take this valise up to your old room?"

"Yes, thank you, Cummings. I'll go right to the hospital. If my husband shows up later, please tell him where to find me."

Without waiting for a reply, Alex hurried outside and sprinted around to the garage. Twilight cast long shadows over the roadway as she gave the powerful car full throttle, flying over the bumps and spitting gravel on the curves. Buck had always hated hospitals. He wouldn't be in one now unless his condition was grave.

Alex had spent most of her life fighting with her father. Only in the past few weeks had she come to realize how much of Buck was in her—the same intensity and drive, the same restlessness, the same need to stand alone and to reach beyond the ordinary. If she could make peace with him at last, she might also be able to make peace with her own demons…and with Rafe.

The hospital was a three-story maze of medicinal green walls and checkered linoleum floors. To Alex's sensitized nose, it reeked of chlorine, carbolic acid, kitchen grease and blood.

An attendant directed her to the third floor, where there were private rooms for those who could afford them. Not seeing an elevator, she started up the stairs. By the second flight, Alex found herself racing. She reached the third floor gasping for breath.

What if she'd arrived too late?

She'd been given the room number, but before she could check the doors she caught sight of her mother coming down the hall. Maude appeared as calm and impeccably groomed as ever, but there was a haunted look about her gray eyes. When she embraced her daughter, a rare gesture, her body felt smaller and more fragile than Alex remembered.

They drew apart. Maude stared at her. "Good heavens, Alexandra, what happened to your face?"

"A little accident. It's nothing. How's Papa?"

"Resting." Maude spoke in a flat tone. "The bullet severed his spine. If he lives he'll be paralyzed."

If he lives... The floor seemed to be dissolving under Alex's feet. Buck had always been there, like a force of nature. It seemed impossible that anything could silence his thundering presence.

"What happened?" she asked.

"Come and sit down. Where's your husband?"

"On his way. He'll be here soon." The words veiled a silent prayer. Alex had never needed Rafe's quiet strength more than she needed it now.

Maude ushered her down the hall to a deserted waiting area furnished with dilapidated armchairs, a sagging leather settee and a ring-stained table with a scattering of well-thumbed magazines.

Maude motioned to the settee. They sat a comfortable distance apart, like two casual acquaintances. "I need to know," Alex said. "Tell me everything. How did Papa get shot?"

"I'm afraid we've had a bit of a scandal." Maude twisted her wedding band. "It was one of our neighbors, Mrs. Maybelle Hampton. She did it at a party in her own home, with her husband's pistol. I wasn't there myself, but there were plenty of witnesses. The police have her in custody."

"May Hampton? But that's unthinkable!"

Actually it wasn't unthinkable. The Bromleys had known the petite, hard-drinking May for years, and Alex had long suspected that she'd been one of Buck's conquests—or that he'd been one of hers. The last time Alex had seen her, May had been storming away from a heated exchange with Rafe. The woman was passionate and volatile. Even so, it was hard to imagine her gunning a man down.

"Why on earth would she do such a thing?" Alex asked, knowing how painful the answer must be.

The papery hands clasped and unclasped. "She…accused Buck of an affair with her married daughter. He was trying to deny it when she shot him."

"Oh, Mama!" Alex reached out but Maude's expression warned her away.

"I'm all right," she said. "I've known for a long time that your father wasn't a saint."

"I've known it, too. But all these years! How could you stand by him the way you have?"

"Isn't that what a good wife does, dear?" She rose, brushing imaginary wrinkles out of her dress. "Are you ready to see him now?"

"I'd like to see him alone if you don't mind."

Maude hesitated, then drew a quick breath. "It's fine," she said. "I'll just get us some tea."

Alex's low-heeled slippers clicked along the corridor. Some of the doors were ajar. Through the narrow openings she glimpsed flickers of light and movement. From one room came the broken sound of weeping.

Outside Buck's door she paused, dreading what lay on the other side. She missed having Rafe beside her, but some paths could only be traveled alone. This, Alex sensed, was one of them.

Steeling her emotions, she walked into the dimly lit room. Her father lay on a narrow iron hospital bed, his head supported by pillows. His injuries were concealed beneath the sheeting that covered him from the chest down. At the foot of the bed, rubber drainage tubes emptied into a big glass jar. Alex willed herself to ignore the stench that had seeped into the air.

Buck's eyelids were closed, his face waxen. The sound of his labored breathing seemed to fill the room as Alex leaned over him and brushed a kiss onto his forehead. "Hello, Papa," she said.

His eyes fluttered open. They were as blue as ever but the fire in them had burned out. "Hello, girl," he whispered hoarsely. "Sorry your old man's not more presentable. Getting shot by a jealous woman's not a pretty way to go, 'specially when she aims low and hits the target." He coughed, pain rippling across his face. Surely the doctors would have him on heavy laudanum, or maybe morphine injections, but he seemed fully lucid. "It's about time you got here. Where's that husband of yours?" he demanded.

"Rafe's on his way. I left Philadelphia ahead of him."

"Well he damned well better hurry. Things I need to tell him, the factory, the war…lot of money to be made. Got to be ready when it comes."

Alex found his clammy hands and clasped them in hers. "Hush, Papa. Don't try to talk so much." She kissed his fingers, wetting them with her tears. "Can you keep a secret?"

"A secret?" One black eyebrow tilted slightly. "A good one?"

"The best. But this is just between you and me. You can't tell anybody else. Promise?"

"Promise…but it better be worth keeping."

"It is." She leaned close, her face a hand's breadth from his own. "You're going to be a grandfather!" she whispered.

"You—?"

"Yes." Alex squeezed his hands. "The doctor was wrong. The next generation of the Bromley line is on its way."

"Well, I'll be damned!" A genuine smile lit his face. "Now I can die a happy man!"

"Maybe you won't die. Maybe you'll be around to see your grandchildren grow up."

"Bullshit!" he exclaimed with a trace of his old spirit. "That Maybelle, she did one helluva job on me. What kind of life would I have, trapped in what's left of this miserable body? When I let go…and it won't be long…know that it's my choice, girl. Just look after your mother, will you? She's a good woman. Better than I ever deserved." He sank back into the pillows with a long sigh, as if the impassioned speech had drained away his strength.

Alex pressed his knuckles against her cheek. "I love you, Papa," she said.

"And I love you, my little Alex. Even when I was behaving like a son of a bitch, you were the queen of my heart. Be good to that husband of yours. He's got a stubborn streak, but I'll warrant he's fine breeding stock…" His voice trailed off. His eyelids fluttered and closed. The only sound in the room was the low, labored rasp of his breathing.

A little after midnight, Buck's life ended as quietly as the stopping of a clock. His wife and daughter flanked the bed, Maude dry-eyed, Alex shedding enough tears for both of them. One of the doctors came in, checked for pulse and breathing, noted the time of death and pulled the sheet over his face. The nurse promised to contact the mortuary. After that, there was nothing to do but walk out of the room and go home to face life without him.

As Alex stepped into the hall, her eyes caught sight of a tall figure on the landing. With a little sob of relief, she hurtled down the long corridor and flung herself into her husband's arms.

Rafe caught her close. He was sweaty and disheveled, and his clothes smelled like the second-class railway coach where he'd found the last available seat. But Alex didn't seem to care. She buried her face against his shirt, holding on to him as if she never wanted to let go.

"Papa's gone," she said.

"I know. I knew it as soon as I saw you." Rafe pressed his lips against her hair. "I'm so sorry, love. And I'm sorry you had to go through this without me."

"If I'd waited, I'd have missed the chance to say goodbye."

"I know. It's all right." Rafe would never tell her about those frantic minutes when he thought she'd left him. "Let's go home. It'll feel good to sleep in our own bed again."

"Oh, but I can't." She pulled away to look up at him. "Mama will be alone. I'll need to stay with her, at least until after the funeral. You're welcome to stay, too, of course," she added, seeing the expression he was too weary to hide.

"Never mind that. I can accomplish more if I stay at our house. Tell your mother not to worry about the factory. I'll see to everything there."

And he would, Rafe vowed silently. But stepping into Buck Bromley's shoes was something he'd never wanted to do. Running the aviation branch was a job he relished. But taking charge of a huge arms factory, especially one that was being converted to make military weapons, would be his idea of pure living hell. Would he have the authority to change things, or would the forces Buck had put in motion be too powerful to stop?

The major decisions, he realized, would rest with Burnsides and Bromley's actual owner. Rafe was familiar with the terms of Joshua Burnsides' will and his contract with Buck. The real holder of power, and his own new partner, was walking down the hall toward them now—a quiet wisp of a woman with the tensile strength of piano wire.

"Thank you for coming, Rafe. We're going to need you in the days ahead," said Maude Burnsides Bromley.

Buck Bromley's funeral was the grandest affair Long Island had seen all summer. It was held in the Garden City Cathedral—probably Buck's first time inside the place. Many state dignitaries attended, as well his neighbors and his senior employees at the factory. The press and curious locals were there as well, drawn like flies to the scandal surrounding Buck's death. May Hampton was set to stand trial for murder, but the rumor was abuzz that her lawyer would get her off on a temporary insanity plea. Given Buck's reputation, it was whispered that no jury would convict her.

Alex sat through the dreary service with her mother on her left and Rafe on her right. Maude, dry-eyed behind her black silk veil, had shown so little emotion that Alex had begun to worry about her. Surely she must be grieving inside. At some point, that grief would need to be released.

As for Rafe, he was doing his best to be a comfort. But Alex sensed the unease in him, the anguish over problems that couldn't be discussed with Maude until Buck was laid to rest. He had shut down the factory until after the funeral. Tomorrow being Sunday, it would be closed for one more day. But on Monday the gates were due to open. By then some wrenching decisions would have to be made.

Two nights ago, after his visit to the main factory, Rafe had sat with Alex on the terrace and poured out his frustration.

"It's a hundred times worse than I ever dreamed it would be," he'd told her. "The sporting guns that built the business are a sideline now. Your father was in the process of converting the whole factory to making military weapons. When I checked the files—bloody hell, the U.S. government contracts were the least of it. Buck had been selling arms to rebels in South America, to warlords in China and mercenaries in Africa, for who knows how long. He had smuggling connections all over the world."

Rafe had stared into the darkness. "I don't even want to think about the cash he was raking in. It's blood money, Alex. I don't want any part of it. But it's tainted everything. My part of the business, my aeroplanes that I wanted to keep so clean and perfect, the whole operation was almost certainly financed with illegal arms sales."

Rafe had stared into the darkness, seething with helpless fury. Alex had suppressed the urge to comfort him, fearing he might snap at her, but to her surprise he'd reached out and caught her hand, pressing it to his cheek.

"I'm sorry, love. I know he was your father. But that only makes things harder. Do we soldier on as if nothing had happened? Shut the place down? Alert the authorities and let them have at it? Buck would expect me to look after you and your mother, and I plan to do just that. But given the mess he left behind…"

"Mama has to be told," Alex had said.

"I know. I'll tell her after the funeral."

"*We'll* tell her. We'll do it together."

The sudden peal of organ music startled Alex back to the present. The service was over, and the pallbearers, Rafe among them, were preparing to move Buck's casket out of the church. As the congregation rose, she took her mother's arm and walked with her up the long aisle. The two had never been close, but maybe, without Buck's overpowering presence, that would change.

Meanwhile, there would be Buck's legacy of arms smuggling to deal with. Maude would take the news hard. But she had the house and her own untainted stash of Burnsides money to fall back on. Financially, at least, she would survive. But it was Rafe that Alex was most concerned about, Rafe whose integrity would not allow him to touch a dishonest dime. Another man might put Buck's ill-gotten money to use and sweep the dirt under the rug. But Rafe wouldn't rest until the last stain was washed away. He would drive himself to ruin, if need be, to clear his name and see justice done.

Alex had come up with a plan. It was a heartbreaking plan, but she could think of no other way to save him.

* * *

By midafternoon the last of the funeral guests had gone, leaving the Bromley household in a state of exhaustion. After Maude had retired to her bedroom, Alex called Rafe into the parlor.

When he walked into the room, she was sitting on the green velvet ottoman, where she'd sat the night he'd asked her to marry him. That night, he recalled, she'd worn yellow. This afternoon she was wearing black. She was pale and red-eyed, and the gash on her forehead was still healing; but his Alex still looked beautiful. What a time she'd been through. If they could make it through this rough patch, he would spend the rest of his life making her smile.

He closed the door behind him. "What is it?" he asked.

"Sit down," she said. "I have a proposition for you."

Rafe might have turned her words into a joke but she looked much too serious for humor. He sank onto the edge of the settee. "What's this all about, Alex?"

"It's about what Papa did at the factory. It's about what it could do to you—to your honor and your reputation, to say nothing of the legal entanglements." She glanced down at her tightly clenched hands. "What I'm proposing is that you walk away. If I ask her, I know Mama will cancel the partnership and return full rights to everything you've designed. With the name you've made for yourself, you could find a new backer tomorrow. It would be a fresh start, Rafe. Garrick and Bromley would no longer exist."

"And what about you?"

Her throat moved as if she were swallowing tears. "I'm a Bromley. And I can't leave my mother alone to straighten out this mess by herself. But you could make a clean break. Do you understand what I'm saying?"

He stared at her, stunned by the implications. Did she mean that they should separate…even divorce?

"This is insane, Alex," he said. "I love you."

"And I love you. That's why I'm giving you a chance to be free of this impossible situation."

"No." Rafe was on his feet now. "I won't hear any more. I married you for better or for worse. We'll get through this."

Rising to face him, she laid a finger on his lips. "Listen to me. I've never been a good wife to you. I've fought you at every turn, put my own selfish ambitions ahead of our marriage and made a shambles of everything I touched. I might try, but I can't promise that I'll ever change. Think about it, that's all I ask. You can give me your answer tomorrow, before we talk to Mama. Now, if you'll excuse me, it's been a dreadful day and I'm worn out. I'm going upstairs to rest."

She glided out of the room, leaving Rafe in a state of shock. He stared at the doorway where his wife had vanished. The whole idea was preposterous. He loved Alex. There was no way he would ever walk out on her. But in order to convince her, he needed to come up with a plan of his own.

He gazed out the bay window, struggling to force his emotions into coherent thought. It was no use. He couldn't concentrate here. He needed a quiet refuge where he could clear his mind and think—the one refuge that had never failed him.

He needed the sky.

Alex was too restless to nap. Even after Rafe had knocked politely on her door and told her he was going to take the biplane up, she'd been unable to close her eyes. She'd tried for another twenty minutes, then swung her feet to the floor, changed into her middy blouse and pongee skirt, laced on her walking shoes and slipped out into the hallway.

Her mother's door was closed and silent. Maude had been exhausted. Sleep would do her a world of good. As for herself, Alex resolved, what she needed most was fresh air.

Ducking under the backyard clotheslines, she set off through the trees. The wilting July heat would be bearable here, on this shaded path cooled by breezes from the Sound. If she went down to the dunes, she might even see Rafe's biplane in the sky.

Had she done the right thing, offering him his freedom without mentioning the baby? Not telling him had been a heartrending decision. But the last thing she'd wanted was to trap Rafe against his will. If he chose to make a new start, she had the means to raise a child on her own. She would even give him a role in their child's life if that was what he wanted.

Such brave thoughts! In truth, the prospect of losing Rafe was ripping her apart. How would she bear the years ahead—waking to an empty pillow every morning, yearning to feel his arms around her, his body filling hers in the night, his love renewing her, making her whole.

Beyond the edge of the trees the sun was blistering. Alex mounted the crest of the highest dune and stood gazing over the Sound. She would hear Rafe's biplane before she saw it, but the air was silent. Maybe he hadn't taken off yet. Maybe he'd flown in some other direction or been distracted by something at the factory. In any case, it was too hot to stand here much longer. She would go back to the house, find something cold to drink and put her feet up until he returned.

Only when she turned around did she see the column of black smoke, rising like a pencil smudge against the distant sky. Alex's heart dropped. The smoke was coming from the direction of the factory.

Heedless of the burning sand she plunged down the lee of the dune and raced through the trees toward the house. The key to the Pierce-Arrow was in her room, and she would need to alert Maude as well.

Her feet flew up the back stairs. What if it was Rafe? What if he was burning to death in the wreckage of his plane? Sick with dread, Alex snatched the key from her bedside table and raced to the closed door of her mother's bedroom. "Mama!" She pounded on the door. When she failed to get an answer she flung the door open.

Maude's room was empty, the bed unrumpled.

There was no time to look for her. Alex dashed down the stairs and sprinted toward the garage. She found the doors open, the Pierce Arrow standing alone in its usual place. Buck's old green Cadillac, the one vehicle Maude knew how to drive, was missing.

As she cranked the big black auto, Alex struggled to make sense of things. Rafe wouldn't have taken the Cadillac. He had his own car. Maude must have seen the smoke first. Not finding Alex in the house, she'd driven off alone.

The powerful engine coughed and roared. Alex sprang into the front seat and shot down the drive. The factory was only minutes away, but today the road seemed a hundred miles long. By now the smoke was billowing upward in a huge black cloud—far too much for a single burning aeroplane. The factory itself was on fire.

The main gate stood open. As Alex barreled through she could see flames leaping from the factory roof. Here and there, explosives stored inside sent rocket bursts into the sky. Parking the auto near the fence, she leaped out and raced closer.

There was no sign of Rafe, his Packard or the green Cadillac. Only a solitary, black-clad figure stood in the parking lot, calmly watching the fire. In her hand was a box of matches.

"Mama, have you lost your mind?" Alex plunged toward her, expecting to see the madness of grief in her mother's eyes. Instead, Maude's face wore an expression of childlike joy.

"Welcome to my own private Independence Day celebration, dear," she said. "This place has been the curse of my life. I won't have it become the curse of yours. I've been wanting to do this for years." Her gray eyes twinkled. "What a shame you didn't bring any frankfurters. We could have ourselves a roast!"

Rafe had wandered east, letting his craft ride the wind as far as Rockaway Beach. Now he turned for home with only one decision made. Whatever the consequences, he would stand by Alex and her mother. He would shoulder the monster burden of the factory. Above all, if it took his entire lifetime, he wouldn't rest until Buck's involvement in the international weapons trade, with all its connections, was wiped out. Tonight he would tell Alex. Tomorrow the two of them would tell Maude and hopefully get her approval.

The plan would consume all his time and energy. He would lose the freedom he'd come to cherish. But of the options open to him, this was the only one he could live with.

He was just leveling out when he saw the smoke.

Even from a distance he could tell it was the factory. The fire was shooting into the sky, pouring out a whole Armageddon of flame and black smoke. What had happened? Everything had been fine when he'd taken off from the field behind the factory.

Minutes of flight brought him over the burning complex. Everything was on fire except the hangars on the far side of the runway. Even his own warehouse was in flames.

His heart convulsed as he spotted the Pierce-Arrow parked near the open front gate. Its most likely driver would have been Alex. Was she somewhere in there, lost in the flames?

But no, he could see her now, not far from the auto. She was with her mother. Both of them were waving. Rafe dipped the wings and circled around to the airstrip. The instant the biplane came to a safe halt he was on the ground, running.

The distance from the plane to the front of the factory was several hundred yards. By the time Rafe rounded the back of the burning building he could see Alex running toward him. She met him halfway, both of them gasping for breath. He caught her as she flung herself against him, laughing and covering his face with kisses.

"Alex, what the devil—?"

"Mama did it! Rafe, she knew! The smuggling, everything, she knew about it! And now it's all gone—the weapons, the contracts, even the cash! We can start over clean, build what we want to! She's already agreed to become a partner with Grandpa Burnsides' money." She kissed him giddily.

Like a man in a dream, Rafe walked back across the vast lot, arm in arm with his wife. Now he could see how Maude had started the conflagration. Too frail to carry a can of gasoline into the building, she had simply driven the heavy Cadillac through the front doors and tossed a match into the tank. He could see the auto's charred rear end sticking out through what was left of the door frame. She'd been lucky to get out of the way in time. As Rafe had long suspected, Alex hadn't inherited all her grit from her father.

Together the three of them watched the factory burn. In the distance they could hear the sound of sirens. By the time the firemen arrived there'd be nothing left to save.

"I've always wanted to see Europe," Maude said. "London, Paris, Rome—all the places I've read about in books. Buck was always too busy to take me. Now I'm going. That's my dream. What about you, Rafe?"

He grinned. "I want to rebuild this place into a business that Joshua Burnsides would be proud of. Aeroplanes for now, maybe other things later. That should be enough to keep me out of trouble for a long time."

"And you, Alexandra?"

Alex wrapped her arms around her mother and her husband, pulling them close. "I'll have plenty of time to make plans," she said. "But right now, I have some surprising news for you."

Epilogue

April 12, 1919

Dressed in grease-stained mechanic's coveralls, Alex walked to the head of her classroom. She always looked forward to the first day of ground school at the Alexandra Bromley Garrick Flight Academy. The new students brought such an air of excitement with them, so much hope and eagerness. All of them were dreaming of the day when they, too, would become pilots.

This day was especially meaningful. In the center seat of the front row sat Miss Jenny Fitzpatrick, the young girl who'd asked Alex to sign her program. Jenny had saved that program for seven years. On her twenty-first birthday she'd sent a letter to the address Alex had given her. Alex had offered her a full scholarship for the three-month course.

It was Jenny who'd first given Alex the idea of opening a flight school. Now, after six years, the academy was a source of pride and joy, as well as a godsend to Alex's personal life. It enabled her to pursue her love of flying and still be close to home for Rafe and their two children—six-year-old Joshua Rafe and four-year-old Harriet Maude. Their household was a lively place, filled with books, games, pets and laughter. How could life be any better?

With Rafe's help she'd set up her school at the new factory, with access to the hangars and runway. The special training model Rafe had designed and produced for her was now being used all over the country.

With a sense of satisfaction, Alex glanced around her classroom. There were photographs and models of planes everywhere, many of them designed and built by her husband. Alone on the far wall was a large, framed portrait of Harriet Quimby at the controls of her Blériot. It was Harriet who'd first inspired her to fly—just as Alex hoped to inspire the young men and women who came to her school. Today the sight of Jenny's eager face filled her with a sense of completion. It was as if she'd come full circle. Jenny Fitzpatrick, she sensed, was going to be a fine pilot.

A hush had fallen over the classroom. The eyes of her fifteen pupils had all shifted toward the door, where Rafe waited to be introduced. Alex liked having him speak to her class on the first day. Meeting the most respected aircraft designer in the country always gave them a thrill. More important, it helped them to see what high goals and hard work could accomplish.

He met her gaze with a barely perceptible wink. The

memory of last night's loving stirred and awakened, bringing a flush to her cheeks. He'd be remembering it, too, the naughty man!

But her students were waiting. Smiling, Alex stepped to the lectern and began.

"Aviation has changed a great deal since I started flying," she said. "But when I look into your faces, I know that one thing will never change. Young people like you will have dreams. With hard work, intelligence and dedication to the art of flying—and it is an art—you can make those dreams come true."

* * * * *

Love Inspired
HISTORICAL

*Powerful, engaging stories of romance,
adventure and faith set in the past—when life was
simpler and faith played a major role
in everyday lives.*

Turn the page for a sneak preview of
THE BRITON
by
Catherine Palmer

*Love Inspired Historical—love and faith
throughout the ages
A brand-new line from Steeple Hill Books
Launching this February!*

"Welcome to the family, Briton," said one of Olaf's men in a mocking voice. "We look forward to the presence of a woman at our hall."

Bronwen grasped her tunic and yanked it from the Viking's thick fingers. As she stepped away from the table, she heard the drunken laughter of the barbarians behind her. How could her father have betrothed her to the old Viking?

Running down the stone steps toward the heavy oak door that led outside from the keep, Bronwen gathered her mantle about her. She ordered the doorman to open the door, and he did so reluctantly, pressing her to carry a torch. But Bronwen pushed past him and fled into the darkness.

Dashing down the steep, pebbled hill toward the beach, she felt the frozen ground give way to sand. She threw off her veil and circlet and kicked away her shoes.

Racing alongside the pounding surf, she felt hot tears

of anger and shame well up and stream down her cheeks. With no concern for her safety, Bronwen ran and ran—her long braids streaming behind her, falling loose, drifting like a tattered black flag.

Blinded with weeping, she did not see the dark form that sprang up in her path and stopped dead her headlong sprint. Bronwen shrieked in surprise and fear as iron arms pinned her, and a heavy cloak threatened to suffocate her.

"Release me!" she cried. "Guard! Guard, help me."

"Hush, my lady." A deep voice emanated from the darkness. "I mean you no harm. What demon drives you to run through the night without fear for your safety?"

"Release me, villain! I am the daughter—"

"I shall hold you until you calm yourself. We had heard there were witches in Amounderness, but I had not thought to meet one so openly."

Still held tight in the man's arms, Bronwen drew back and peered up at the hooded figure. "You! You are the man who spied on our feast. Release me at once, or I shall call the guard upon you."

The man chuckled at this and turned toward his companions, who stood in a group nearby. Bronwen caught hold of the back of his hood and jerked it down to reveal a head of glossy raven curls. But the man's face was shrouded in darkness yet, and as he looked at her, she could not read his expression.

"So you are the blessed bride-to-be." He returned the hood to his head. "Your father has paired you with an interesting choice."

Relieved that her captor did not appear to be a high-wayman, she pushed away from him and sagged onto the wet sand. "Please leave me here alone. I need peace to think. Go on your way."

The tall stranger shrugged off his outer mantle and wrapped it around her shoulders. "Why did your father betroth you thus to the aged Viking?" he asked.

"For one purported to be a spy, you know precious little about Amounderness. But I shall tell you, as it is all common knowledge."

She pulled the cloak tightly about her, reveling in its warmth. "This land, known as Amounderness, once was Briton territory. Olaf Lothbrok, my betrothed, came here as a youth when the Viking invasions had nearly subsided. He took the lands directly to the south of Rossall Hall from their Briton lord. Then, of course, the Normans came, and Amounderness was pillaged by William the Conqueror's army."

The man squatted on the sand beside Bronwen. He listened with obvious interest as she continued. "When William took an account of Amounderness in his Domesday Book, he recorded no remaining lords and few people at all. But he did not know the Britons. Slowly we crept out of hiding and returned to our halls. My father's family reoccupied Rossall Hall. And there we live, as we should, watching over our serfs as they fish and grow their meager crops. Indeed, there is not much here for the greedy Normans to want, if they are the ones for whom you spy."

Unwilling to continue speaking when her heart was

so heavy, Bronwen stood and turned toward the sea. The traveler rose beside her and touched her arm. "Olaf Lothbrok's lands—together with your father's—will reunite most of Amounderness under the rule of the son you are beholden to bear. A clever plan. Your sister's future husband holds the rest of the adjoining lands, I understand."

"You've done your work, sir. Your lord will be pleased. Who is he—some land-hungry Scottish baron? Or have you forgotten that King Stephen gave Amounderness to the Scots, as a trade for their support in his war with Matilda? I certainly hope your lord is not a Norman. He would be so disappointed to learn he has no legal rights here. Now, if you will excuse me?"

Bronwen turned and began walking back along the beach toward Rossall Hall. She felt better for her run, and somehow her father's plan did not seem so far-fetched anymore. Distant lights twinkled through the fog that was rolling in from the west, and she suddenly realized what a long way she had come.

"My lady," the man's voice called out behind her.

Bronwen kept walking, unwilling to face again the one who had seen her in her humiliation. She didn't care what he reported to his master.

"My lady, you have quite a walk ahead of you." The traveler strode forward to join her. "I shall accompany you to your destination."

"You leave me no choice, I see."

"I am not one to compromise myself, dear lady. I follow the path God has set before me and none other."

"And just who are you?"

"I am called Jacques."

"French. A Norman, as I had suspected."

The man chuckled. "Not nearly as Norman as you are Briton."

As they approached the fortress, Bronwen could see that the guests had not yet begun to disperse. Perhaps no one had missed her, and she could slip quietly into bed beside Gildan.

She turned to go, but he took her arm and studied her face in the moonlight. Then, gently, he drew her into the folds of his hooded cloak. "Perhaps the bride would like the memory of a younger man's embrace to warm her," he whispered.

Astonished, Bronwen attempted to remove his arms from around her waist. But she could not escape his lips as they found her own. The kiss was soft and warm, melting away her resistance like the sun upon the snow. Before she had time to react, he was striding back down the beach.

Bronwen stood stunned for a moment, clutching his woolen mantle about her. Suddenly she cried out, "Wait, Jacques! Your mantle!"

The dark one turned to her. "Keep it for now," he shouted into the wind. "I shall ask for it when we meet again."

* * * * *

Don't miss this deeply moving story
THE BRITON
Available February 2008
From the new Love Inspired Historical line

And also look for
HOMESPUN BRIDE
by Jillian Hart
Where a Montana woman discovers that love
is the greatest blessing of all

Texas Hold 'Em

When it comes to love, the stakes are high

Sixteen years ago, Luke Chisum dated
Becky Parker on a dare...before going
on to break her heart. Now the former
River Bluff daredevil is back, rekindling
desire and tempting Becky to pick up
where they left off. But this time she has
to resist or Luke could discover the secret
she's kept locked away all these years....

Look for

TEXAS BLUFF

by *Linda Warren*
#1470

Available February 2008
wherever you buy books.

Romantic
SUSPENSE

**Sparked by Danger,
Fueled by Passion.**

When Tech Sergeant Jacob "Mako" Stone opens
his door to a mysterious woman without a past,
he knows his time off is over. As threats to Dee's
life bring her and Jacob together, she must set
aside her pride and accept the help of the military
hero with too many secrets of his own.

Out of Uniform
by Catherine Mann

Available February wherever you buy books.

REQUEST YOUR FREE BOOKS!

Harlequin® Historical
Historical Romantic Adventure!

2 FREE NOVELS PLUS 2 FREE GIFTS!

YES! Please send me 2 FREE Harlequin® Historical novels and my 2 FREE gifts. After receiving them, if I don't wish to receive any more books, I can return the shipping statement marked "cancel." If I don't cancel, I will receive 6 brand-new novels every month and be billed just $4.69 per book in the U.S., or $5.24 per book in Canada, plus 25¢ shipping and handling per book and applicable taxes, if any*. That's a savings of close to 15% off the cover price! I understand that accepting the 2 free books and gifts places me under no obligation to buy anything. I can always return a shipment and cancel at any time. Even if I never buy another book from Harlequin, the two free books and gifts are mine to keep forever.

246 HDN EEWW   349 HDN EEW9

Name _____ (PLEASE PRINT)

Address _____ Apt. #

City _____ State/Prov. _____ Zip/Postal Code

Signature (if under 18, a parent or guardian must sign)

Mail to the **Harlequin Reader Service®**:
IN U.S.A.: P.O. Box 1867, Buffalo, NY 14240-1867
IN CANADA: P.O. Box 609, Fort Erie, Ontario L2A 5X3

Not valid to current Harlequin Historical subscribers.

Want to try two free books from another line?
Call 1-800-873-8635 or visit www.morefreebooks.com.

* Terms and prices subject to change without notice. NY residents add applicable sales tax. Canadian residents will be charged applicable provincial taxes and GST. This offer is limited to one order per household. All orders subject to approval. Credit or debit balances in a customer's account(s) may be offset by any other outstanding balance owed by or to the customer. Please allow 4 to 6 weeks for delivery.

Your Privacy: Harlequin is committed to protecting your privacy. Our Privacy Policy is available online at www.eHarlequin.com or upon request from the Reader Service. From time to time we make our lists of customers available to reputable firms who may have a product or service of interest to you. If you would prefer we not share your name and address, please check here. ☐

HH07

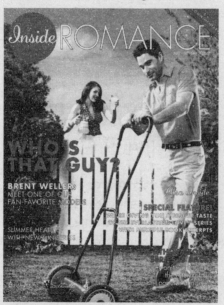

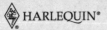

COMING NEXT MONTH FROM
HARLEQUIN®
HISTORICAL

- **OUTLAW BRIDE**
  by **Jenna Kernan**
  (Western)
  Bridget Callaghan is desperate to save her family, stranded in the Cascade Mountains, but the only man who can help her is condemned to hang. With a posse at their heels and the mountain looming, Bridget wonders if the biggest danger might be in trusting this dark and dangerous man.
  Jenna Kernan brings us not only a sensual romance, but also a thrilling Western adventure!

- **THE WAYWARD DEBUTANTE**
  by **Sarah Elliott**
  (Regency)
  Eleanor Sinclair is thoroughly bored by high society. Sneaking out one night, dressed as a servant, to avoid yet another stuffy party, she meets the most handsome man—but her innocent deception will lead her to a most improper marriage....
  Sarah Elliott's defiant heroine will enchant you!

- **SCANDALOUS LORD, REBELLIOUS MISS**
  by **Deb Marlowe**
  (Regency)
  Charles Alden, Viscount Dayle, is desperately trying to reform—and the outrageously unconventional Miss Westby is a most inappropriate choice to help him. But Charles just can't seem to stay away from her!
  Witty and sparkling—enjoy the Regency Season in Golden Heart Award winner Deb Marlowe's sexy debut.

- **SURRENDER TO THE HIGHLANDER**
  by **Terri Brisbin**
  (Medieval)
  Growing up in a convent, Margriet was entirely innocent in the ways of the world. Now, sent to escort her home, Rurik is shocked to be tempted by the woman beneath the nun's habit!
  Surrender to Terri Brisbin's gorgeous Highland hero!